80 DAYS OR DIE

ALSO BY PETER LERANGIS

MAX TILT: FIRE THE DEPTHS

THE SEVEN WONDERS SERIES

THE LOST GIRLS TRILOGY

THE DRAMA CLUB SERIES

THE SPY X SERIES

THE ABRACADABRA SERIES

THE ANTARCTICA SERIES

THE WATCHERS SERIES

39 CLUES: THE SWORD THIEF

39 CLUES: THE VIPER'S NEST

39 CLUES: VESPERS RISING
(WITH RICK RIORDAN, GORDAN KORMAN, AND JUDE WATSON)

39 CLUES: CAHILLS VS. VESPERS: THE DEAD OF NIGHT

80 DAYS OR DIE

PETER LERANGIS

HARPER

An Imprint of HarperCollinsPublishers

Library of Congress Control Number: 2018941365
ISBN 978-0-06-244103-4

Typography by Andrea Vandergrift
18 19 20 21 22   CG/LSCH   10 9 8 7 6 5 4 3 2 1
❖
First Edition

Αιωνία η μνήμη
In loving memory of my dad, Nicholas P. Lerangis.
He is in every word
and always will be.
1921–2017

PROLOGUE

NO one ever paid attention to the man with the drooping eye. He moved swiftly through the London streets like a stale wind. Sometimes he mumbled, and sometimes he broke into a dance that resembled a fit of electrocution. He smelled oddly sweet and moldy, and his skin was like parched paper. These traits were fine for a book but not so much for a human.

So of course people avoided him. On a gray August morning when he stopped short on a crowded sidewalk, they walked politely around the man as if he didn't exist. They kept their eyes on their phones. They minded their own business.

Hearing a noise, the old man looked up. Even in the summer he felt cold, always cold, and he pulled his thin black raincoat tight around him. He'd lost the belt years ago, a great disadvantage on a damp, cloudy day. He trained his good eye on a neon orange-and-black jet emerging from the clouds. His sight was weak, but he could make out the name emblazoned on the tail.

TILT.

It was a strange name for a jet, to be sure. But that did not explain the old man's reaction.

"By the ghost of Gaston!" he squealed. Then he leaped into a complex little jig, his legs twirling and twiddling like rubber sticks. It would have been an impressive display, but as no one was watching, there was no one to be impressed.

Fishing a flip phone from his pocket, he tapped out a message. They're here.

The answer came back immediately. Yes, I noticed. Not modest, are they?

With a grin, the old man shoved the phone back into his pocket. As he shuffled quickly through the grim and growing crowd, he smiled. He was in a good mood now, so he muttered merry greetings.

But he got no replies.

No one ever paid attention to the man with the drooping eye.

A FEW DAYS EARLIER . . .

MAX hadn't planned on drifting off into space. Space found him.

To be more precise, what found him was a conveyance *into* space.

It was just sitting in a field behind his school. A lot of other things were sitting in the field too, like a dozen trailers, a roller coaster not quite fastened down, three wooden stages, stacks of metal risers and chairs, tools and tape, and a garish sign that said Midsoutheastern Ohio State Fair Coming in August.

Conveyance was a word that meant "a way of getting someplace." It was a better word than *vehicle* or *vessel*. That was a fact, and Max was fond of facts. His home-made drone Vulturon was a conveyance, but that had been crushed in the hatch of a submarine in the Atlantic Ocean.

This conveyance, the one in the field behind the gate, was, in fact, a balloon. A big hot-air balloon.

Now, outside of the land of Oz, it is not normal for a hot-air balloon to be sitting in a field all ready to go. It is even less normal for a balloon to beckon to a human being. But a day earlier, Max had looked out his bedroom window and seen the balloon floating high above his house, trailing a banner to advertise the fair. In its basket were a man and woman in old-timey clothes, waving to the roofs below. In the center of the basket, a thick flame shot upward through a hole at the bottom of the balloon. The hot air was lighter than the cooler atmosphere, which caused the balloon to rise. That was another fact.

Max had nearly dropped his iPad in his rush to get to his window and wave back, but they hadn't seen him. Maybe they'd been looking at the roofs. Shingles were interesting, if you really took the time to read about them. But Max had had the weird feeling that the balloon itself had noticed him. It had seemed to turn toward him, dipping in the direction of his house. As if it were bowing.

Now, standing outside the field in the wee minutes before sunrise, Max decided to investigate. He didn't always take sunrise walks, but sometimes he had insomnia, and this seemed as good a thing to do as any. He didn't feel unsafe. He was, after all, thirteen and could take care of himself. And ever since he and his cousin Alex had found the treasure hidden by the famous author Jules Verne, everyone in Savile had become supernice to him. That included the Fearsome Foursome, who used to make fun of him for being "on the spectrum," which wasn't a bad thing when you realized that rainbows were spectra and they were pretty much perfect. Also most people didn't know that spectra was the plural of spectrum, a fact that Max liked very much.

As he strolled closer to the field, he realized the gate was open.

It occurred to him that it shouldn't have been left open, and that someone had probably stumbled out of one of those trailers, forgotten to shut the gate, and was now fast asleep, facedown in a plate of scrambled eggs at the Nightowl Diner on Ash Street. But open gates, as far as Max was concerned, were meant to be walked through. Which he did.

He stepped around the platforms and metal beams and piles of this and that. "Hi, thanks for inviting me," he said as he approached the balloon basket. He knew this was silly because balloons do not really make invitations, but saying it made him smile because it sure felt that way. The basket was smaller than he'd expected. He could have just stepped over the edge into it, but there was a door with a latch, so he used that. Metal bars rose up from the sides of the basket to form a kind of frame that came together a foot or so over his head, making a small platform. In the center of the platform was a contraption that looked a little like a gun and a little like a miniature barbecue, pointed upward. This was called a *brazier*. Max wasn't sure how he knew that, but a steady diet of facts did that to you sometimes. Above that contraption was the balloon material, limp like a pile of blankets. It was made of a special kind of fabric, but Max couldn't remember what that was called.

He spotted a pair of gloves on the basket floor, which he put on. He reached up, grabbing a handhold at the base of the gun-like contraption. His index finger came to rest on a switch, so he snapped it down. It sparked.

That seemed pretty cool.

He tried it again and again—until finally a flame burst upward from the contraption. That caused him to pull his hand back with a start. It seemed like the flame should have burned the balloon material or melted it. But that didn't happen.

Instead, the fabric began to move, as if it were alive, waking from the night's sleep. It shifted around slowly, and then a little faster. The flowing pattern of the fabric's motion was so fascinating to watch that it took a while for Max to realize that the stuff was actually rising.

Max knew that it would continue to rise until it assumed the shape it had been sewn to, which in this case was a balloony sphere. But he did not want that to happen *at all*. He grabbed the handhold again but couldn't figure out how to turn it off. Whatever he was doing only seemed to make the flame stronger.

He considered running away. But it wouldn't be right for the balloon to float up and away from the state fair, to be lost in the atmosphere. That was like stealing.

Max pressed buttons, flicked levers, twisted, yanked, and turned anything he could. He concentrated so fiercely on the contraption above him, that he wasn't really noticing what the balloon itself was doing.

Rising.

The fabric reached its balloon shape faster than he expected. He felt the basket teeter, and he almost fell out. As he left the ground, he gripped the edge of the basket wall. The field below him began to recede. He could see the roof of his school. Fear of heights was called *acrophobia* and he didn't have that, but he did have unlimited-rising-into-space-with-no-way-to-control-it-phobia. And he was beginning to move fast.

"He-e-e-e-ey!" he shrieked. *"He-e-e-elp!"*

But even before the sound left his mouth, a door flew open in the side of a trailer, and a large barefoot man in a T-shirt and checked boxer shorts was racing outside, spitting out some very bad words.

"Throw up, dope!" the man shouted. At least that was what Max thought he said, until he repeated it and Max realized it was "Throw out the rope!"

Max hadn't even noticed the rope coiled in the corner of the basket. It was thick and heavy, but he managed to hoist it out over the edge. As the coil hurtled downward, the basket tipped again. Max clutched tight to the rope, his knuckles white.

The smell of fish rushed into his nostrils. For reasons no one knew, Max always smelled fish when he was afraid.

The end of the rope slapped against the ground, and the man in the T-shirt grabbed onto it. He was shouting something, but Max couldn't hear it. Now another man had joined him. That guy was shouting too. Max held tight to the rope as the guys pulled and pulled the other end. The basket was tipped almost horizontal now. On the positive side, that caused the flame to angle away from the hole in the bottom of the balloon, which helped keep it from rising. And the men were strong, pulling

Max and the balloon closer.

On the negative side, Max was about to fall.

He felt his feet sliding along the now-horizontal basket. He tried to hang tight to the rope, and at this distance he could hear the men clearly. They were saying, "Don't hold onto the rope!"

Now they were telling him.

Max let go. The basket juddered. But the sudden upward thrust of the edge caught him at the knees and he flipped upward.

And over.

Max screamed. As he dropped toward the ground, he caught a glimpse of the horizon, and it occurred to him it would be the last sunrise of his life.

2

"YOU did what?"

Smriti Patel's voice sounded different in the Tilts' new kitchen. It was bigger than the old one. They were standing in the part that used to be a driveway, before the Tilts had bought the house next door and torn it down. Now the Tilts had a beautiful garden, a humongous kitchen, and a glassed-in study for Mom that was protected by a Hulk action figure Max had made with his 3D printer. Also a bathtub shaped like a battleship, Sonos in every room, furniture from Italy, toilets from Japan, two Teslas, a private jet, and a framed portrait of the science-fiction writer Jules Verne hanging in their living room.

These are the kinds of things that happened when you found a secret buried treasure on an island off the coast of Greenland. Which Max and his cousin Alex did, due to finding a hidden note in their attic left by Verne, who was Max's great-great-great-grandfather. After his adventure, Max was ready to have a normal life without mortal danger and media attention. He didn't mean for his balloon escapade to happen. But Smriti was the first person who had actually noticed the bruises on his arm.

"I fell off a trampoline," Max said in answer to her question.

He and Smriti and their friend Evelyn Lopez were making cupcakes for Max's mom's birthday. Not long ago it had looked like she might not see the day. But doctors had found a way to make her cancer-free, so this was the most special birthday of all time, and it needed the most special chocolate cupcakes of all time.

Smriti was Max's best friend. She lived across the street. Evelyn was Max's partner in robotics class and was just about as addicted to facts. One fact about her was that she had a condition called scleroderma. It made her skin waxy and hard and forced her to use a wheelchair. Basically, all her organs were hardening and there was no cure, so things were either going to stay the same or get worse, but those were facts they both preferred not to think about. Evelyn had a great nose for things that weren't facts too, so Max was not surprised when she said in response to his trampoline comment, "I don't believe you."

"Yeah, that's a lie," Max said, taking a heavy bag of peanut M&M's out of the cupboard. They'd already put cinnamon, white chocolate chips, and bananas into the cupcake mix, but it needed more. "But that's what I promised I would say. The state fair people didn't want me to admit what happened. They thought it would be bad for their reputation."

"So what's the truth?" Smriti said.

"I took a ride in a hot-air balloon."

They both gave him the LSS Look. Long, Silent, Stupefied. Max didn't understand that look, but he knew that people had ways of thinking that didn't exactly connect with his, which was OK. Sometimes they just drifted off into a confused silence and figured it out later, and Max was patient.

Dumping some M&M's into the mix, he snuck a quick glance at the clock—6:37. Mom's book club buddies were scheduled to bring her to the house at seven o'clock for the surprise. The cupcakes would take twenty minutes to bake.

"Perfect," he said. "Let's do this."

Together, the three ladled the mix into cupcake tins. As Max shoved the tins inside the oven, a scream rang out from the doorway behind them: *"I cannot believe they did this to us!"*

It was his cousin Alex, that's all, but she had a habit of getting overexcited, and Max jumped. His wrist touched the oven edge, which was a couple of degrees short of a gazillion. *"Yeoow!"*

"Ohhhh, sorry!" she said. "Let's get that wrist under cold water."

She was holding her phone, so she set it near the sink and shoved Max's wrist under the cold water tap. Alex was eighteen, five years older than Max, with a luxuriant explosion of curly hair courtesy of her African-American mother and piercing green eyes from her French-Canadian dad. But right now, her face was a shade of deep crimson.

"Is he going to be OK?" Evelyn asked.

"We can always do a wrist transplant," Smriti said.

This, Max knew, was a joke. He could tell by the way the left side of Smriti's lip curled.

"Finish baking the cupcakes first, then surgery," Max said through gritted teeth. As Smriti shut the oven door, Evelyn wheeled herself closer and glanced curiously at Alex's phone screen. "You just complained that some-body did something to you. But all I see is an obituary."

Max leaned over and looked:

—BASILE WICKERSHAM GRIMSBY—

Beloved uncle, brother, colleague of many, Mr. Grimsby was a man of diverse talents: singer, cartographer, sea captain, marine biologist. He perished undersea after the malfunction of his submarine, while saving the lives of the two young American heirs to the Jules Verne fortune. Memorial service to be held Sunday, August 21, 11 a.m., at the Alfred P. Twombley Funeral Parlor, London.

"Basile is the guy who saved our lives," Alex said. "When the submarine ran out of fuel, we could have been sucked into a whirlpool. But he made us all swim to safety. Max and I barely survived. He didn't. He sacrificed himself for us."

"His last name was *Grimsby*?" Max said. "He never told us that."

"Check out the date," Alex said. "August 21! Two days from now. Did we know? No! No invitation, no nothing. What's up with that?"

"You could send flowers," Smriti offered.

"Are you allowed to Skype into a funeral?" Max asked.

"You could just go," Evelyn said. "I mean, what good

is owning a jet if you don't use it?"

"Ding ding ding ding!" Max's dad chimed, which he always did when he wanted attention. He popped into the kitchen and announced: "Mom is on her way!"

Max cast a quick, panicked glance at the oven clock— 6:44. "She can't," he said. "She's not supposed to be here till seven. The cupcakes won't be ready."

His dad shrugged. "Nothing we can do now. Her book club buddy just texted me. Guess their dinner ended early."

"They must have been discussing a lame book," Alex said.

Max opened his mouth to protest, but Alex, Dad, and Smriti were already rushing out of the kitchen. Evelyn rolled back toward the opposite side of the kitchen. "I'll join you guys in a minute. I think I need to take some meds."

But Max was focused on the stove. This sequence of events was all wrong. Mom was supposed to see the cupcakes when she opened the door. Smell them. That was the plan, and plans were supposed to work. Max was getting angry, which meant he smelled cat pee, and that wasn't too pleasant when it was mixed with chocolate.

"Max, are you OK?" asked Evelyn from behind him.

Give up the things you can't change, Max told himself,

which was something his therapist was always getting him to work on. *Breathe deep. Close your eyes.* "Fine," he said.

A few last-minute giggles erupted from the living room, followed by a flurry of *sssshhh*es. Max opened his eyes. He glanced toward the front of the house, then at the stove.

Before joining the others, he quickly flicked the oven temperature all the way up.

The living room lights were out. Everyone whispered nervously, hiding behind furniture. On the coffee table was a cookie-dough ice-cream cake with a sugar-photo of Mom, Dad, and Max. It was inscribed HAPPY BIRTHDAY, MICHELE! WE LOVE YOU!!! MAX, ALEX, & GEORGE. Streamers hung everywhere, along with collages of favorite family photos.

"I see them—quiet!"

At the urging of Max's dad, the room fell silent. Outside, a car engine grew louder, then stopped. Footsteps clomped up the front walk. A key was thrust into the lock, and the door slowly opened. Dad counted to three by holding up his fingers, then . . .

"Surprise!"

There was Mom, standing in the doorway with her book club friends behind her. A knit cap covered her short but growing hair. Her brown suede coat was still a bit too large, but Max could tell she was putting on weight. She just stood there for a long moment, framed by the door, her face pale in the porch light. Max expected her to burst out laughing.

Instead, she began to cry.

She wasn't supposed to cry. He'd only seen her cry once—on the day he found out she had cancer. That was one of the worst days of his life. He pushed his way through the living room, shoving aside the partygoers to reach her. *"Mom?"* he called out. *"Mom?"*

She swept him up in a hug. He felt his feet leave the ground. He hated both of these things normally but he sometimes made an exception with Mom, in small doses. "Thank you, sweetie!" she said.

"Are you sick again?" he asked.

Sometimes she gave him the LSS Look too, like now, but it never lasted long. Now she was crying and laughing at the same time. "I'm fine, Max. I'm crying because you and Dad make me so happy!"

Max nodded. As he touched his head to her shoulder, he caught the scent of something burning. "I smell smoke."

Alex and Smriti were hugging Mom now, catching Max in the middle like a big, uncomfortable sandwich.

Alex laughed. "Smoke? That's a new one. I know fish for fear, gasoline for embarrassment, ham for confusion . . . What does smoke mean?"

"It means I smell smoke."

Smriti's face fell. "So do I."

"Could it be the cupcakes?" Alex said. "You didn't touch the oven, did you, Max?"

"I had to," Max said. "I turned the temperature up to the highest, so the cupcakes would cook faster."

As the smoke detector's shrill beeping rang out, the guests fell silent.

"Max, you can't broil cupcakes!" Alex shouted, running back to the kitchen.

Max sprinted after her. The entire room was engulfed in black-gray smoke. As Alex yanked open the oven, a thicker cloud belched out. Coughing, she pulled out the cupcake tins with a potholder and threw them onto the counter. Smriti, Dad, and Mom were pushing the windows open as far as they could go.

Alex waved away the smoke. The cupcakes looked like little lumps of charcoal.

"I can scrape off the burned parts!" Max said, rummaging through the kitchen drawer.

He grabbed a kitchen knife and turned. But no one was looking at him or the cupcakes.

Evelyn was in the corner of the kitchen, exactly where he'd left her. But she was clutching her coat in her lap and staring at Max's mom with wide eyes. Her face was nearly white. "Ha—happy . . . birth—" she rasped. "Couldn't get . . . to the stove . . . sorry. Gotta go home . . ."

Max knelt beside her, taking her hand. "Evvie? What's up? Are you OK?"

"Fine," Evelyn said. "I . . . j—just need to get . . ."

She never finished the sentence. Her eyes rolled back into their sockets, and her head slumped onto the back of the wheelchair with a solid thump.

THE clock in the waiting room at Savile General Hospital showed 8:53 a.m. Seven whole minutes till morning visiting hour. Max paced in front of Alex and an elderly woman. He'd barely slept the night before. For about the twentieth time, he rearranged the flowers in a vase he'd brought for Evelyn.

"Are you OK?" Alex asked. "You look upset."

"I smell garlic," he announced.

The elderly woman looked up from a magazine. "I smell roses."

"He smells garlic when he feels guilty," explained Alex. She was sitting hunched over a coffee table, typing on a laptop. "Which he shouldn't, because he has no reason to."

"I see," said the woman, although her face said *I don't*.

"The smoke made Evelyn sick, Alex," he moaned. "From the burned cupcakes. So it's my fault."

Alex reached out and touched his hand. "Max, Evelyn has a serious condition. It's unpredictable. She spends a lot of time at the hospital, and it has nothing to do with smoke. Come on. Chill."

She patted the seat next to her and Max sat. He drummed his fingers on the chair's arm as Alex went back to her work. "I finally finished translating that last note Grandpa Julesy left," she said. "I'm checking it now. It's just as weird as all the others."

Next to the laptop was a note scribbled in French on a yellowed sheet of paper—the last message left by Jules Verne, which they had found at the bottom of the treasure.

They'd found a whole series of them, not long after Max's parents had left for his mom's cancer treatments at the Mayo Clinic. One message had led to another. Together they took Max and Alex on a journey that Verne himself had made, a wild submarine chase that he used as research for his famous novel *Twenty Thousand Leagues Under the Sea*.

As usual, this message was in his native French. Alex was fluent, but with all the post-adventure excitement, she'd only now had a chance to finish translating this one.

She turned her laptop toward Max.

THE LOST TREASURES

—PART FOUR—

. . . What follows from my adventure with Nemo is a wonder greatly surpassing the glitter of earthly wealth. For wealth, as we know, does not travel with the possessor after death.

As it happens, death itself was the subject of my further adventure. Namely, the reversal thereof. There exists in human biology a vexing problem: cells within the body so vigorous, so alive with growth, that they devour all around them and destroy the very body they occupy.

This condition goes by the name of the greedy beast visible in the night constellations, Cancer the Crab.

Who knew that my tragic voyages with Nemo would bring into my possession one specimen (among thousands collected) that would lead to a discovery too powerful to expose to the world in my lifetime. A cure to that disease which knows no mercy.

For this, reader, one cannot begin without *Isis hippuris*.

For years had I read fantastical accounts of the properties of *Isis hippuris*, a type of rare deep-sea coral also known as "sea fan." Rumors abounded about this substance—some said it would cause human cells to correct their own defects.

Or that diseases would be reversed. Or it must be ground into a powder and rubbed on the feet. Or digested by a weasel and then excreted. Or, if immersed in holy water, it could cause age itself to stop! Such rumors were powerful enough to send the great explorer Ponce de León on a failed search for the Fountain of Youth.

When a person of science hears the cries—*Magical powers! Instant healing!*—skepticism is in order. I thought it no more than an amusing tale, and I added it to my growing list of possible ideas for a novel.

On the day I was shot by my nephew Gaston, everything changed. My beloved physician decreed that I had three months to live!

I pause here to declare that the pain of the gunshot was excruciating. Yet I blamed not Gaston. For he had an illness of the mind, a malady eating his brain alive. I felt for his pain as well as mine. If only, I thought, there would be a cure for us both.

In my fevered state, I thought again of *Isis hippuris* . . .

And the idea of altering human cells . . .

My desperation got the better of my skepticism. If this claim were true, what boundless possibilities! This miracle substance might not only cure cancer but all maladies! I buried myself in research. Among much failed scientific speculation were the reports of the brilliant, neglected American scientist Kinsey Loren Steele, who claimed to have released the healing properties of

Isis hippuris by immersing it in a combination of waters derived from many remote and inaccessible parts of the world. The substance was destroyed in a laboratory fire, but after great sleuthing and greater expense, I recovered a carefully written list, documenting the locations of these waters.

I knew that replicating these results would require a great deal of travel. This, of course, necessitated funding.

And that, dear reader, is when I approached some English financiers at the Reform Club. It took many weeks for them to reach a decision. They had certain demands:

1. I must create a record of my account, solely for their use and not the public's.

2. I would have a time limit for the successful completion. After much discussion this was set at eighty days.

3. If I failed I would return the money.

Harsh, but arguably fair, thought I. Still, how could I—a writer of some renown!—not proclaim to the public about what promised to be such a dramatic journey? Yet how could I not agree to such a fantastical voyage?

Above all, this question: upon the (quite likely) failure of this endeavor, how would I survive the financial ruin?

My nephew concocted a solution: write two books! One would be a novel—with the locations and incidents wholly made up. Complete fiction. The other would be the true account for our financiers. Gaston pointed out that if our mission failed, and the money were returned, well then, the novel would sell enough copies to reimburse the author! With great pride, he volunteered to write the latter.

What guile and brilliance! The nephew who attempted my murder would be my helpmeet, my literary manservant! With great cheer I struck an agreement with the wealthy English gentlemen. I secretly set to work on my novel, inventing my character Phileas Fogg. His manservant Passepartout was modeled after Gaston himself. The book, *Around the World in 80 Days*, indeed succeeded beyond my dreams.

But enough of vanity! I see your impatience as you read this. Verne, you ask, was this voyage—the real voyage—a success?

Yes, I say.

And no.

The substance exists. But there is no longer any trace.

But do not lose hope, dear reader, for with my guidance you may find it. To do this, one must begin with the true account of our voyage, as written by loyal Gaston.

It remains under lock and key with the LeBretch Forum.

"LeBretch Forum?" Max said.

"That's what he wrote—letter for letter, not even translated," Alex replied. "I Googled it, and I found nothing. But I've read *Around the World in 80 Days*. It's amazing. The main guy, Phileas Fogg, is a little like you, super-OCD, efficient, smart, unflappable. He's at his club in London one day with his BFFs, smoking cigars and stroking beards and saying *Well, fuff fuff fuff, old fellow,* and they come up with this idea—"

Max giggled. "They said, 'fuff fuff fuff'?"

"They're English," Alex replied. "Anyway, Fogg brags he can travel around the world in eighty days. Which now seems like yeah-big-whoop, but back then? With no airplanes, no phones, no internet, maybe a few railroads? Unthinkable! So of course these guys are like *Ho ho, what a fool!* They bet him a crazy amount of money he can't do it, and Fogg's trusty sidekick, Passepartout, is like, *No, master, this is impossible!* But Fogg is cool as a witch's nose in Hades. He says yes to the bet, and off they go. But—cue sinister music!—they don't realize they're being followed. Seems there's this police chief who thinks Fogg is a bank robber, and he vows to track him to the ends of the Earth. Literally."

Max could barely sit still. "Wait. So Verne just made that story up to make money, while he actually went around the world looking for a secret formula to heal himself? If he found it, how come no one knows?"

"He didn't lie to us about the secret treasure," Alex said, scratching her head. "He had his reasons for hiding that. We can't know what his reasons are here. He could have used the healing formula on himself, Max. We know he didn't die from that gunshot wound." She shrugged. "There's only one way to find out."

"No," Max said.

"No, what?" Alex replied.

"No, we're not going off on a crazy chase again. We almost died the first time."

"We have a jet now, Max. And we have experience decoding Verne's messages. We can do this."

"Don't you have to go home to Quaflac?" Max asked. "And write a best-selling novel, and go to college?"

"It's *Quebec*," Alex said. "And yes, I do. But this could be world changing, Max."

"Then do it yourself."

In the opposite corner of the room, the old woman blurted out, "Oh dear! Oh my gracious!"

Max and Alex had been so deep into their conversation, they'd forgotten she was there. And now she'd heard every word of their conversation. "Don't pay attention to anything we said," Max told her. "It's fake news!"

"I overheard you saying *Jules Verne!*" she exclaimed. "I know you! You're the young people I saw on the evening news! I know this is . . . oh, I'm so embarrassed to ask . . . but may I have a selfie to show my granddaughter?"

As she fished in her purse for a phone, a nurse stepped into the waiting room and announced, "Ms. Lopez is ready to see you."

Max and Alex jumped out of their seats and followed. The nurse was a thin, smiling young man with a badge that read Arthur Ramos. "Does that happen to you a lot?" he asked. "The celebrity treatment?"

"Too many times," Alex replied.

Max spotted Evelyn's name in a frame outside a door at the end of the hallway. He raced ahead to the room and peeked in. Evelyn was sitting up in bed, an enormous, striped stuffed animal by her side.

She was smiling.

"Zebra?" Max asked.

Evelyn smiled and gave the animal a hug. "Quagga. It's extinct. I love extinct animals. One of the perks of having a mom who works for a conservation society." She picked up an iPad and showed Max a collection of images. "I've been adding to my Pinterest page on endangered species. If I die, Max, promise you'll never torment or kill an endangered animal or plant."

Alex rushed around Max to hug Evelyn. "You're not dying. You look so much better!"

"Thanks, I feel better," Evelyn replied. "Did you bring me a cupcake? I love the taste of charcoal."

"Was that sarcastic?" Max was very good at facts but not so good at sarcasm.

"Yes."

"But the promise about endangered species was not sarcastic?"

"No, that was serious."

"OK, I promise." Max cringed as Evelyn signaled him to come close. "Do we have to hug?"

"Don't worry. I just have to tell you something, that's all."

Max stepped forward and leaned down, turning his ear to Evelyn's mouth. When she spoke, he could feel her breath on his ear. This made him smell mint, and then gasoline—mint for excitement, gasoline for embarrassment that he was smelling mint.

"My dad helped me on the details of our experiment," she said softly.

"The new drone?" Max asked.

Evelyn shook her head. "The other one. Charles the flying robot."

"Uh-oh. Nerd break," Alex murmured to the nurse.

In robotics class, Max and Evelyn were called the Genius Twins, which Max never understood because they were neither geniuses nor twins. Evelyn had helped Max develop Vulturon. Charles was their new project, a hang-gliding robot.

"Dad checked our calculations about Charles's collapsible wings," Evelyn said. "We were right. It won't work. They're too heavy."

Max sighed. "Back to the drawing board."

"Not so fast." With a grin, Evelyn pulled a small duffel out of her backpack. "Voilà. This is for you. Happy belated your-mom's birthday!"

Max unzipped the duffel. Inside was a tangle of thin plastic sheeting and folding poles, tied tightly with a cord. "A tent?"

"It's the whole glider, Max—with harness too," Evelyn said. "Dad's company made a prototype, using our design. He said it was perfect. Ready to strap onto Charles the robot. If we ever finish making him."

"Wow . . ." Max lay the glider on the floor and unwrapped the cord. The wing fabric was attached to a lightweight skeleton of folded aluminum rods, which in turn was attached to a harness. As Max lifted it, one of the aluminum poles shot outward with a loud *sshhhhhickk*. The fabric went taut and a wing sprang into shape, its tip clanging against a metal cabinet. "Sorry!" he said.

Max stood and leaned over Evelyn's bed. "Thanks!" he said.

"You're . . ." She yawned. Her eyelids were heavy. "Welcome. Arrrgh, I get so tired. This sucks."

Nurse Ramos looked at his watch. "All right, you two, I'm afraid we need to leave."

"Go ahead, I promise I'll be OK," Evelyn said. "By the time you come back . . . from London . . ."

"London?"

"The funeral." Evelyn stared levelly at Max. "You are going, right?"

"I—I—" Max's breath caught in his throat. He looked nervously at Alex. "We haven't talked about it."

"Well, talk about it. It's important to remember people after they go. That's how they live on, inside you." Evelyn smiled. Her eyes fluttered and she nestled back into her pillow. "When you come back . . . we'll take those gliders . . . you and me . . . and we'll . . ."

Her voice drifted off as she fell asleep.

Nurse Ramos took Alex and Max both by the arm and quietly led them out of the room. Max's head felt light and spinny. Evelyn hadn't finished her sentence, but in his brain he imagined her voice saying the last word, over and over.

Fly.

As they walked down the hall, he stuffed the glider into his backpack and slung it over his shoulder. On the trek to the elevator, neither of them said a thing. But Max couldn't stop thinking about what was happening to Evelyn. And what she had said.

It's important to remember people after they go. That's how they live on, inside you.

"I'm scared," Max finally said, stopping in the hallway.

"Me too," answered Alex.

"When we started this project, she was walking," Max said. "Back then, when she had to be in a wheelchair, she turned it into something cool. Even though we were making the hang gliders for the robot, we really planned to test them ourselves."

"She's a fighter," Alex said.

Max nodded. "But now she's talking like she's dying. She never did that before. She's afraid we're not going to remember her. I want her to know she's important. I want to do something for her."

"There's a nice gift shop in the lobby."

"I was thinking about Basile's funeral. Evelyn wants us to go. She knows it's important to us. Even though she's so weak, she's thinking about *us*. So we should honor that."

Alex took his arm and started toward the elevator.

"I'll talk to your dad. Maybe he can get us a pilot."

"We had the jet painted," Max said. "It would be a shame not to show it off."

"Good point," Alex said. "And afterward you'll go back home—and I'll go off following the words of Jules Verne, all by myself."

"Are you being sarcastic?" Max said. "Because finding that secret potion thing is scientifically unlikely."

"And Evelyn's fate is scientifically certain." Alex sighed. "Sorry. That's harsh."

"But it's a fact," Max said softly.

"I'm not being sarcastic. About finding the formula. I want to do this. I don't see a downside, Max."

Max pushed the elevator button. "When we followed Jules Verne's last note, we were kidnapped, attacked by a killer squid, tied to a snowmobile and pushed into the sea, and marooned on an island in the Arctic Circle. That's the downside."

"But look what we got out of it!" Alex said.

"No, no, and no." As the elevator door opened, Max went in first. "Just the funeral. Not the search."

"Are you sure?"

"No," Max said. Because he preferred to tell the truth unless he was saying he fell off a trampoline.

Alex smiled. "Well, it's a start."

"**YOU** can't make this thing roll?" Max asked the hired pilot, whose name was Brandon. "Or do a loop? Or plunge?"

Max had expected the private plane to feel like a Starfighter, but it was closer to a giant, noisy tuna can. Which got really old when you were going all the way across the Atlantic.

Brandon glanced over his shoulder at Max and smiled. "Actually, I can do all of those things."

"But you won't," Alex piped up, gripping the pilot's arm. "Because you do not want to scare the person who hired you."

The reason she could grip his arm was because she was sitting in the copilot seat. This made no sense to

Max. For one thing, there was a perfectly nice seat next to him and behind Brandon. For another, Alex didn't know the first thing about copiloting.

So Max sat behind them all alone, in a navy blue suit that felt like a blanket of invisible mosquitoes. He and Alex had gotten lots of cash at the bank before leaving. He had a wad of Euros the size of a small animal in his pocket. All of which made it hard to concentrate on reading *Around the World in 80 Days*.

"Liking the book?" Alex asked.

"The best," Max said. "Fogg is awesome. So is the suspense. But when they're in India, they ride elephants. They shouldn't have been doing that. It's painful for the elephants."

"They're cheap to feed, though," Brandon said. "Wait for it . . . It only costs peanuts!"

He cracked up at his own joke.

"Will you tell him to stop talking?" Max grumbled. "He's not funny."

"Does he mean me?" Brandon said.

Alex's face turned red. As she touched Brandon the Pilot's arm, the plane jolted. Max's book slipped off his lap onto the floor and slid across the cabin.

Alex gasped and tightened her grip on Brandon's arm. "What's happening?"

"Just a little turbulence as we descend to our final destination," said Brandon.

"That's a *little*?" Alex asked.

"I'm smelling fish!" Max cried out.

"Excuse me?" Brandon said.

"He smells fish when he's afraid," Alex explained.

"What?"

"Synesthesia," Max said. "Where you associate smells with emotions. I was born with it. Like you were born with an abnormal body temperature."

Alex's face was turning red. "Max, don't go there—"

"I don't understand," Brandon said.

"Alex said we had to hire you because you were hot," Max said.

Alex groaned, shrinking into her seat. "Where's the Ejector button?"

"You said that?" Brandon asked.

"No!" Alex said. "I mean, yes. No!"

Brandon's eyes were focused ahead, but he couldn't hide a big smile. "Don't worry, we're coming out of that weather pattern pretty quickly, guys. It'll be clear sailing from here on in."

Max could swear he heard Alex say, "That's what you think." But he wasn't sure.

Outside the windshield, the clouds were breaking,

and Max could see an airport emerging in the distance. Brandon and Alex were silent the rest of the way.

A line of stretch limos waited just beyond the tarmac at Heathrow Airport. But only one was pink.

Alex paused as she emerged from the plane. "Don't tell me . . ."

"This was the only color on the drop-down list that wasn't boring black," Max said, starting down the ladder. "I call the copilot seat this time! Last one there is a rotten egg."

As he got close, a craggy-faced limo driver in a crisp gray uniform shook his head and pulled open the rear door. "No copilots, laddie. Driver in front, celebrities in back. Rules of the game."

Max veered to the left and got in. He expected Alex to be close behind, but she was still chatting with Brandon at the base of the ladder. He was fishing a business card out of his pocket.

"We're late!" Max called out.

Alex took the card, ran to the limo, and slid in next to Max. "Sorry. I needed to get his contact info for the return trip."

"You didn't kiss him," Max said, waggling his eyebrows.

Alex slammed the door shut. "Stop it. I thought you didn't understand sarcasm."

"It's not sarcasm," Max said. "It's teasing."

"And that's better?"

As the car sped toward the Heathrow exit, Max and Alex belted themselves in. "Not to put any pressure on," the driver called over his shoulder, "but according to my schedule, the event begins about now. Just sayin'. So when you're late, you won't blame old Gerrold, eh? Heh heh."

Max was firing up his GPS app, watching as it calculated the fastest route. "At this hour, we'll get there faster if we take the neighborhood streets."

Gerrold let out a big guffaw. "In a pink car? We will attract a lot of attention."

"We're used to it," Max said.

"Turn left now . . ." chirped the app.

The car exited the airport and shot out onto the left side of a London street. "You're driving on the wrong side of the road!" Max shouted.

"Here in England, driving on the left is right—ha! See what I did there?" Gerrold said.

The streets quickly became narrower. Brick buildings crowded either side, all jammed together. Through the car windows wafted some amazing smells, some sharp and some sweet. Alex breathed deeply. "Yummm."

"Coriander, masala sauce, curry," Gerrold said. "That is the hazard of these streets. They make you hungry!"

A pair of smiling kids ran after the car, asking for a ride. A sage, old woman paused during a very slow walk, eyeing the car and applauding. Shopkeepers came out of their front doors. People waved from windows. Gerrold waved back. "Ha! This limo is doing wonders for my popularity! Isn't this fun?"

But Max's eye was on his watch, which was clicking past 11:00. "The service has already started!"

"I'm a driver, not a miracle worker," Gerrold replied. "Hang on, we're very close."

"At the next corner, turn right," the app said.

Gerrold sped up to make a yellow light. A stocky brick building blocked the view to the right of the intersection. The tires squealed as they lurched through the light and veered right.

The intersection was empty. But just beyond it, a figure moved across the street, a phone pressed to his ear. Not walking exactly but *dancing*, his shoulders swaying, his feet tracing out a complicated little pattern. As if there were no traffic for miles.

"Blimey . . ." Gerrold said. *"Crazy old sod!"*

He slammed on the brakes. The car slid. Alex and Max lurched forward, screaming. The seatbelt pressed against Max's chest.

Max let out a scream, and the old guy spun around. His face loomed closer through the windshield, his eyes wide with shock.

Well, one of the eyes was wide.

The other drooped.

THE old man seemed to move in slow motion, leaping high like a ballet dancer. As the limo fishtailed, he floated above the roof, then landed on the sidewalk, just past the driver's side door.

"You nearly killed him!" Alex screamed.

"I didn't see him, ma'am!" Gerrold's eyes flickered up to the rearview mirror. "He's picking himself up like nothing happened. He's fine . . ."

The driver's knuckles were white as he navigated the turn and pulled up to the front of the Alfred P. Twombley Funeral Parlor.

As Max got out of the car, the building was vibrating. Or maybe that was Max. Alex quickly took his arm, and they headed toward the door on a rain-slickened brick sidewalk. From the front window, grim but curi-ous faces stared out at the pink limo. The low clouds and steady drizzle seemed to wash out all color, making the neighborhood seem black and white. At the front door, a sour-faced man said, "The Grimsby service, I assume. You'll find it in the large room to your left. And . . . my sincere condolences."

Max shook off the shock of their near accident. The front hallway smelled of mothballs, mildew, stale cigars, and old wood. People quietly and glumly milled about, but he felt the hair on the back of his neck prickle. "This feels weird," he whispered.

"It's a funeral, it should," Alex replied.

"More than that," Max said. "I keep thinking we'll see you-know-who here."

"Who?" Alex answered.

"The Evil Guy with the Skunk Hair and Missing Pinkie Who Must Not Be Named. I can't really think about Basile without thinking about his boss."

"Spencer Niemand is in a jail in Greenland, halfway around the world."

Max cringed at the sound of their kidnapper's name. "Don't say that again."

"What—Spencer Niemand?"

"Stop!"

In front of the room for the service was a huge portrait of Basile on an easel, his smile just as big and friendly as it was in real life. As they stared at it, a voice boomed out through the open doorway. A big-bellied man with a trim beard was standing in front of a closed coffin, addressing a room packed with people: "There was I, on the stage of La Scala opera house, before an adoring crowd, when I first heard the voice of dear, deeeear Basile—in the first row, eating popcorn and shouting, *'Louder, my good man! And funnier!'"*

A big laugh erupted through the dense shoulder-to-shoulder throng. There were massive men with wild, curly hair; women in sequined gowns who looked like they'd come through a time machine from the seventies; people with pink and purple hair and full-arm tattoos; at least three men dressed as women and two women dressed as men.

"Definitely Basile's kind of peeps," Alex said with a smile. "I love this."

"Let's invite them to *our* funerals," Max suggested.

It was so crowded, they could only take a few steps into the room. They stood near a girl about Max's age. Her face was beaded with sweat, her blonde hair pulled back with a headband. She wore a black dress that matched the one worn by a chic-looking red-haired woman standing next to her. With their broad faces, steel-blue eyes, and thick noses, they looked like thinner, female versions of Basile.

"Don't stare at people," Alex whispered.

"Sorry," Max said. "They look sort of lumpy like Basile, that's all."

The woman's eyes snapped up from a program, pinning Max with a sharp glare over a set of half glasses. As she pulled the girl closer to her side, people began turning toward Max and Alex. The silence gave way to murmuring voices:

"The Americans . . ."

"Found their way to the submarine . . ."

"Filthy rich . . ."

"If it weren't for them . . ."

Alex clutched his hand. Now she was sweating too.

"Ahem!" The speaker cleared his throat loudly, then boomed out over the crowd: "As I was saying! Dear old Basile was not afraid to speak his mind, but he was never less than kind and helpful. And under that gruff, tough exterior, he was a barrel of monkeys!"

A bearded man shouted, *"Hear, hear,"* and the crowd applauded.

"He was not!" Max muttered to Alex.

Alex took his arm. "That's an old-timey expression, meaning 'a lot of fun.'"

"But it makes no sense," Max shot back. "The monkeys would be angry and claustrophobic and maybe violent. They'd spit and scratch and scream."

"Max, chill!" Alex hissed. "These people here? They already don't like us. They're blaming us for Basile's death."

The blonde girl turned and smiled at Alex. "We don't blame you. We're really grateful you took the trouble to come." She stuck out her hand to Max. "Basile was my uncle. I'm Bitsy. And this is my mom. You're right, we do look like him, and we're proud of it."

Max shook Bitsy's hand, which felt like a cold octopus. "Why is your hand so wet?" he asked.

"Max!" Alex snapped.

Bitsy laughed. "That's OK. Honesty is refreshing. I suffer from a very bad fear of crowds. I hide it as best I can. But my sebaceous glands don't lie."

"Me too!" Max said. "And I know what sebaceous means. Sweat."

"Bitsy does very well managing her fear," said her mother. "I am Gloria Bentham, Basile's younger sister. From Kensington."

Alex smiled at them both. "I'm Alex, and this is Max. We're cousins. I'm from Canada. He's from Ohio."

"Darling girl, we *know* who you are," sniffed Gloria Bentham.

As the speaker rattled on, another laugh rippled through the crowd. Behind Max, more latecomers were filing in. The room seemed to be getting warmer, the air thick as porridge. "I smell sweaty feet," he muttered.

"Excuse me?" Bitsy said, looking downward at her shoes.

"Not yours. He smells sweaty feet when he feels smothered." Alex took Max by the hand. "Come on, cuz, let's get you some air."

"Oh, good Lord, what a sensible idea," Bitsy said. "I'll join you."

Gloria turned to her with a weary glance. "Darling Bitsy, the only way to confront your fears is to—"

Her voice faded into the din of the crowd as the three kids elbowed their way toward the back door. Max squeezed around a woman in a wheelchair, only to be blocked by a scrum of old couples in tweed coats and skirts. He was beginning to feel light-headed. *"Sweaty feet!"* he shouted. *"Sweaty feeeeet!"*

An elderly man stared at Max in confusion, until his wife pulled him away. "It's the fungus, my dear," she said. "Next time, use your powder."

Now Alex had Max's arm. His eyes were beginning to see swirls instead of people, but he did manage to spot Bitsy racing for the restroom. He took in deep breaths and stumbled over the lip of a thick carpet. His hand slipped out of Alex's and he tripped, bumping into the back of a thin, shabby-looking man.

"Max!" Alex shouted.

The man leaped aside with a graceful little spin. Max scrambled to his feet, to face two black-suited funeral directors heading briskly toward him. One of them veered toward the old man with a stern expression. "Pardon us, sir, are you a guest at the Grimsby service?"

"In a manner of speaking, yes." The old man's voice was hoarse and oddly high-pitched as he turned toward Max with an elaborate bow.

That was when Max noticed his face. And the droopy left eye.

"Y-Y-You're the guy in the street," Max stammered. "The dancer—"

"Who the heck are you?" Alex asked.

"Well, to you, I suppose I'd be Uncle Nigel!" the old man said, pulling a yellowed card out of his jacket pocket.

"I don't have an uncle Nigel," Max said.

"Fifth cousin twice removed, I believe, is the exact

relationship," the man said. "And how long are you planning to stay, my children?"

"Why do you ask?" Alex said.

"Just for the funeral," Max said, giving her a nervous look.

The two funeral directors gripped the old man's arms. "This way, old chap."

"As you wish." The man who called himself Nigel held out the card to Max. "But you may want to reconsider your plans."

6

FIRSYM'R KURS KUTOR
V-2 (WHY YES)
C+1

MAX sat on the front steps of the Alfred P. Twombley Funeral Parlor, the rain dripping off his brow and onto the old man's note. "What the heck does this mean?"

"I don't know, but give it a couple more minutes in the rain and it'll be a nice abstract watercolor," Alex said.

The door opened behind them and Bitsy emerged. "There you are! Here, I brought you some brollies."

"I'm not hungry," Max said.

"It's another word for *umbrellas*," Alex explained. She took one and handed another to Max, but he just laid it down on the stoop. "Maybe Bitsy knows what this means. It's a note the old guy gave us."

Bitsy opened Max's umbrella and handed it to him while looking over his shoulder. "Looks like some sort of maths equation. Is that his name—Kutor? Hungarian, perhaps? Polish? Czech?"

"It's gibberish, from a crazy person," Alex offered.

"He said he was our uncle," Max replied.

"If he said he was the Easter Bunny, would you believe him?" Alex asked.

Max scratched his head. "I don't know, this looks like a code. Was it a coincidence that we nearly ran him over and that he came to the funeral? Maybe he *is* related. Jules Verne was all about codes. Our family is cool that way."

"I do the *Times* crossword puzzle every Sunday!" Bitsy squealed. "Let's have a look. But not in the rain. Won't you join me for a quick spot of tea? There's a lovely place around the corner. Mummy won't even notice."

"There's a mummy in here?" Max said.

"That's what she calls her mom," Alex said.

"Honestly, it'll be refreshing to be away from her,"

Bitsy said. "Not to be disrespectful. She is wonderful, but I believe she missed the memo that I grew up." She let out a laugh and leaned in, her eyes dancing with curiosity.

"You sound like you're about forty years old," Max said.

"Max, that's rude!" Alex turned to Bitsy. "Don't mind my cousin. You'll get used to him."

"Oh, I love him already," Bitsy said. "Tell me, did you really find a note from Jules Verne and follow the voyage of the *Nautilus*? I want all the details. I adore Verne. My favorite book is *Twenty Thousand Leagues Under the Sea*! So very thrilling to find out that it was actually true!"

"How about *Around the World in 80 Days*?" Max asked. "Is it thrilling? I was supposed to read it on the plane, but I couldn't concentrate because Alex was flirting with the pilot."

"That's a lie!" Alex said.

"Why do you ask?" Bitsy lowered herself to the stoop. Her umbrella locked with Max's and Alex's, forming a kind of tent. "Have you found that *Around the World in 80 Days* is true too? Oh, I hope so. All those fabulous locales and adventures!"

"No!" Alex said.

"Yes," Max countered. "In a complicated way."

"Max . . . no . . . TMI . . ." Alex said through clenched teeth.

"You needn't worry about me," Bitsy said, crossing her heart. "I'm brilliant at keeping secrets."

"OK, technically it's not a true story," Max said, despite Alex's wild waving of her hands. "Which is a relief, because it includes elephant abuse. In reality, Jules Verne was being paid to follow a different path."

Bitsy's eyes widened. "By the toffs at that old men's club!"

"Yup, the Reform Club," Max replied. "Those guys wanted his real story exclusively, which was actually a search for some magical waters. So that's why there were two books. *Around the World in 80 Days* was the fictional one. The other trip was written in secret."

Alex smacked her forehead. "Well, it's not secret anymore. Hear that thump in the direction of France? That's your old great-great-great-granddad Jules turning in his grave."

"It doesn't matter," Max insisted. "The book doesn't exist anymore, because the place where it was hidden doesn't exist anymore."

"What place was that?" Bitsy asked.

"The LeBretch Forum," Max replied. "We Googled it—nada."

"Oh dear, I've lived here all my life and never heard of it." Bitsy pulled a pen and an envelope out of her purse. "I will make it my mission to do further research. How do you spell it?"

As Max spelled out the name, he watched Bitsy write LEBRETCH FORUM in perfect, neat capital letters on the back of the envelope. Jet lag was beginning to kick in, and the letters seemed to be dancing before his eyes.

Max loved letter games. And the first thing he noticed was that three of the letters spelled *the*. Which could be a coincidence, but it made him wonder about the other letters.

And something became instantly clear.

"Wait." Max sat up straight, snatching the envelope and pen from Bitsy's hand.

"Dude . . . manners?" Alex said.

"Please and thank you," Max replied, staring at the words. "Verne liked codes. Maybe there never was a LeBretch Forum. But I see a *the*, and *forum* is close to *form*, which is close to . . . wait . . . can you hold the umbrella over me?"

"Yes, milord," Bitsy said.

Steadying the envelope on the palm of his left hand, he began writing with the right:

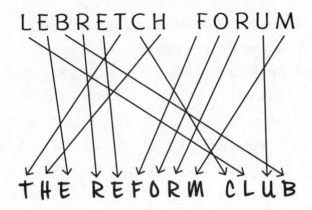

"Voilà!" Max said, then turned to Bitsy. "That's French for 'bingo.'"

Alex's eyes were wide. "Wow. Max, that is impressive. But does the place still exist?"

"Yes," Bitsy said. "I can take you there. I'm sixteen. I just got my permit. If we're quick, Mummy won't notice. Her Volvo is parked just up the street. She'll be hobnobbing at Uncle's service for a while."

"This is awesome!" Alex said. "I'm in."

"We came for a funeral," Max said. "Not another mission."

"Max," Alex said. "We talked about this."

"And I said no."

"You said maybe."

"I'll wait here. I'll talk to Basile's picture. You go to

the Reform Club and let me know what happens."

Even though people were wandering out of the service now, Max stood up from the stoop and headed back inside. Behind him he could hear Bitsy whisper, "Is he always this way?"

"He's stubborn," Alex replied. "When he thinks he's right, he's impossible."

He kept walking. But he was starting to smell ham. He smelled ham when he was confused.

As he entered the lobby of the funeral home, he caught sight of the photo of Basile on the easel again. His face was framed in a bushy beard, his eyes all crinkly as if he'd just told a joke. Max smiled. He didn't trust people easily, but there was something about Basile. When the submarine was stuck, Basile had taken him for a walk on the ocean floor in a pressurized suit. Max had learned the name of every specimen they'd seen. Basile had broken off exotic pieces of coral for Max. Including a very special yellow one that looked like a mass of fingers. *"Isis hippuris . . ."* Max murmured. "Sea fan."

As he got closer, he realized that Basile's eyes were staring straight back at him. He could have sworn they had been looking off to the left when he first saw the photo.

It had to be a trick of the light.

He felt his skin prickle. Really, it was more than his eyes. Basile's entire face was sharper, more vibrant. It radiated warmth, as if the pixels had been swapped out with real flesh, bone, and blood. It looked so alive, Max half expected Basile to burst from the easel with a big "Haw!"

People were swarming past either side of the photo now, leaving the service, talking solemnly, checking their phones. Max caught a quick glimpse of Gloria Bentham, still in the room where the service had taken place. A sour-looking man walked past him, complaining to a companion about how long the service had taken. None of them—not one—was talking about Basile.

"You were an explorer," Max whispered to the still, smiling portrait. "That's why you worked for Niemand. You called him Stinky. But you didn't want to make people slaves, like he did. You wanted to find new things. You wanted to do good and help people—even when you were sick." He paused, as if the photo would answer him back, which felt a little silly. "I'm not brave like you. Alex wants me to do this crazy thing. But I don't know . . ."

Max stood motionless, his eyes locked on the portrait's. In his mind, he heard Evelyn's words. *It's important to remember people after they go. That's how they live on, inside you.*

But he was hearing them spoken with Basile's voice.

Max turned. He pushed his way back out the door and began running as fast as he could after Bitsy's green Volvo, which was climbing a hill to his left.

"Wait for me!"

7

NOT knowing what exactly to say to a room full of cigar-smoking old men in red leather chairs surrounded by bookcases, Max opted for the first question that popped into his head. "Who farted?"

"Beg pardon?" said Howell, the tuxedo-clad man who had let them into the Reform Club. His eyes were wide with shock, his face tilted stiffly as if to balance strings of hair combed across his bald head like a musical staff.

An elderly man, who seemed to have melted into his seat, raised his sleepy head. His face was papery and mottled, and he cast a glassy-eyed look at Max. As if he'd saved up all his energy for this moment, he spat out a loud *"Ha!"* Then he sagged again, his eyes falling shut.

"Well, you excited Queasly with that remark," said a broad-shouldered man with a trim brown beard and tightly gelled hair. He stood from his seat and held out a hand to Max. "That counts for something. Afternoon. I am the club's vice chairman and chief archivist, W. Prescott Wooster."

"That's your first name, *W*?" Max asked.

Alex gave him a swift kick in the shins. "He's Max Tilt. I'm Alex Verne."

"And I'm Elizabeth Crowninshield Bentham," said Bitsy, holding out her hand. "But please call me Bitsy."

Walking toward them was an older man with a shock of silver-white hair that rose thickly on his head like a coconut muffin. "To what do we owe the pleasure of a visit by these American gold diggers?"

"Glimp, be a gentleman," said Wooster.

The other men in the room were coming to life now, murmuring to one another. Max couldn't hear the words but it sounded like "Humph humph . . . grabble grabble . . . fuff fuff fuff."

"You were right, Alex," he said. "They *do* say that!"

Glimp raised a monocle to his eye and stared at Max. "Whot whot?"

"May I interject?" said Bitsy. "My friends have come with a simple question. It seems they've found evidence of a manuscript lost to the ages but perhaps secreted right here at the Reform Club. It was left by none other than Jules Verne."

The men all fell silent. Max could feel their glares burning into his and Alex's faces.

"What she said," Alex squeaked.

"I assume you want to sell it, do you? One tidy fortune isn't enough?" hissed Glimp, stepping closer to Max. "What has the world come to? You, young man—I'd think you would be a bit young for this class of shenanigans."

As Max backed away, Wooster stepped between them. He pulled a gold-chained watch from his pocket and announced, "Gentlemen! I believe our customary glorious lunch is served in the Corinthian Room."

Grumbling, the men rose from their seats. Two of them flanked old Queasly's chair and began shouting into the old man's ear.

"Up and at 'em, young fellow!"

"Today's your dancing day!"

"Dolores . . ." Queasly muttered in his sleep. "Is that you, Dolores?"

As the two men laughed, Wooster turned away. "Come," he said over his shoulder.

He led Max, Alex, and Bitsy out of the drawing room

and into a smaller empty chamber. It smelled of cigars, its dark-green walls festooned with framed paintings of hunting scenes and basset hounds. The patterned carpet was thick but badly worn out, and at the center was a solid oak table surrounded by six chairs. "I apologize for the frosty reception," Wooster said. "We don't reveal our ages here, but I regret that some of these men behave as if they were alive during the nineteenth century, when your ancestor Jules Verne graced these old rooms. Some grudges die hard, I'm afraid."

"What grudges?" Alex asked.

"He made an agreement to write two books," Max added. "And he did it—didn't he?"

Wooster took a deep breath. "Very good. You've done your homework. One of those books was *Around the World in 80 Days*, to everyone's delight. But the other book—the actual account of his voyage—*that* was a bit of a problem. Verne did not do the writing himself, but assigned it to his nephew Gaston, who accompanied him."

"I could have told you that," Max said.

"This trickery may have been forgiven, all things considered," Wooster went on, "but as it happened, this Gaston provided not a book but a one-page list. He said the list contained hints to the secret findings of the voyage. However, upon opening it, the club was dismayed to see that it was utter gibberish! A secret code, Verne claimed. The club would need a cryptographer—not even for the book, mind you, but for a list of findings! The whole thing was a mockery. You can imagine the perplexity of the club officers. And here is where things went very wrong. Verne demanded a payment, otherwise he would withhold the key to this code. Only if the club solved it would he release the book. In other words, a ransom!"

"I would have given him the money," Max said.

"Indeed?" Wooster said. "Well, we are gentlemen, and gentlemen do not welsh on agreements. Nor do they extort money."

"Did anyone try to break the code, without the key?" Max asked.

"The members, at that point, had lost faith in Verne," Wooster said. "They did not believe his story. If Verne had succeeded in finding the so-called magical waters, why would he ask for this money? The club had agreed to share any profits, and a discovery of this magnitude would have made him rich beyond his wildest dreams! The club reasoned that Gaston, being a deranged fellow, may have filled the pages with doodles, blatherings, meat drippings—and Verne was too embarrassed to admit it. But most likely he had simply failed to find the mystical serum. After all, no one ever saw it! By asking for a payment he knew the club would not give, Verne would save face. No one would expose him as a failure. And he would never have to provide a key that did not exist."

"What if the club had called his bluff?" Alex asked. "What if they'd given him the money?"

Wooster shrugged. "If, if, if. We can never know *if*, can we? The club held on to this infernal list, in the hopes that Verne might relent. Surely if his voyage *was* successful, if he'd indeed found this miraculous cure, he would come clean. But this did not happen. The list was deemed worthless and forgotten. It eventually made its way into the archives. Of which I am the current keeper."

"Can we see it?" Max asked.

Wooster gave him a sharp look. For a moment he said nothing, as if searching for words. Then he reached into his pants pocket and pulled out a thick ring of keys. "If you insist."

They followed the man to the opposite end of the room, where he opened a padlock on a thick wooden door. A musty smell wafted out as he flicked on a light switch and then descended a stairwell. Max followed first, with Alex and Bitsy behind him. The rickety stairs creaked loudly, swaying side to side, as Wooster batted away cobwebs. At the bottom, he turned on another switch. Before them, lit by harsh fluorescent lights, was a low-ceilinged basement with tightly arranged rows of shelves. On the shelves were musty books, wooden and cardboard boxes, and bundled stacks of paper.

The lights let out a soft buzz as Wooster led them around the stairs and into an open area. In the center was a simple table that contained a thick, leather-bound book. Around it were several metal chairs, and against the wall was a set of dark wooden cabinets.

Wooster flipped open the book. "I apologize. We intend to digitize these records in the coming years, but it's been hard to drum up support among the members. They're used to the old system. It suits them."

Max, Alex, and Bitsy gathered around, looking over Wooster's shoulder. "About fifty years ago," he went on, thumbing quickly through the pages, "the archives surpassed the limits of this space. Papers were stacked floor to ceiling, a real fire hazard. It is rumored one of the members died down here and wasn't found for weeks. So the club undertook a cleanup. Anything deemed inferior quality was purged. The rest was organized precisely so every item could be easily found."

He lay the book open and pointed to an item on a long list.

RCQ Cleanup Records V1/2Q Row 34 Box 115

"That's Gaston's list?" Max asked.

"It is the record of how the archives are arranged," Wooster said, jogging away into the catacombs of the basement. "I shall be right back."

"This is *thrilling*!" Bitsy squealed. "May I join you? I love old catacombs."

"No harm in that!" Wooster said.

As she scooted away, Alex gave Max a look that was excited but also wary. "Do we trust her?" she whispered.

"I thought you did," Max said.

"She's a stranger," Alex said.

"Her mom is Basile's sister. We like Basile."

"But Basile worked for you-know-who. That puts the Benthams one degree of separation from him. I just don't like it. Let's keep our eyes and ears open, OK?"

Max shrugged. "Sure."

In a moment, Wooster and Bitsy returned. He was carrying a white box secured with a string, which he quickly untied. Inside was a stack of spiral notebooks. He fingered through and picked out one labeled *VOLUME 1, SECOND QUARTER* and set it on the table.

He opened it to the first page. Max's eyes went right to the handwriting on top:

The Reform Club
London
Organizational Report of Archival Consolidation
Roderick Chesterton Queasly, Scribe

"Queasly?" Max said. "Is that—?"

"The old fellow upstairs who appears to have become part of the furniture?" Wooster said. "Yes. In his time, he was a clever and useful fellow. He masterminded this entire project. This is a record of what happened to all the items during the cleanup."

Under the writing was a list in carefully written, tiny letters.

Misc. photos taken in clubhouse, 1897–99..........................Storage

Annual expense records, 1816–20...........................Row 17, Box 30

List of club menus, 1931–52.....................Taken by G. Schermerhorn

Notes on club history, 1916, Clive Stoughton.............Row 3, Box 9

Volume, bawdy poetry, Festus McFadden.......................Incinerated

Oil painting, Smythe family paddock, Devonshire....Sold at auction

"There's an index in the back." Wooster took the book, flipped to the end, and said, "Ah, here we go . . ."

He set the book down, open to a page in the middle.

Max didn't need to ask where the information about the manuscript was. His eyes went right to it.

Manuscript attributed to Gaston Verne.........................Incinerated

"My deep regrets, old chap," Wooster said. "Looks like your manuscript has gone up in smoke."

"WE'LL *flip a hook in the whale, and hoist it up o'er the rail!"* The men in the large room upstairs were singing loudly and out of tune, as Wooster led Alex, Max, and Bitsy up from the basement.

"Good Lord, lunch is served and the lads are in the parlor singing sea chanteys?" Wooster said with a laugh and a shake of his head.

Max was barely hearing any of it. As he followed the others up into the meeting room, all he could think about was Evelyn, slumped over. A moment ago, he had been full of hope, but now he smelled cat pee. Which always happened when he was really, really angry.

Behind him, Alex murmured, "Cheer up, Max. We can keep looking."

"Where?" Max asked. "Incinerated means burned."

They walked through the dark meeting room into the parlor, where three club members had gathered around Queasly. The old man was leaning forward over a glass table. The men were trying to lift him to his feet, but he was batting them away, his hands trembling as he reached for a pencil.

"What on earth are you chaps doing?" Wooster called out.

"Haw! The question is, what's Queasly doing?" one of the men bellowed. "We're just trying to get him to lunch so he doesn't wither away!"

But Queasly was now writing something on a napkin, his hands shaking. The men seemed to be finding this incredibly funny, shouting at the same time:

"Struck by inspiration, is he?"

"Writing a love poem to his dear, departed Dolores?"

"A novel, I think!"

"Good God, if that's the case we'll be here until we're all as old as he is!"

With a bemused smile, Wooster turned to Max, Alex, and Bitsy. "Well, you have a flavor of our jolly life here. All in good fun. So sorry we weren't able to get you what you need."

But Bitsy was heading straight into the parlor, her

brow tightly furrowed. "Oh honestly, you call yourselves gentlemen? Stop teasing that man like he's some sort of trained monkey!"

The men backed away uncomfortably. Queasly looked up at Bitsy, his gray eyes magnified by thick glasses. Lifting the note from the table, he held it out toward her. The men chimed in once more:

"He always had an eye for a pretty lass, the old dog!"

"A proposal of marriage, I'll wager!"

"Lucky girl!"

As they all burst out laughing again, Bitsy took the note from the old man. She gave it a quick look, then bowed slightly. "Thank you for this, Mr. Queasly. I am sorry you are not respected by these men who claim to be your friends. And thank *you*, Mr. Wooster, for your help."

It looked like Queasly was nodding, but it was hard to tell.

Max let out a deep exhalation as they exited to the sidewalk. The clouds were beginning to lift, revealing weak columns of light from the midday sun. As they trudged wearily to the corner, where the car was parked, Alex looked over her shoulder at the stately brick club building. "You were awesome, Bitsy," she murmured.

"What a curious place," Bitsy remarked. "They burn their important documents, and they are unpleasant to their elders. Do you suppose they would be that way if the club admitted women?"

"No way," Alex said.

"What's the note say?" Max asked.

"Nothing," Bitsy said, opening up the napkin. "Appears to be artwork. Like a child. That dear, dear old man. He can barely move his fingers."

"Is that supposed to be a portrait of you?" Alex asked.

"It looks like a scarecrow with indigestion," Max remarked.

"Lovely." Bitsy crumpled up the napkin and threw it into a trash basket on the street corner. "So then, I assume you'll be going back to the States?"

Max looked at Alex. His mood was crashing hard. He was surprised at how heartbroken he felt. As much of a long shot as it was, he felt like he was letting Evelyn down. "Yeah, I guess."

"If you don't need to leave in a hurry," Bitsy said, "won't you take lunch with Mummy and me? She is diabetic so she must eat soon."

"Max?" Alex said.

But Max was staring at the little note in the trash can. He couldn't get Queasly out of his mind. The guy was trying so hard. Why?

"Don't you think it's weird that we've been in London for one day, and two old guys randomly slipped us messages?" he asked.

Alex shrugged. "Weird is the new normal for our lives."

Bitsy's phone chimed, and she glanced down at the screen. "It's Mummy," she said. "Wondering where I went with the car. I can tell she's cross. Come. I insist you stay for lunch, or perhaps tea. Or both! If only to blunt the impact of Mummy's wrath."

Max slid into the back seat. Once again, Alex was in front. He stared out the window as the car wound its way through streets lined with neat brick buildings. Soon they'd be eating lunch and then boarding the plane back to the States.

Max took out his phone and sent a text to his dad and mom.

Max
london is cool how is evelyn doing?

In a moment his dad texted back:

Dad
Still in the hospital. Holding steady.

Max
what does steady mean? what do drs say?

Dad
Well. It's not good news, Max.

Max
i can take it.

Dad
They're giving her 11 to 12 weeks.

Max
to live???????

Max didn't wait for the answer. He snapped the phone off.

"What happened?" Alex asked, turning from the front seat.

"Evelyn is worse. The doctors say she only has eleven to twelve weeks to live," Max said.

"What?"

Max swallowed. He was smelling skunk and fish and cat pee and ham, and the sadness, fear, anger, and confusion felt like it was going to smother him, so he smelled sweaty feet too.

Eleven to twelve weeks.

Which was, more or less, eighty days.

MAX felt numb as Bitsy's car wound its way through the London streets. "Maybe it's a sign," he said.

"That it's eighty days?" Alex said gently, turning around. "I thought you believed in facts, Max. Not omens."

Max nodded. "Yeah."

"I mean, if we had a lead, somewhere to start, a reason to keep looking, we could stay," Alex pointed out. "But . . ."

Her voice trailed off, and Max looked through the car window. They passed a shabby older man sitting on a park bench. He was feeding a flock of pigeons with crumbs from a thick plastic bag marked ST. DUNSTAN

HOUSE OF WELCOME. For a moment Max thought it might be the old guy with the droopy eye, Nigel. But the clothes were much more threadbare, the face thinner and more rugged.

The thought of Nigel reminded him of the strange note. He fished it out and gave it another look.

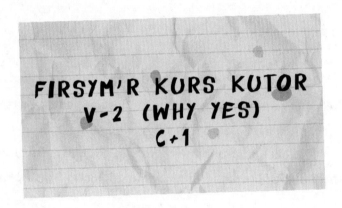

"That thing again?" Alex said, looking over her shoulder. "Max, it's just silliness."

"If it's a code, I want to solve it," Max said. "I thought you liked codes."

"You just had some sad news," Bitsy reminded Alex. "This could take your mind off it."

"Yeah, guess so." Alex sighed and unbuckled her

belt. She swung her leg into the space between the front seats, and then squeezed into the back next to Max and glanced at the message for a few moments. "Well, there's an apostrophe followed by an *R*. Lots of words end in apostrophe-*s*, like 'That's cool.' So maybe we should substitute *S* for *R*."

Max nodded. "*S* is one letter after *R* in the alphabet. That's got to be it. We substitute the next letter over, for all of them!"

"So how would you solve *Z*?" Alex asked.

"There is no *Z* in the message," Max said. "But if there was, it would become an *A*. You'd go to the beginning."

He carefully wrote out the top line with all the substituted letters:

GJSTZN'S LVST LVUPS

"That's even worse," Alex groaned.

"You know, words end in apostrophe-*t* also," Bitsy piped up, "like 'I can't stand asparagus.' Also apostrophe-*d*—'Where'd you get that coat?'"

"OK . . . if apostrophe-*R* becomes apostrophe-*T*, that's two letters over," Max said, counting in his head, "and if it becomes apostrophe-*D*, that's . . . fourteen letters back."

He tried it both ways:

go over 2 letters for each—
HKTUAO'T MWTU MWVQT

go back 14 letters for each—
RUDEKY'D WGDE WGFAD

"Like I thought," Alex said. "The guy is a nut job."

But Max was staring at the rest of the message. "There's stuff below the letters. It says 'V minus 2 (why yes),' then 'C plus 1.'"

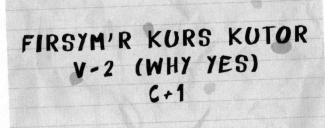

"Plus and minus . . ." Alex said. "That sounds like what we've just been doing. But it turned out wrong."

"So maybe you substitute only the Vs and Cs?" Bitsy guessed. "Backward two with each V and forward one with each C?"

"Look at that top line," Max said. "It has no V or C in it. I'm thinking V and C might stand for something."

"'Very' and 'Crazy,'" Alex replied.

"Or something to do with words?" Bitsy said. "V could mean 'Verb.' And C . . . um . . ."

"'Cadjectives?'" Alex said.

Max shook his head. "Or letters. V could be 'Vowels,' C 'Consonants.'"

"So . . . V *minus two* would mean 'go two vowels back in the alphabet,'" Alex said.

"It says 'why yes'!" Max blurted. "That's another clue. Get it?"

"Actually, no."

"It's not 'why'—it's the letter Y!" Max said. "Y can be considered a vowel or a consonant. So *why, yes* means 'yes, Y is a vowel'!"

"Brilliant!" Bitsy exclaimed, braking hard for a red light.

"We need to stay alive for this," Alex said.

"OK, so *V* minus two . . . take each vowel and go two vowels to the left," Max said softly. "And we have *AEIOUY* to work with. So, like, *O* would be *E* . . ."

"And *C* plus one means for each consonant we go forward one," Alex said. "*Ucchhh!* I think we need to write out a substitution key."

She quickly wrote out what each letter would be:

vowels:
a e i o u y =
u y a e i o

consonants:
b c d f g h j k l m n p q r s t v w x z =
c d f g h j k l m n p q r s t v w x z b

Carefully Max substituted each letter in Nigel's note:

FIRSYM'R KURS KUTOR

GASTON'S LIST LIVES

Alex let out a scream.

Bitsy slammed on the brakes, nearly colliding with a parked car. "Good God, what is it?"

Max could barely sit. He was bouncing on the seat. "The list—the one they burned—it exists!"

"Really?" Bitsy turned. "We have to find that fellow then—Nigel."

"No," Max said, a thought churning up in his head. "Not yet. We have to get back to the Reform Club."

"What?" Alex said.

"Just drive!" Max commanded. *"Now!"*

Bitsy's car squealed to a stop in front of the club, causing a poodle on a leash to nearly leap a foot in the air.

"Sorry," Max said as he pushed open the car door.

He ran to the trash can and reached in, as the poodle sped off down the block with its owner close behind.

"Dear boy, will you explain yourself?" Bitsy asked.

Max pulled out a fistful of papers, orange rinds, and candy wrappers. Shaking loose the debris, he held up a wilted, stained napkin. "The note Queasly gave us."

"Ew, Max," Alex said. "Just ew."

"Think about the facts," Max said, pacing. "Fact: this guy Nigel knew we were going to be at the funeral. He's related to us—well, OK, we don't know if that's a fact. Anyway, somehow he has this information about Gaston's book—"

"So maybe Gaston is his ancestor," Alex said, "the

way Jules Verne is ours!"

Max nodded. "That's what I'm thinking. So fact: he gives us the note, but we don't know what it means. Another fact: we go to the actual place where Jules Verne made the deal to produce two books, his novel and Gaston's nonfiction book about the secret, real cure. To keep that book secure, the two Vernes keep it away from the club but tease them with a list—which has info about the ingredients for this formula. Fact: because no one can read it, the club guys get angry and throw it into their files—and years later, old Queasly burns it. But wait— the note from Nigel says the list still exists. Which means someone rescued it . . ." Max grinned. "And there's only one person that someone could be."

If Max had had popcorn, Alex's and Bitsy's open mouths would have been perfect targets.

"Queasly . . ." Bitsy said.

"Right," Alex said. "He knew we were curious about Verne. He saw us go to the basement with Wooster. And he saw us coming back up all disappointed. So he must have figured that Wooster told us about the incineration."

"And he got all agitated," Bitsy said. "But not because I was so incredibly beautiful. Because he had something to tell us!"

"Bingo," Max said, holding up the napkin. "So he wrote this note."

"Bingo," Bitsy said with a nod.

"That's Alex's word," Max said. "Meaning 'voilà.'"

They gathered around to look at the note.

"Everything you said makes sense," Bitsy said. "But I don't understand what this mess could possibly mean."

"It's got to mean something," Max said. "Maybe . . . 'the Gaston manuscript is hidden inside a scarecrow'?"

"He's old," Alex said. "Like, *old* old. You saw the way his hands shook. Maybe this isn't a drawing. Maybe he was trying to write something. . . ."

She turned the napkin sideways and then upside down.

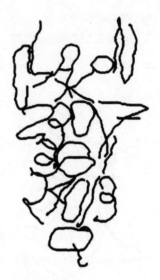

"Wait," Max said. "That looks like letters and numbers."

"He needs to take handwriting lessons from Uncle Nigel," Bitsy said.

"I'm thinking that top line is a word," Max offered. "The swoop looked like a C, then an $L\ldots A\ldots$"

"Looks like an X tucked underneath, then an $O\ldots N\ldots$" Alex said.

"Claxon?" Bitsy piped up. "That's the name of a street."

"And those squiggles underneath it," Alex said. "They look like numbers—two, three, nine, seven. And a group in the middle—three, six, one."

"And then way at the bottom, two, four, zero, one, three," Max added.

Alex smiled. "He signed it at the bottom, with the letter Q. That's cute."

"I'm no Sherlock Holmes, but I would say the address is either 361 or 2397 or 24013 Claxon . . ." Bitsy said, shaking her head. "But no one in the Reform Club would be caught dead in the neighborhood of Claxon Street. Mummy would kill me if she knew I even thought of going there."

But Max was already checking his GPS. "The address 2397 Claxon is the only one that exists, and it's a little over a mile away," he said. "I can walk."

Bitsy grabbed his arm. "I will not be responsible for your early demise. Let me text Mummy we'll be late."

As she took out her phone, Alex ran to the car and slipped into the front passenger seat. That meant Max had to ride in back, but this time he didn't mind. *"Woo-hoo!"* he screamed, punching his fist into the air.

"Mummy, it's very important," Bitsy was saying softly into the phone. "I know you prefer voice to text, so I thought I'd . . . yes, it has to do with an important matter . . . I will tell you later . . . I think you will be pleased . . ."

Max stuck the napkin into his pocket. But as he ran around the back of the Volvo, he stopped short.

The sun, struggling to appear among the clouds, cast a weak beam of light against an ornament on the trunk of the car. Its gold-and-black logo glinted dully at him.

It was a sleekly designed NE.

Niemand Enterprises.

MAX had worked hard his whole life to express himself in words, but expressing himself in grunts and eye rolls and whistles and shoulder taps was much harder.

"Max, what are you trying to tell me?" Alex said, turning from the front seat to look at him.

He angled his body, darting his eyes toward the trunk. All he could think about were Alex's words: *Basile worked for you-know-who. That puts the Benthams one degree of separation from him. . . . Let's keep our eyes and ears open. . . .*

All he needed was his eyes. The last time Max had seen the Niemand Enterprises symbol was on the side of a submarine—right before Niemand had kidnapped them.

Alex had been right not to trust Bitsy. "Hmmm . . ." he mumbled. "N . . . E . . ."

"Any what?"

"Hmm hmmm . . . logo . . . *logo* . . . *trunk* . . ."

"What's he saying?" Bitsy asked.

"Nnnnn . . . eeeeeee!" Max said.

"Please excuse my cousin," Alex said. "He has unique ways of showing his excitement."

This was hopeless. Max turned to Bitsy and blurted, *"Where are you taking us?"*

"You already know where I'm taking you," Bitsy said with a confused laugh, as she squinted through the windshield. "To 2397 Claxon. And we're almost there. . . ."

The car was slowing down as Bitsy swerved around potholes. On either side of the street, boarded-up buildings alternated with rubble-strewn lots like broken teeth. A rat peeked over a toppled brick, grabbing a tossed-off chunk of pizza on the other side. On the next block was a long parking lot ringed by a razor-wire fence. Just beyond it stood a stout brown-brick building with faded white letters on the wall: PRESTIGE STORAGE.

"That's the place," Bitsy announced.

"A storage facility . . ." Alex said. "OK, this is making sense. I'm figuring the club told Queasly to burn the list, but he didn't want to. He knew that the men were just acting out of anger. It was crazy to just destroy it. So he reported it 'incinerated' to the archives. But he really snuck it away to this place. Does that sound right?"

"Spot on," Bitsy said.

"And storage lockers have locks." Alex was looking at Queasly's note again. "If the numbers in the middle are the street address, then these other numbers, at the bottom of Queasly's message? Maybe they're a combination!"

"Lo . . . go . . ." Max squeaked, pointing toward the back of the car.

As Bitsy drove up to the gate, an imposing sign stared back at them, reading Admission Only to ID Holders with Appointment.

"We don't have an appointment," Alex said. "Or an ID."

"We'll just have to convince them to let us in." Bitsy waved her fingers to a guard who approached them from a side door.

"Us!" Max blurted, pointing to himself and then Alex. "Us! *This* us!"

"Pardon?" Bitsy said.

"Alex and me us!" Max said. "Just Alex and me. Alone."

Alex looked at him oddly. "Max, what has gotten into—?"

"Because . . . Bitsy has to go back to her mummy!" Max said. "She's really angry!"

Bitsy sighed. "Well, you know, he does have a point."

The guard was a short, heavy man with thinning hair and a nose that twisted and turned like a ski slope. As he lumbered toward them, Bitsy rolled down the window. "We're looking for the security guard."

"That would be meself," the man growled, pointing to a badge on his chest that read PRESTIGE STORAGE SECURITY: GUS. "Do you have your ID?"

"Oh, I'm sorry, Mr. Gus," Bitsy said with a laugh. "I saw you, and I just assumed a modeling agency worked here."

The guy's face contorted into a pained expression that Max realized was his smile. "Aw, well, heh heh, people do say that sometimes," Gus said. "Me mum does anyway."

"Would you be a love and let us in?" Bitsy said. "Sadly, sweet Grandmama has left us, and it will be such a comfort to retrieve her effects for the memorial service."

"*Sweet Grandmam—?*" Max blurted, but Alex put her hand over his mouth.

"Of course, lass, so sorry," Gus said, as he inserted a key into a metal box.

The gate slid open and Bitsy quickly drove through. She pulled up to a door at the side of the building marked

Entrance and said, "Will you text me when you're finished? I'm ever so eager to learn what happens!"

Max nodded. He thought his heart was going to bust right out of his chest.

He and Alex left the car and walked into the building. Just inside the door was a grimy-windowed office, where a white-shirted woman gave them a bored wave. "Max Tilt, what was that all about?" Alex demanded as they walked down a hallway. "Bitsy has been helping us, and you're acting like a goon!"

"Did you see the back of her car?" Max rasped, trying not to shout.

"Why would I look at the back of her car?"

"Well, I did. There's a Niemand Enterprises logo on the trunk! She's working for . . . *him.* He who must not be named! Even though I just did."

Alex stopped. "Wait. *What?* Really?"

"I should have known this would happen," Max said, pacing the corridor. "I don't know why I opened my big mouth. I shouldn't have trusted her. Or her mother. They make me nervous. 'The *Times* crossword puzzle' . . . 'a quick spot of tea' . . . 'Mummy' . . . 'old toffs' . . . they both sound like they're in a movie."

"They're English! They think we talk funny too." Alex pulled him toward the elevator. "Now are we going to figure out what to do next or just wander around this place arguing?"

Max gulped, looking at a directory above the elevator buttons.

FLOOR 1: 100–199A
FLOOR 2: 200–299A
FLOOR 3: 300–399B
FLOOR 4: 400–498

"There are two numbers left from this note—24013 and 361," Max said. "I'm guessing 361 is the locker number."

Alex pressed 3. "OK, Max, let's be like Max. Think this through. Why would Gloria Bentham have a Niemand Enterprises car?"

"She is Basile's sister," Max said. "Basile worked for you-know-who. It's a degree of separation! That's what you called it. So maybe Basile got her involved in the company."

"Or vice versa. Gloria might have gotten the job first, then gotten Basile involved. It doesn't always start with the guy."

Max nodded. "Plus, she's old and smart and well-dressed and all. So she probably had an important job.

Like vice president or something."

Alex groaned. "This may be worse than we thought."

"How?"

"Think about it. After Stinky is thrown in jail, the other officers of the company move up in rank. So there's a chance Gloria Bentham is now . . ."

Her words hung in the air, and Max nodded. "The boss," he said softly.

"If Niemand Enterprises was so eager to find the treasure," Alex said, "they're going to be all over this. And we're giving it to them."

"That's what I was trying to tell you!" Max said.

As the elevator opened to the third floor, they walked quickly down a cement floor. Their footsteps echoed hollowly against the walls of floor-to-ceiling lockers, until they stopped at number 361. A thick combination lock hung from the handle. "We get this thing and we leave," Alex said.

"Right to the plane," Max agreed. "And Brendan."

"Brandon," Alex said.

Max pulled out the note from Queasly, checked the numbers, and carefully spun 2, 4, 0, 1, 3. "Cross your fingers," he said.

With a deep breath, he yanked downward, but the lock didn't budge. "Wait. Maybe the numbers are supposed to be grouped. Like 24, 0, 13."

He tried 24, 0, 13. And 2, 40, 13. And every single other combination of the digits, until finally he threw up his hands. "What are we doing wrong?"

"It's old," Alex said. "It needs oil."

"Did you bring any?" Max asked.

"No, but I brought this." Alex stepped back, let out a roar, and gave the lock a sharp kick.

The clang echoed down the hallway. *"Yeeeeeow!"* Alex screamed, hopping away and holding her leg.

From inside the locker came a dull thump. The lock swung left and right. Max cupped it in his hand, and it fell open with a soft *click*. "That," he said, "was awesome."

"They . . . teach . . . martial arts . . . in Canada too. . . ." Alex said through a grimace.

The door let out an angry squeal as Max pulled against cranky, rusted hinges. He planted his feet and gave it a solid yank. With a deep *GRO-O-O-CK*, the door opened. Out of the shadows inside, a massive, jagged shape hurtled toward him. It had a face and wide, glassy eyes.

11

MAX leaped backward, hitting his head against a solid metal locker. Alex screamed. He scrambled to his feet and ran. When he got to the end of the hallway, he stopped.

Alex's scream had turned into raucous cackling. *"What's so funny?"* he cried out.

"I'm sorry!" Alex was squatting on the floor, holding her stomach and laughing so hard she was almost crying. Next to her, cocked at a strange angle, was the head of a reindeer with broken antlers. "I must have kicked the locker pretty hard. Looks like I shook loose Blitzen here."

Max dusted himself off and walked back to the locker. Already a bump was growing on the back of his head. Ignoring Alex and the reindeer, he peered inside the locker.

Against the back wall, piled at least two deep, were tightly packed wooden file cabinets topped by stacks of white cardboard boxes marked REFORM CLUB. On top of those boxes were dusty old relics that looked like they'd been thrown in at the last minute—lamps, books, a bicycle wheel, several rusted spray cans, a fake beard, a basket of plastic fruit, a stack of old hats, and a solid black metal box.

A space remained, about the size of a mounted, stuffed reindeer head. Max did not have the urge to put it back.

"We'll never find it in all this junk," Alex said.

But Max's eye was on the black box. It had a combo lock on it too. "Maybe we won't have to look that far," he said.

"Oh, sweet, another combo," Alex said.

"Well, there's one more thing in Queasly's message," Max said, reaching into his pocket.

Alex stepped into the cramped space. She watched as Max unfolded the note. "The letter Q," he said. "Where he signed it. Or started to."

Alex nodded. "Those guys were being so mean to

him. He was trying so hard. He didn't have a chance to finish."

Max eyed the combo lock. Around the circumference, instead of numbers, were the twenty-six letters of the alphabet. He spun the dial, and then settled on the letter *Q* and pulled. "Ognib," he said.

"What?"

"That's *bingo* backward. *Bingo* would mean, 'Yay, it works!' *Ognib* means the opposite. 'Boo, it doesn't work.' Want to give the box a kick?"

Alex thought a moment. "Maybe I don't have to. Why would he be signing his name, Max? Just for grins? *Queasly* has seven letters. What if we try them?" She took the lock from Max and spun out *Q*, *U*, *E*, *A*, *S*, *L*, and *Y*.

With a solid click, the lock fell open. "Sometimes," she said, "it's easy."

Max held his breath as Alex pulled out a manila envelope. In it were a few sheets of paper, held together with a rusted, old paper clip. The sheet on top fell to the floor.

Alex and Max both stooped to get it, but Max got to it first. He brought it out to the bright light of the hallway, where they both sank to the floor to read it, their backs against the lockers.

The Reform Club
London

To Whom It May Concern,
I write this with the full knowledge that it may
only be read after I have shuffled off this mortal coil.

"Queasly danced on coils?" Max said.
"*Shuffled off this mortal coil* means 'died,'" Alex replied.
"He thought no one would read this until he died."

I certify here that as club archivist, I have always
discharged my duties loyally and without question.
But I fear I have been forced to take action against a
sea of ignorance.
For more than a century, the club has possessed an
extraordinary work, left to us as part of an agree-
ment with one Jules Verne—a list that summarized
the account of a secret voyage, written in English,
the fruits of which were to be shared by the club
and Verne. Verne assigned the task to his nephew,
Gaston.
It has been said that Verne held back the trans-
lation of this list, and by extension the release of the

entire book, until an extortion payment was received. If true, this would have been a dastardly deed!

But, dear reader, it was not true. My grandfather, Septus Queasly, was a club vice president who kept the facts about this incident to himself. He knew Verne to be a fair, scrupulous man. No, in fact, it was our hallowed Reform Club that sought to cheat Verne of his payment! Half was promised before he left, and it was indeed paid. The other half, however, was promised upon delivery.

Verne was merely seeking what was due to him.

While Verne was on his voyage, it seems, the men had other ideas about the promised money. Rather than being held for Mr. Verne, every last farthing was spent on cigars, venison, parties! What to do upon Verne's return? A plot was concocted. Verne was informed that the club would need to read the manuscript first. They would pay him only if "its findings could be successfully replicated"—in other words, only if he or someone else could perform the search successfully again.

Verne was aghast! Insulted! He knew the club meant to avoid paying him. So he turned the tables.

He held on to Gaston's work and instructed Gaston to produce a brief list—merely the basics—in code. Only if the club paid him—as agreed!—would Verne reveal how to read the text. In angry response, the club consigned the list to the chaos of its basement.

Whereupon I enter the story. Years later, upon the purge of documents, I was tasked with the destruction of this precious but cryptic work.

I could not do it. I have served the inebriated toffs of this organization with loyalty for my entire life, and they reward me with scorn and condescension. If they cannot comprehend the value of this list, it is up to me to preserve it.

The key to the reading of this has been lost to the ages. It was said that only one copy of this cipher existed. It was in the possession of Verne's nephew, Gaston Verne, who alas descended into a terrible dementia. Rumor has it Gaston's son inherited his possessions, which allows for the possibility that it still exists, passed down through the generations.

And the possibility that you, dear reader, will be the one to discover its secrets.

"Is this for real?" Alex said.

Max let the letter fall to the floor, reached into the box, and pulled out two sheets of paper, clipped together. They stared at the top one.

ZOUMF SGO SQAO IBBYAMS YD I
LUQIBAKYAR VYQKC TYEIFO
ZE YMO HAKOR TOQMO

"It's gibberish," Alex said.

"It's code," Max said. "If we can figure it out, we'll know everything about Jules Verne's search."

"Any ideas how to get a code key that went missing generations ago?" Alex pointed out.

Max smiled. "Well, according to Queasly, we would have to find Gaston's son's son's son. Or son's daughter's daughter's daughter. Or son's daughter's son's daughter. Actually, there are five more permutations—"

"Yes, and . . . ?" Alex said impatiently.

"And . . ." Max smiled. "One of those permutations might be the dancing guy with the droopy eye."

He took Nigel's note from his pocket and spread it out on the top of the cabinet.

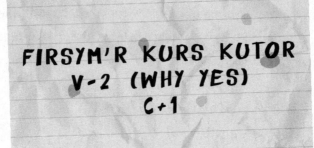

"OK, that key decoded *his* message," Alex said. "How do you know it's going to decode this one?"

"I don't," Max said, fishing in his pocket again. "But let's give it a try. We'll need that little cheat sheet we made."

He pulled out one last piece of paper.

vowels:

a e i o u y =
u y a e i o

consonants:

b c d f g h j k l m n p q r s t v w x z =
c d f g h j k l m n p q r s t v w x z b

Alex's phone beeped, but she silenced it and stared at the two notes and the manuscript page.

"Here's what I'm thinking," Max said. "Say I'm Nigel, OK? I'm descended from this guy Gaston. My family has inherited the code key, so it's been around now for generations."

"If no one threw it out," Alex pointed out.

"Exactly," Max said. "So way back, Gaston's kids or grandkids are like, dudes, we can decode this secret message—only they don't say *dudes*, maybe more like *old chums*. They figure the feud with Verne is over, so they go back to the club. But the club guys get all fuff fuff-y and say 'You can't have it!' When the family keeps trying, the club says leave us alone, we burned it! The family goes bonkers. But somebody learns the truth—maybe Queasly drops a hint, whatever—that the list exists, somewhere unknown. Boom, cut to the present. I, Nigel, hear that two kids found one of Jules Verne's big secrets. I also hear about Basile's funeral and I figure the kids will show up—which they do! These kids are so smart, maybe they'll find the book. So I give them the code key—"

"And write a note using that code," Alex continued. "A note that says 'Gaston's list lives.' So number one, the kids will know the truth. Number two, in order to learn it, they will have cracked the code. And number three, cracking the code will make them ready to decode this list! That's brilliant! Go for it, Max. Substitute those letters!"

Max took a pen from his pocket. "Each vowel shifts two vowels earlier, each consonant one consonant ahead . . ." Looking at the key, he replaced each letter, one by one:

~~ZOUMF SGO SQAO IBBYAMS YD I~~
BEING THE TRUE ACCOUNT OF A

~~LUQIBAKYAR VYQKC TYEIFO~~
MIRACULOUS WORLD VOYAGE

~~ZE YMO HAKOR TOQMO~~
BY ONE JULES VERNE

"WOO-HOO!" Alex grabbed the two sheets and began dancing. "Do you realize what this means?"

"Whoa . . ." Max said softly. "We might be able to save Evelyn."

"It's in English!" Alex screamed. "I don't have to translate!"

"OK, keep going . . ." Max said. "Next page."

Alex pulled it out, and they both stared.

Hkcta nbk Hgyci Yozzgncut ul Krnxguxjctgxcfs Iuzvfcignkj Kpktny, Fkgjcta nu nbk Jcyiupkxs ul g Yohyngtik ul Otyvkgeghfk Xkpufoncutgxs Czvuxngtik nu nbk Bozgt Xgik

Yohzcnnkj hs Agynut nbk Zgatclciktn

Hkact qcnb Cycy bcvvoxcy, ghupk gff gtj qcnbuon qbcib tunbcta igt bgvvkt.

Gjj nbk ygfohxcuoy gtj igngfsncigffs zgxpkfuoy kllkiny ovut nbcy yohyngtik, jkxcpkj lxuz nbk luffuqcta qgnkx yuoxiky:

* Vxkykxpkj qcnb nbk nctinoxk ul iucf joyn lxuz nbk Eumbcz Xcpkx

* Krnxginkj lxuz nbk xkj iugn ul nbk gticktn qkn xcpkx buxyk lxuz nbk yuoxik ul nbk Xcpkx Ynsr

* Ngekt lxuz g aufl hgff y iktnkx ct nbk lgn zuotngcty ul Zkrciu

* Jkxcpkj lxuz nbk hfgie yzkgx ul knkxtcns lxuz Gxzgtju ul Egnbzgtjo

* Xkyiokj lxuz g bun igpk ct nbk quxfjy iufjkyn fgtj zgyy

"Yuck," Max said.

"It's really long," Alex agreed. "We'll be here till next month."

"But you translated Verne's messages pretty fast."

"Yeah, but those were word by word, not letter by letter!"

Max shrugged. "I'll try some. I'm dying of curiosity."

Quickly he began substituting in the first line:

*Hkcta nbk Hgyci Yozzgncut ul Krnxguxjctgxcfs
Iuzvfcignkj Kpktny, Fkgjcta . . .*
Jldvu pcl Jhoda Oebbhpdiv . . .

"What the—?" He paused in midsentence and checked his work.

"Well, that's a big help," Alex said.

"This is a different code than Nigel's note."

"Oh, great. They changed it page to page?"

Max shrugged. "I guess."

"Which means there's only one thing to do," Alex said.

Max shot her a look. "Find Nigel."

Alex's phone beeped again, and she pulled it out. "It's Bitsy. She's waiting by the gate to pick us up."

"No!" Max said, gathering up the papers. "Tell her we died!"

"If we died, how could we be texting her?" Alex asked.

Max shoved the papers back into the box and slammed it shut. "Tell her I stepped in dog poop. Massive poop that will contaminate her car and eat through the floor. *I don't know, tell her anything!* We can't trust her, Alex. She's driving a Niemand Enterprises car. We can't give this secret to the enemy. Let's find a back exit and text Gerrold."

"Max, think. Avoiding her would be suspicious. She knows everything—why we're here, what we're looking for. But she doesn't have to know what we just found. Put the papers in the box and put the box in your backpack. I'll tell her we're on our way. We'll play it cool, say we found some old photos, then we'll figure out a way to get rid of her."

"OK. Right. OK." Max let out a breath like an Arctic wind. He nearly busted a zipper trying to stuff the box into his backpack. Together they took the elevator out of the building.

Bitsy's car was idling at the curb. She waved to them with a broad smile. "Helloooo! I convinced Mummy to let me pick you up. Did you find it?"

"No!" Alex and Max said at the same time.

"Just pictures," Max said, as he pulled open the rear door. "Old pictures. A box of old pictures. A box of old pictures that can't be opened."

"How curious," Bitsy remarked. "If it can't be opened, how do you know what's inside?"

Alex shot Max a panicked look. Now both Alex and Bitsy were staring at him.

Fish. Fish sauce. Fish cakes. Fish rain. Max's fists were clenching and unclenching. Alex gave him a warning look. Which just made things worse. "You . . . *you lied to us!*"

"Beg pardon?" Bitsy said.

"Max!" Alex snapped.

"The logo on the back of your car!" Max blurted. "Tell us about that."

"Oh dear, *that* thing," Bitsy said. "I suppose you could say it's one of the perks of working for old Stinky."

Max whirled toward Alex. "See? She works for him, and she's the enemy!"

"Oh, dear Lord, is that what you're getting all barmy about?" Bitsy asked with a baffled smile. "This was Mummy's company car. After all, she *was* married to him."

Max swallowed hard. "Wait. So . . . you're his daughter?"

Bitsy threw her head back in a laugh. "Mummy had been married before. When things were dire, I'm afraid Stinky came along and swept her off her feet with lofty dreams of changing the world."

"Right. Underwater cities . . ." Alex murmured.

"Needless to say, those dreams died quickly. After the divorce, all she got was a modest house . . . and this car." Bitsy reached out, taking Max's hand and Alex's. "I am so, so sorry to have made you fearful. I've asked Mummy repeatedly to have that awful insignia removed. To me it is like looking at a swastika. But she claims pulling it off would leave holes in the boot. She's vain."

Max let go of her hand. "You make me smell fish."

"I had a tuna sandwich for lunch," Bitsy said, covering her mouth.

"It means he's afraid," Alex said.

"It means I don't trust you," Max added.

"I see . . ." Bitsy thought for a moment. Then, slowly, she unclasped and pulled off her necklace. On it was a large silver locket, which she turned around to show Max.

Engraved on the back was a message. The letters were so teensy, Max had to hold the locket right up close to his eye:

FOR MY KINDRED SPIRIT

ON HER 13TH BIRTHDAY

FIGHT THE POWER

LOVE AND SMILES, BASILE

"The power was Niemand," Bitsy said gently. "I knew how much Basile hated him. My uncle wanted to overthrow that tyrant, but he was too gentle a soul to do it. He considered me the daughter he never had, and his fight was mine. So you see, I've been at this longer than you. Please understand, whatever I can do for you, I will. Just name it."

Max turned away, looking at the locket. *Kindred spirit* meant 'soul mate.' Basile had a terrible singing voice and sometimes bad breath, but he had a really good soul. Max trusted him. And it sure looked like Basile trusted Bitsy.

Max handed the locket back to Bitsy. "Do you still smell fish?" she asked with a smile.

"I think it must be the tuna sandwich," Max replied.

"Max?" Alex said. "Are we good?"

Max nodded.

Taking a deep breath, Alex said, "OK, I think we may have an uncle too, Bitsy. One we never knew. That old guy who slipped us the note at the funeral home . . . we need to find him."

"I never did actually see him," Bitsy said. "What did he look like?"

"Old," Max said. "Not much hair. Skinny."

"Well, that narrows it down to half the men in London," Bitsy drawled.

"A few minutes before we got to the funeral home, our driver almost hit him in the street by accident," Alex said. "Somehow he managed to get out of the way. Amazing reflexes. Like an acrobat. Or a dancer."

"He told us his name was Nigel," Max added.

Bitsy's frown loosened. She pulled out her phone, did

a quick search, and held out the screen to them. "Was it this fellow?"

Max and Alex gazed at a black-and-white image of a bare-chested ballet dancer in midleap. His chest muscles gleamed, and he stared into the camera with a confident smile. Printed across the bottom of the image was the name NIGEL HANSCOMBE.

Alex pinched the photo out to look at the face. "That's him, I think!" Max blurted. "A lot younger."

"So he was a famous dancer?" Alex asked. "What happened?"

"His fame didn't come from dancing, exactly," Bitsy said, flipping into the article that accompanied the photo. "He was second understudy for the corps de ballet in the Northeast Swansea Terpsichorean Troupe. What made him famous was the thing that cut his career short. It was an errant trapdoor in a production of *Swan Lake*, which opened when it was supposed to stay shut. Injuries all over his body, his left eye nearly lost. After that, Hanscombe disappeared."

"Bummer," Alex said.

"Go back to the search," Max said. "Can we get some contact information?"

Bitsy's thumbs began working the phone again. As she scrolled down a list of hits on Nigel's name, buried among all the ballet references was a link that read ST. STEPHEN'S EPISCOPAL CHURCH SHELTER AND SOUP KITCHEN, 55 WESTBY LANE, OPEN 7 DAYS A WEEK, REV. JONAS P. MUDGE, MANAGER N. HANSCOMBE.

Max smiled. "Bingo."

THE Saint Stephen's Episcopal Church basement smelled of cabbage, which might have explained the puckered-up face of Reverend Jonas P. Mudge. "And what exactly is the nature of your business with Mr. Hanscombe?" he sniffed, peering through thick glasses at Bitsy, Max, and Alex. "We are quite busy here, and—"

From behind him a voice called out, "Let them in, Jonas, fiddledeedee, lunch is over and I'm a free man."

"As you wish, Nigel," the reverend said, stepping aside.

Down a dim, narrow corridor walked a bent but quick-moving silhouette. As he emerged into the light of the open door, he smiled. One eye drooped, but the other shone as brightly as in the photo of his younger self. Looking from Max to Alex, the eye quickly became moist with emotion. "Glorious," he said. "So my instincts about you were correct. Please. Come in, children. Reverend, we shall be in my office."

He led them into a small side office with no windows. Flicking on a light, Nigel gestured to the corner, where several folded metal chairs were propped against the bare wall. Max, Alex, and Bitsy unfolded three of them as the old man sat on a battered wooden desk. With a smile, he thrust out his arms joyously. "What a banner day this is! How utterly enchanting to see you again—"

"We need facts," Max said. "Are you really who you say you are—a relative of Gaston, the nephew who shot Jules Verne?"

Nigel's face flinched with surprise. He focused on Max, his good eye steel-gray and steady. "Well, we don't stand on ceremony, do we? The facts. Yes, Gaston is my ancestor."

"Did you know about the list that Queasly had saved?" Max pressed.

"A list?" Nigel replied. "I thought Gaston had written a rather long work."

"I think that's probably lost," Max said. "The club never got it. But Gaston made a short summary. You didn't know that?"

"No."

"So you didn't know where it was hidden?"

"No. Did you find it?"

"I'm asking the questions," Max said.

Nigel let out a high-pitched squeak of a laugh. "You drive a hard bargain, young man. I like that."

"Did you know you gave us a code that only worked on one page?" Max pressed on.

"Not exactly. I don't really know how the codes work."

"Do you have any other code keys?"

Nigel's eyebrows shot way up. "Well, well . . . I believe I do." He nearly floated off his desk, spinning around to sit in a chair. From a file cabinet he pulled out a metal box of his own and spun a combination lock to reveal another metal box, which he unlocked with a key. Inside that was a third box guarded by a finger pad, and from that he pulled out an unmarked manila envelope. His fingers were shaking. "You will forgive my nerves. I had given up hope, and as I have no children, these documents would have died with me."

He spilled out a small stack of papers, each about the size of an index card. Max recognized the one on top. "V minus two, C plus one," he said. "We used that one already. It decoded the first page."

"Ah," Nigel said. "That would explain why the card is labeled on the back with a 1. Code one for page one."

"Splendid!" Bitsy said. "Where is the one for page two?"

Max quickly found the card labeled 2, then turned it to the front.

AN ARROW
MZ HUB

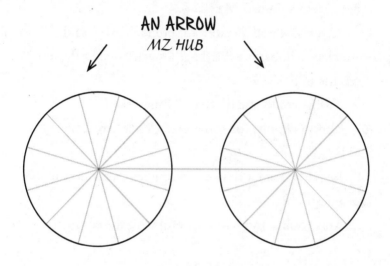

"What on earth—?" he murmured.

"Wagon wheels," Bitsy said. "How . . . eccentric."

Alex groaned. "How is this supposed to help us?"

"This one," Nigel said, "has remained a mystery."

Max drummed his fingers on the table. They let out a dull *pudududum . . . pudududum . . .* "I'm not getting why there's a drawing of wheels. This is a code. A code is about letters."

"Yes, lad, I have looked at this many times," Nigel

said. "I can only assume that the text on top is crucial. It refers to 'an arrow' . . ."

"But there are two arrows," Bitsy said.

"It also says 'MZ hub'—whatever *MZ* means—and there are two hubs," Max said.

"Aren't *M* and *Z* random letters?" Alex said. "Two letters, two hubs? Maybe that's a start. You put the letters into the hubs?"

"Why would you do that?" Bitsy asked.

"I don't know, for some crazy, code-y reason?" Alex said.

Nigel opened a drawer and pulled out a pencil. "Be my guest."

Max took it and wrote carefully on the card:

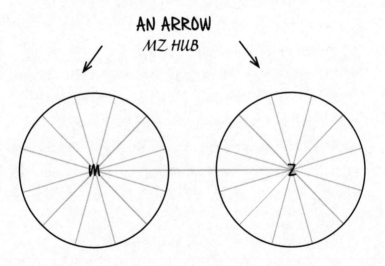

Max stared at it a moment. "So what does 'an arrow' mean?"

Pudududum . . . pudududum . . .

"Will you stop that?" Alex snapped.

"Perhaps the arrows indicate which way to spin the wheels?" Bitsy suggested.

"This is a code, not a toy," Nigel said.

Max slapped his hand down on the table. "Maybe it's not 'an arrow'! *M* and *Z* are two random letters, right? Two letters, followed by their location—'hub.' So maybe *A* and *N* are meant to be two random letters too. Then that top line could mean '*A*, *N* arrow.'"

"So if we put the *M* and the *Z* in the hubs," Alex piped up, "we can put *A* and *N* where the arrows are!"

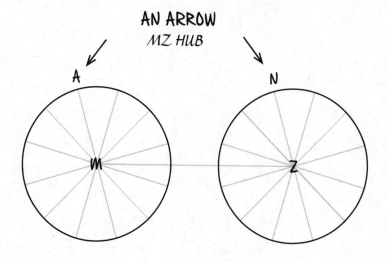

AN ARROW
MZ HUB

"Clever!" Bitsy said. "Looks like the circles are dividing the alphabet. The first one is *A* through *M*, and the second circle is *N* through *Z*."

"Where do the other letters go?" Max murmured. *Pudududum . . . pudududum . . .*

Alex smacked her hand down over Max's. "Max, there are twelve lines in each circle. M and Z are in the middle, so there are twenty-four letters left. So if you had a letter at each end, they'd all fit!"

Max nodded. "The first half of the alphabet in the first circle, the second half in the second circle . . . letters arranged around the circumference, like numbers on an analog clock . . ."

He quickly filled in more letters:

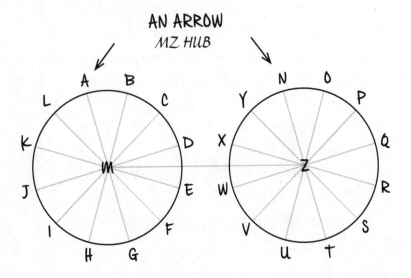

AN ARROW
MZ HUB

Max jumped up from the table. "Y-y-y-yes! Got it!"

"It's . . . lovely," Nigel said. "But what does it mean?"

Alex peered at it. "I'm thinking it's a substitution. You swap each letter with the letter on the opposite side of the circle, connected by the line—so *A* for *G* and *G* for *A*. Same with *B* and *H*, *C* and *I*, and so on. The ones in the middle, *M* and *Z*, swap with each other."

Bitsy leaned over the desk, pulling out page 2.

Hkcta nbk Hgycí Yozzgncut ul Krnxguxjctgxcfs Iuzvfcignkj Kpktny, Fkgjcta nu nbk Jcyiupkxs ul g Yohyngtik ul Otyvkgeghfk Xkpufoncutgxs Czvuxngtik nu nbk Bozgt Xgík

Yohzcnnkj hs Agynut nbk Zgatclciktn

Hkact qcnb Cycy bcvvoxcy, ghupk gff gtj qcnbuon qbcib tunbcta igt bgvvkt.

Gjj nbk ygfohxcuoy gtj igngfsncigffs zgxpkfuoy kllkiny ovut nbcy yohyngtik, jkxcpkj lxuz nbk luffuqcta qgnkx yuoxiky:

* Vxkykxpkj qcnb nbk nctinoxk ul iucf joyn lxuz nbk Eumbcz Xcpkx

* Krnxgcnkj lxuz nbk xkj iugn ul nbk gticktn qkn xcpkx buxyk lxuz nbk yuoxik ul nbk Xcpkx Ynsr

* Ngekt lxuz g aufl hgff'y iktnkx ct nbk lgn zuotngcty ul Zkrciu

Jkxcpkj lxuz nbk hfgie yzkgx ul knkxtcns lxuz Gxzgtju ul Egnbzgtjo

Xkyiokj lxuz g bun igpk ct nbk quxfj'y iufjkyn fgtj zgyy

"This will take forever," Bitsy said. "You have to replace every single letter?"

"Ugh," Alex groaned.

"Can we have a bite to eat first?" Nigel asked.

But Max was already writing. "Eat all you want. I'm working."

14

Hkcta nbk Hgyci Yozzgncut ul Krnxguxjctgxcfs
Iuzvfcignkj Kpktny, Fkgjcta nu nbk Jcyiupkxs ul g
Yohyngtik ul Otyvkgeghfk Xkpufoncutgxs Czvuxngtik
nu nbk Bozgt Xgik
Yohzcnnkj hs Agynut nbk Zgatclciktn

Being the Basic Summation of Extraordinarily Complicated Events, Leading to the Discovery of a Substance of Unspeakable Revolutionary Importance to the Human Race
Submitted by Gaston the Magnificent

Hkact qcnb Cycy bcvvoxcy, ghupk gff gtj qcnbuon
qbcib tunbcta igt bgvvkt.

Begin with *Isis hippuris*, above all and without which nothing can happen.

Gjj nbk ygfohxcuoy gtj igngfsncigffs zgxpk-fuoy kllkiny ovut nbcy yohyngtik, jkxcpkj lxuz nbk luffugcta qgnkx yuoxiky:
Add the salubrious and catalytically marvelous effects upon this substance, derived from the following water sources:

    * *Vxkykxpkj qcnb nbk nctinoxk ul iucf joyn lxuz nbk Eumbcz Xcpkx*
    * Preserved with the tincture of coil dust from the Kozhim River

    * *Krnxginkj lxuz nbk xkj iugn ul nbk gticktn qkn xcpkx buxyk lxuz nbk yuoxik ul nbk Xcpkx Ynsr*
    * Extracted from the red coat of the ancient wet river horse from the source of the River Styx

    * *Ngekt lxuz g aufl hgff'y iktnkx ct nbk lgn zuotngcty ul Zkrciu*
    * Taken from a golf ball's center in the fat mountains of Mexico

* *Jkxcpkj lxuz nbk hfgie yzkgx ul knkxtcns lxuz Gxzgtju ul Egnbzgtjo*
  * Derived from the black smear of eternity from Armando of Kathmandu

  * *Xkyiokj lxuz g bun igpk ct nbk quxfj'y iufjkyn fgtj zgyy*
  * Rescued from a hot cave in the world's coldest land mass

A slap on the desk woke Alex up. She lurched up from a curled-up position on her chair. Her back hurt, and each click of the old clock on the wall sounded like a bone breaking.

"*Brrrmff!*" snorted Nigel, who had been slumped over his desk, also asleep.

"*Chhhhh . . .*" snored Bitsy, who was on the floor, using her coat as a mattress.

"Read it . . . read it . . ." sang Max as he danced around the room, singing to an old Michael Jackson tune.

With a groan, Alex picked up the decoded page and read. Nigel leaned forward and angled the paper so he could see it. Now Bitsy was staggering over too. "He finished?" she said. "How long have we been here, a week?"

But Alex was barely hearing her. The message was turning her brain inside out. "This is amazing, Max."

"Brilliant . . ." the old man said.

"Well, *Kathmandu* is familiar because I know someone there," Bitsy said. "But what does the rest mean? *'Isis hippuris'*? 'Coil dust'? 'Wet river horse'? 'Golf ball's center'? 'Black smear of eternity'?"

"Isis hippuris is a type of coral that's also called sea fan, which we already have," Alex said. "No idea about the rest."

"This doesn't scare you?" Bitsy said.

"We'll figure out the locations," Max said. "Kathmandu is a start. It's in Nepal and Nepal has yaks, and yaks are my favorite animal."

Alex burst out laughing. "Uh, Max . . . ?"

"What?"

"You said you never wanted to travel again."

"I don't. I want a normal life." Max sighed. "But Evelyn wants a normal life too. And she can't have one."

"Evelyn?" Bitsy asked.

"Max's friend," Alex explained. "She has a condition called scleroderma."

"It makes scar tissue form on your skin, like you had an injury—only it happens for no reason, and the skin stays hard and stiff," Max said. "It can form over large parts of your body. It ends up affecting the blood vessels. And then the blood stops flowing. There's no cure for what she has. Odds are one hundred percent she'll die soon."

"That's harsh," Bitsy said.

"It's a fact," Max replied. "I don't know what the odds are for this whole mission to succeed. But even if it's like one percent possible, that's better than zero. What if we can make it work, and then get scientists to make more of the formula? All we need to do is find these ingredients and give it a try."

"Five ingredients from all over the world, in places we can't even figure out," Bitsy reminded him. "The information we have is coded, vague, and brief. It's just a list. There are no instructions of what to look for and look out for. Are you sure you're ready to do this?"

Max closed his eyes and recited in a monotone: "'Sometimes you can't be ready to do the things you really need to do. You just do them. And that makes you ready.' It's the Alex Verne motto."

"I can't believe you remember that," Alex said.

"You are one remarkable lad," Nigel said, wiping his brow. "You give me faith in humanity. But you and your cousin are young. May I suggest the obvious—that you would benefit from adult guidance and expertise?"

"You mean, *you*?" Alex asked.

As Nigel nodded, Alex gave Max a look. She didn't know what to say. She hadn't really imagined taking on this adventure with anyone but Max. "I don't think so. Max and I are kind of a team."

"Tell me, do you know where the Kozhim River is?" Nigel asked.

"Not offhand," Max said. "But it's easy enough to—"

"Russia," Nigel shot back. "In one of the northern republics—Komi, I believe. As a dancer I traveled the world, and I speak fluent Greek, Russian, Spanish, French, German, and Mandarin. Also a smidgen of Tibetan and Nepali. I may be advanced in years, but I am agile! Crafty too—without old Nigel you never would have decoded the message at all."

"Oh, it does sound ever so exciting," Bitsy added, her eyes wide and hopeful. "I would love to help. Would you consider expanding to four? I've spent summers trekking through Arabian deserts, rock climbing, scuba diving, and such. I won't tell Mummy, if you're uncomfortable about her connection to Stinky. I'll say you've invited me on a little Mediterranean jaunt in your private plane. That's the truth, after all—sort of."

"Stinky?" Nigel said.

"Long story." Alex took Max by the arm. "This is

kind of confusing. Give us a minute. Talk among yourselves."

Together they left the room, and Alex pulled the door
shut. "What do we do, Max? It's one thing to solve codes
together, but so far it's been just you and me."

"We could just run now," Max replied.

"I don't even know if we *can* do this," Alex said, pulling out her phone. "It's a small jet."

She quickly texted Brandon:

> hey. wd there be rm on jet for 2 more peeps?

"What if he says yes?" Max said.

Alex took a deep breath. "I don't know, maybe they'd
be a help. Everything they said makes sense. We could
use the skills and brainpower. And we don't have time
for do-overs, not if we're going to help Evelyn."

"But what if they try to steal our discoveries?" Max
said.

Alex nodded. "I guess it's a risk. But the waters won't
do any good without the *Isis hippuris*. And we have that,
Max. In Ohio. The waters won't work without it."

From inside the closed room, Alex heard a sudden,
"Ha!"

Then Bitsy's voice, slightly muffled: "What is it, Nigel?"

Alex and Max both inched closer to listen.

"'Extracted from the red coat of the ancient wet river horse from the source of the River Styx . . .'" Nigel's voice replied. "I believe I know where that would be."

"River Styx led to the underworld," Bitsy said. "It's not a real place."

"Ah, but like many legends, it was based on something observed," came Nigel's answer. "Scholars believe the journey began when the dead entered a boat on a river in the northern Peloponnese called the Mavronéri, which means 'black water.' But it is in the southern entrance, at the caves near Pirgos Dirou, where the locals believe the underworld actually began! Yes, that would be a splendid place to start. I will collect some vials. We will need different sizes. And I believe I can conjure up a large collection canister that will hold them all. . . ."

Max sighed. "I don't know what to think. Can you tell me what to think?"

Alex laughed. "Would you listen to me?"

"This time, yeah," Max said.

She closed her eyes. The voices on the other side of the door were rising—Bitsy and Nigel, brewing up all kinds of ideas. Collecting things for the trip.

They're not Spencer Niemand, she thought. They weren't André and Pandora and Niemand's other wicked cohorts.

She and Max had succeeded despite that bunch of criminals. It would be amazing to have smart people on their side. Good people.

"Yeah," she said softly. "I think we should do it. With them."

"Then I think so too," Max replied.

Alex felt her phone vibrate in her palm, and she looked at the message.

yup. 7-seater. works fine. can b ready 2 go anytime. at this short notice only cleared for athens ok?

"Your boyfriend?" Max asked.

Ignoring him, Alex opened the door and barged into the room. "Wheels up in twenty," she announced. "Everybody's invited to the party."

15

MAX was glad he had forgotten to eat that day, because he would have lost it all on the drive up the Peloponnesian mountains of Greece.

The road was steep and narrow, barely wide enough for one car. It wound in tight, switchback turns against a steep rock wall with zero visibility. To the right was a small grassy shoulder and a sudden drop-off to . . . nothing. Well, not exactly nothing. Way below, barely visible in the distance, were clusters of houses and shops. Separated only by an expanse of blue sky.

"Grigora, ippos!" Nigel grunted as he floored the accelerator.

"What does that mean?" Alex shouted. "'We're about to die'?"

"Sorry, practicing my Greek!" Nigel shouted back. "*Grigora* means 'go faster,' and *ippos* is the Ancient Greek way of saying horse. Which is what this jalopy feels like— an ancient horse!" The uphill angle was getting steeper, and Nigel floored the accelerator. "Got to get momentum or she'll stall! Hang on!"

Max slammed back into his seat. The car groaned in protest, picking up speed. The rock wall whizzed by on one side, inches from his window. Max tried not to look toward the other side, but as they neared a blind turn, he couldn't help it. On the road's shoulder was a smattering of white crosses decorated with flowers and ribbons, as if they'd sprouted from seeds. *"What are those for?"* Bitsy demanded, her fists clutching the dashboard.

"Each cross is where someone died, driving this road!" Nigel shouted. *"A Greek tradition!"*

Max could see Bitsy's face grow about three shades whiter. Alex took his hand but he pulled it away.

Nigel leaned into the sharp turn. Max could hear the roar of another engine, somewhere. A horn blasted. Nigel slammed on the brakes. The car's rear end jack-knifed right . . . left. . . . From around the wall came a sharp, eye-level glint—the grill of a cobalt-blue tour bus.

"Slow down!" Bitsy screamed.

The bus swerved to the right, just missing a collision.

Its deafening horn did not drown out Alex's and Bitsy's screams in the car.

Max could feel the rush of wind as it sped by inches away. The smell of fish was so powerful, he couldn't breathe. *"Let me out! I changed my mind. I don't want to do this trip!"*

Max reached for the door handle but Alex yanked him back. *"Max, you can't do that, you'll die!"*

"We're going to die anyway!" Max said.

"I've got this!" Nigel shouted. "I did this trip many times, when I was touring with the Swansea-Hellenic ballet exchange! Oh, the memories!"

"Stop remembering—and slow down!" screamed Bitsy.

A red convertible screamed toward them around the next turn. Max nearly barfed. The driver, a dark-haired guy with sunglasses, waved to them as if this were a lazy Sunday drive in Ohio.

Max unhooked his belt and sank to the floor of the car. There he could see nothing but the worn black floor pads of the rented car and the scuff marks from other people's shoes. He stared and stared at those patterns. If you looked at them a certain way, they resembled a herd of giraffes. Giraffes were a nice thing to think about. They took his mind off the drive.

He heard Alex gasping about something and heard

a *whoosh* from another car. But they were alive, and the giraffes hadn't noticed a thing.

"Let me know when we get there," Max said.

Max must have fallen asleep, because when Alex tapped his shoulder, the car was stopped.

"Are we dead?" he asked.

"I would hope not," came Bitsy's voice, "though we are positioned near the entrance to the underworld."

Alex was leaning in through the open window. She waved a sugary, sweet-smelling bread pastry under his nose. "You missed a great bakery in Sparta and a really pretty town called Diros. But we saved this for you."

From behind Alex came Nigel's voice. "Ah, the sleeping traveler wakes!"

Max didn't realize how hungry he was. He sat up and shoved the pastry into his mouth. It was still warm, with a strong taste of cinnamon and a faint smell of . . . *ocean*?

He turned and looked out the car window. They were no longer on the side of a mountain. Across the road, the land sloped gently to an expanse of vast, dark sea. In the distance, small villages dotted the coastline, and beyond them loomed a green-gray mountain. Their car was parked in a small lot against a tall, scrubby hillside. A few yards to their left, also against the hill, was a small outdoor waiting area under a metal roof—a gate, a booth, a map, some plastic seats, and a doorway. A few dozen tourists were walking past their car, milling about, talking in languages Max didn't understand.

He stepped out, squinting his eyes against the blazing Greek sun. A man in white clothing strolled by holding out small baskets of green and purple fruit. "Sicko?" he said to Nigel.

"He drives like one," Max said.

"That is the Greek word for 'fig'—*syko*," Nigel said. "Shall we get some?"

"I don't like them unless they're Newtons." Max squinted at a brown-and-white sign attached to the roof, which said Cave of Vlihada. "At least you didn't get us lost."

"Wait," Alex said. "I thought the place was called Piggos. . . ."

"Pirgos Dirou is the name of the town we drove through when I was sleeping," Max said. "Technically, it's Diros, but there's a famous tower. *Pirgos* means 'tower.' *Dirou* means 'belonging to Diros.' Vlihada is the name of the cave site."

Bitsy stared at him, slack-jawed. "Have you thought of competing on *Jeopardy*?"

"I looked it all up on the plane. I love factoids."

Max shot Alex a glance. "I would have learned more if Brandon had better Wi-Fi. Anyway, this is a vast underground waterway that goes through a network of caves, with sections that have still not been explored. Vlihada was the first section to have been opened to the public. That was in 1949. But it had already been explored for years by rock scientists. Don't ask me their names. I know, but I can't pronounce them."

"Thank you, Encyclopedia Brown," Nigel said. He looked behind him toward the entrance, then lowered his voice to a near whisper. "While you were asleep, old boy, I arranged for two of the guides to give us a private boat tour. We will split into two boats. They will be smaller and easier to navigate through the narrow limestone passageways. We will be careful of stalagmites and stalactites, as some of the latter hang very low to the water surface. They will take us wherever we ask them, as the rules allow."

"Do we even know what we're looking for?" Max said.

"The 'red coat of the ancient wet river horse,'" Alex said. "Duh."

"In other words, no," Bitsy added.

"I guess we'll find out," Max said. He picked up his backpack and opened it. Inside was a thin cylindrical case where he'd packed his collapsible hang glider. It weighed the pack down, but it reminded him of Evelyn. Quickly he pushed it aside and removed the lid from a large rectangular collection canister labeled ST. STEPHEN'S. Inside were several empty glass vials wrapped in bubble plastic. "Nothing broken. We are locked and loaded."

They walked to the little ticket area under the metal roof. Two men rose from plastic seats as they approached. The shorter of the two was heavy and balding, with a shaved head and a gap-toothed smile, and an old T-shirt that said I ♥ MILWAUKEE. The other, a thin, craggy-faced guy with hair like a stack of scorched hay, was dressed in a rumpled, navy linen suit that appeared to have done double duty as pj's. "Kosta," the thin guy said, and then pointed to the other: "Kosta."

The other man let out a noise like a car horn, which Max figured was a laugh. "They have the same name?" he asked.

"Kontonikolaos, me," the man continued, "and Doundoulakis, him. Last names."

"Well, that makes it easier," Bitsy said.

"I dub thee Kosta K. and Kosta D.," Nigel said. "Come."

The two guides led them through the waiting crowd. They stopped before a modest-looking closed wooden door. "We can skip the restroom," Max said. "I'll wait."

"It's not the restroom," Nigel said. "It appears to be the entrance to the cave."

"Really?" Bitsy said. "I would expect something a little grander. Festive lights. Picture windows."

Kosta K. pulled the door open to reveal a small room with a slanted rock wall. He muttered something in Greek, moved inside, and began to sink downward.

Peering in through the open door, Max realized that the room was actually the landing atop a stone staircase that sank deep into the earth. He followed Kosta K. down to a smooth, dimly lit rock floor. A group of small blue rowboats floated lazily in shallow water, moored to metal hooks in the rock. Orange life jackets were arranged neatly on the boat's narrow benches.

At the bottom, the stairway wall gave way to a wide-open cavern. Max stopped motionless on the stairs, causing Alex to nearly tumble into him from behind. Maybe she complained, maybe she didn't. Max wasn't noticing.

He wasn't moving either. He couldn't.

Seeing the Cave of Vlihada wasn't really *seeing*, in the ordinary way. It was more like an all-points bulletin to the senses.

Wet alabaster columns oozed down from the ceiling like the beards of a thousand petrified giants. A pool of black water meandered into the blackness among jagged, warty monster arms reaching upward. It seemed like sound itself had been squeezed out of existence, save for a tiny series of drips like the soft stroking of the highest key on a hundred distant pianos.

Behind them, Kosta D. burped. Which was just as well, or Max might never have moved.

"Wow," was the first thing that left his mouth, and honestly it felt like the dumbest thing he'd ever said.

"It's so . . . so . . ." Alex said, "underworld-y."

"*Ffffffuhhh . . .*" exhaled Bitsy. "*Gllrp.*"

"Bits?" Alex said softly. "Are you OK?"

Bitsy was taking deep breaths. A thin film of sweat formed above her brow. "Yeah. Just a bit of, you know . . ."

Alex nodded. "Claustro—"

"Don't say that word," Bitsy said.

"Really?"

Bitsy laughed. "Really. I know the word exists. I can easily put it out of my mind. But if I hear it aloud, I kind of freak. It's weird, right? I know it's weird. Don't judge me. I can do this."

"You don't have to come along, you know," Alex said gently. "You can wait for us on the beach. It's a beautiful day."

"I'm feeling clau—feeling it too," Max said.

"Thank you," Bitsy said. "But the show must go on. Am I right, Max?"

Max nodded.

"We need to face our fears," Bitsy said. "If Max can do this, so can I. To the river, then!"

"Sto potamós!" Nigel said, eyeing the walls with awe.

"I'm guessing *sto* means 'to' and *potamós* means 'river,'" Max said.

The two Kostas each untied a small boat. Bitsy was shaking as Kosta K. took her hand to help her into the boat. "Is good," he said. "Is no be afraid."

"Ahhhh-choooo!" Nigel sneezed. "Sorry, allergies."

Alex gave Max a look. "I'm not feeling good about this," she whispered.

As they stepped into their boat, Max thought maybe she was right. He missed traveling as a duo.

It had its advantages.

16

USING their wooden oars, the men pushed off from the stone dock. As they floated away in the two boats, Kosta K. spoke in rapid Greek. Nigel nodded patiently and then spoke aloud, his voice easily heard in the other boat. "Our boatman does not speak English well and has asked me to translate. You will notice that the lighting system is quite clever. High wattage lamps are placed strategically behind some of the wider stalagmites, making it appear as if the caves are magically lit."

Strategically didn't seem like the right word, Max thought. You didn't need strategy to light this place. You could put a lamp anywhere. It was all crazy impossible. Walls of green-and-white stone seemed to undulate in the light like curtains. Just beyond them were clusters of tapered columns that mirrored each other, thrusting upward from the floor and dropping from the ceiling, as if two city skylines had grown over the ages and fused in the center. Vast islands rose up like forests of candles lumped with wax. None of the columns were alike, some thick and treelike, some stubby and broken, others as fine as needles. They were like baseball bats, like bones, like fingers, like icicles, like unruly hair that defied gravity.

All sounds were muffled in the close space. Together they were like gentle music—the dripping of water, Kosta K.'s rhythmic Greek speech, the occasional plash of oars in the water, and the gentle *thunk . . . thunk* as the boatmen pressed their oars against the rock columns to steer the boats.

"Fascinating," Nigel said. "The gentleman explains that all of this rococo beauty is caused by the action of water dripping through the mountainside. It carries limestone from the soil, right down to this cavern. Over thousands of years, the microscopic bits of limestone collect at the ceiling, like a roof with a billion leaks. Slowly stalactites form. Then they drip to the bottom, where the remaining limestone collects once again. The limestone itself is largely white, but in different areas, the water will pick up other minerals in the soil, resulting in the blues, greens, and reds. Little by little, in this manner, stalagmites grow upward toward their brothers and sisters on the ceiling."

"I could have told you that," Max said.

"How do you remember which *ite* is which?" Alex asked.

"*Stalagmite* has a *g* for 'ground,'" Max replied. "*Stalactite* has a *c* for 'ceiling.'"

"Awesome, eh?" grumbled Kosta D. with a little laugh.

"You can say that again," Max murmured.

"Awesome, eh?" Kosta D. repeated.

"Is it warm in here?" Bitsy asked from the other boat, wiping her forehead with a handkerchief.

"I find it actually rather cold," Nigel said.

Alex leaned toward Max. "I'm worried about her. She's going to freak at any second. We may have to go back. Do you see any . . . I don't know . . . wet river horse shapes? Like the clue?"

"I don't know! How can you tell?"

As the boat moved out of one vast chamber and into another one, Kosta K. began mumbling in Greek to Nigel again. The formations in this area were superfine, like rock candy crystal. They glowed with a lighter, green-blue tint.

"Some of these things look like monsters, or animals." Alex pointed to a chaotic mass of knotted rock, jammed into a curve in the wall. "OK. That formation. What do *you* see?"

"Three giraffes throwing a beach ball? That's definitely not it." Max squinted at another formation. "How about that one?"

"I see Grumpy the Dwarf crushed by fallen bicycles." Alex exhaled. "Who knows what Gaston saw? It's all so subjective. Could be a rhinoceros or a swan. Maybe 'ancient wet river horse' is some kind of code, I wish we had more information!"

"OK, OK, let me think," Max said.

There were rules to solving a problem. *Break it down into its components.* It made complex things seem simpler.

Red. Coat. Ancient. Wet. River. Horse.

Everything down here was ancient. And wet. And on a river. That narrowed it down to red coats and horses.

Which didn't really help.

Now Nigel was lecturing from the other boat: "Our dear friend Kosta—*ahhhh-choo!*—is telling me that the early Greek explorers found bones down here. Occasionally they were the remains of buried human beings, but mostly—you'll find this amusing—bones of hippopotami!"

Kosta D. let out a honking laugh, and he gave Max a tap on the shoulder. "*Ippopotamos*, eh?"

"Aaahhh!" Max blurted, nearly toppling the boat.

"Eh?" said Kosta D.

"No, aaahhh," Max replied. "As in, aaahhh, maybe that's it!"

"What's it?" Alex said.

"Not a horse *shape*—horse *bones*." Max turned to the other boat and called out, *"Nigel, ask Kosta K. if they ever found horse bones!"*

When Nigel asked Kosta K. the question in Greek, the boatman burst into laughter and looked at Max as if he were a cute but slightly annoying toddler.

He took that to be a no.

As they approached a sharp turn, Kosta K. pushed his oar against a stalagmite to change course, all the while speaking Greek to Nigel.

"Our intrepid guide has noticed you're interested in the bones," Nigel said. "And he thought you'd like to know that many of those bones were found in this very area just ahead!"

Nigel gestured to a chamber beyond a stone archway, which glowed with an eerie pinkish light. "Apparently this is an unusual cavern, even for the Cave of Vlihada. In the soil directly above, there is a rich source of copper. The rainwater has carried this mineral into the limestone, which gives the formations here a distinct hue."

Max sat bolt upright so sharply the boat teetered.

Red. The room was red.

"Max . . ." Alex said.

Kosta K. muttered something in Greek to Nigel, who shrugged.

But Max's eyes were focused on the walls of this new, high-arching chamber. The color was subtle, closer to pink really. The walls were a complex construction of ancient twisted limestone, but behind them were small, shadowy holes in the cavern wall.

Max had his eye on a dog-sized opening in the wall just at the edge of the light. A yellow rope was drawn across the opening, along with a sign with very small print. He squinted. Half of it was in Greek, the other half in English, but the English part was coming into focus:

SPELEOLOGICAL SITE. PLEASE KEEP OUT!

"I need you to make a distraction," Max said to Alex. "Now."

Alex spun around. *"What?"*

"Ssssh." The other boat wasn't too far ahead of them, but Kosta K. was droning on and on. No one seemed to be hearing Max and Alex's conversation. Max hooked his arm under the strap of his backpack. He looked for the hole against the cavern's opposite wall, but it had disappeared behind the formations. "Alex, do you remember what Nigel said when we first got down here?"

"No. It was Greek!"

"*Sto potamós!*"

"I can't believe you remember that."

"*Potamós* is the Greek word for 'river.'"

Alex cocked her head. "Right . . . and *river* is one of the words in the clue."

"Exactly! OK, so I was thinking, earlier today when Nigel was trying to accelerate up the mountain, he called his car a *horse*. Only the word he used for horse was the Ancient Greek one, *ippos*." Max leaned closer to his cousin. "Put those two words together, Alex."

"*Potamós-ippos?*"

"*Ippopotamos!*" Max said. "Stick on the *h* for good measure. *Hippopotamus* comes from the Greek word for 'river horse.' So you plug that into the clue. 'The red coat of the ancient wet river horse' really means 'the red coat of the ancient wet hippopotamus'!"

Alex's eyes were as bright as lamps. "Max, any animal that's ancient is dead. And a dead animal is a skeleton. And a skeleton is *bones*. So we're looking for hippo bones with some kind of . . . red coat."

Max nodded. "If the bones exist down here, in this

room, they would be coated with red from the copper."

"We approach what is known as the Great Gate . . ." As Nigel's voice echoed in the silence, Bitsy daubed her forehead with a handkerchief.

"They can't see me do this," Max said. "Distract them!"

"OK, OK!" Alex said. "I'm thinking."

Max began slipping on the backpack. Alex stood, her eye on Bitsy, as Nigel droned on: " . . . so called because it appears that these two massive columns were constructed specifically to mark the—"

"*Claustrophobia!*" Alex blurted out.

Bitsy's body went stiff.

Nigel fell silent. "My dear?"

"Wow, this ceiling is low . . . and I feel *claustrophobia!*" Alex said. "Do you feel *claustrophobia?*"

"Ohhhhh . . ." Bitsy moaned. She was reaching for the sides of the boat, her hands shaking. "I have to go back!"

"*Ti?*" Kosta K. said.

"I'm sorry," Bitsy said. "I can't do this. I'll go back by myself. In the water. It's shallow. I'll be fine. You guys go ahead."

"Bitsy, dear, you can't *walk* back," Nigel said.

As Bitsy tried to step over the side of the boat, Kosta

K. took her by the arm. Bitsy threw off the boatman's hand. *"You leave me alone, or I'll have you in an international court by Tuesday!"*

Now Kosta D. was frantically poling the boat toward Kosta K.'s. Max shot a look at Alex. She winked back.

And Max, with the pack on his back, slipped into the waist-high water.

MAX was fine until the shadows.

The water itself was warmer than he'd expected. The floor was slippery but made of solid rock, and the limestone content made it impossible for fish to live there. These were facts. So it made absolutely no sense to see monsters and disembodied arms and black holes large enough for a human.

But in the shadows, he did.

"My fears are not the boss of me," Max said to the water.

Talking to water itself didn't make sense, which made Max smile. Smiling was a great way to stop feeling fear. He wished he could tell Bitsy that. He felt bad for her. She was still screaming. Maybe Alex should have thought of a better distraction. Claustrophobia was a bad thing. He knew that, because he was fighting it every step of the way himself.

The hole in the wall. Look at the hole, he told himself. He could see it now, lit by the cavern lamp. He stepped slowly along the slippery rock floor and reached out to the wall for support, but the wall felt like it had been constructed of dead lizards.

To get to the hole he would have to pass into the light briefly, and he might be visible to the boats. But once he crawled inside, he'd be out of sight again.

"Max?" echoed a voice. "Blast it, lad, where did you go?"

Nigel.

He turned but couldn't see the boats. They were still in the chamber where Max had left them. But it was only a matter of time before they returned.

Max waded into the light. He could read the sign clearly now:

SPELEOLOGICAL SITE. PLEASE KEEP OUT!

Speleological meant 'having to do with the study of caves.' You didn't see that word too often. Learning weird words was great, because you could store them up and remember them later. And remembering stuff was another method to keep away fear. But the sign also said "Keep Out," which meant *keep out*, so the two things canceled each other out.

The hole had a ledge, maybe four feet high. Max hoisted himself up and looked inside. He could see nothing in the pitch-black. He pulled out his phone, which had gotten a little wet.

It was on, which was a good sign, so he activated the flashlight feature and shone it into the hole. It was bright enough. It would work fine.

The hole went deep into the wall. But the light didn't reach far enough to show where the tunnel ended. Still, Max figured, if this was a site, that meant there was something important inside, *somewhere*. And if it was true that the speleologists had found hippo bones here in this part of the cave, this would be the most likely place.

"Honestly, where is that boy?"

Nigel's voice seemed superclose.

"Max?" Bitsy called out.

"Wait, I think I saw him *back where we were!*" Alex said. *"Maybe we should turn around and go back to the other chamber!"*

Max grimaced. Alex was trying to cover for him. But she was never going to win a Golden Globe acting award.

Quickly, silently, he slid the backpack into the hole.

He knew he wasn't supposed to enter, but then he thought about Evelyn and that was enough. He crawled in, but he was only able to stay on his knees for a few feet before the ceiling sloped downward. He had to flatten out, but the slimy surface made it pretty easy to slide along. He was thankful for that, even though the surface was gross. Sweaty feet were gross too, and he was smelling them, which was not a good sign at all. He knew he could only take a few moments of feeling smothered like this before he freaked out like Bitsy. And the last thing the team needed was twin freak-outs.

"Here, hippo hippo hippo," Max said, which was kind of funny but kind of not. There were lots of not-funny parts. Like what if his hunch was just wrong? What if this was not the bone site, and the tunnel led nowhere? What if the old sign was a relic from the sixties? As he crawled along, he could feel the limestone dripping on him. What would happen if he got stuck? Would the drips harden all over his body, pinning him helplessly between stalactites and stalagmites? Would ads of the future promise a look at the Famous Petrified Boy from Savile, Ohio?

"*Stop thinking,*" Max said to himself. "*Stop stop stop stop stop . . .*"

At the fifth *stop* his phone slipped out of his hand. As he picked it up, the light swung left and right. And he caught a glimpse of something that glinted back.

Something metallic. About twenty yards ahead.

He took a deep breath, which didn't feel as refreshing as he wanted it to. The air was too thin. He edged himself along, using his elbows and knees. Soon the walls of the tunnel flared out, making it easier to move, until he lifted himself back into a crawl.

He stopped when he reached a ledge.

Swinging his legs around, he was able to draw himself into a sitting position. He shone the phone downward carefully, slowly.

He was at the top of five steps, cut into the stone walls of the chamber. They led down to a roughly round area, big enough to maybe fit his house's living room but not much else. The walls were tiered with circular ledges all the way around, like some kind of small stadium. Strewn about on the floor below were hammers, chisels, brushes, and a bunch of strange curved tools Max had never seen before.

And on the ledges, collected into neat little piles, were bones.

Max stood, inching closer to a pile to his right. The bones seemed pretty small, but they were definitely tinted red. Under them was a handwritten card that said γάτα, which did not look like *hippopotamus*.

He widened his circle of light and saw another pile, much bigger, laid out on the very top tier. The air was already feeling clammy and warm. "Please be a hippo," he said.

This pile's ID card was jammed under the pile. Max grabbed it and pulled. Some bones slipped and fell off the tier. Max instinctively reached out to catch them, just as something round and large rolled toward him, stopping on the ledge.

A human skull.

Max choked back a scream. He could see the place from where the skull had fallen now—the bones were actually the skeleton of a short person laid out head to toe. The skull's jaw only contained about half its teeth.

It looked like it was laughing.

"Sweaty feet . . . *sweaty feet* . . ." He backed away. Deep breaths. He had to take deep breaths or he would fly away to nothingness, disappear from the earth. It was *a scientific site,* he reminded himself. Scientific sites were not scary. They were about collecting knowledge. He would be fine. His back smacked against the opposite ledge. Another pile of bones clattered to the floor. Great. He was going to destroy everything. Max, the Great Disrupter of Greek Science.

Something square and light-colored fell to the floor, and Max shone his light on it.

A card. He squinted at the writing:

ιπποπόταμος

He stooped to lift it. Max couldn't read Greek, but English letters were influenced by Greek. Fact. The shape and pattern of these letters . . . well, they seemed pretty clear. Except π. But that was pi. He knew that from math. The word was *hippopotamus*.

Moving the phone to the right, he looked at the bones directly above the spot from where the card had fallen.

They were thick and stubby. And deeply coated with red.

"Thank you . . ." he murmured. "In hippo language."

Max grabbed one. It was the size of a knuckle.

OK, he had the artifact he needed. But this wasn't only about the artifacts. It was about the water too. From what he figured, they would need both. He opened his pack and rummaged through the vials Nigel had given him. Three of them were big enough to fit the bones. He dropped one into each. Then he dipped each vial into the water at the bottom of the cave and sealed the tops tight.

"Sorry, hippo spirit," he whispered, "but it's for a good cause."

As he zipped the pack shut, its weight felt reassuring. He hooked it on and smiled.

Score one for the team.

He began spinning around in a little dance. He couldn't help it. But when he stopped, the room had gone pitch-dark. He needed to refresh the phone's light.

He touched the screen and nothing happened. Then he pressed the Power button. Nada.

His phone was dead.

MAX looked around in a panic. He opened his eyes as wide as they could go. "Alex? *Ale-e-e-ex?*"

Nothing. Not even an echo.

Max felt around for the wall. If he followed its contours, he would get to the tunnel. Fact. He'd been through the tunnel, and he already knew what was in it, which was an absence of anything. So there was nothing to fear. Fact fact fact. There was comfort in facts.

A droplet bounced off his nose, and he flinched. That flinch sent his phone flying. He heard it clatter to the ground.

Hold yourself together. Find it.

OK. The sound of the clatter would tell him where it fell. To the left, and close by. He got on his hands and knees. Slowly. Because he knew there were tools on the ground. He'd seen them, and some of them had looked sharp.

More facts: It was dark. Darkness sucked, but darkness was the absence of light. It wasn't the addition of anything. And things did not just appear out of nothing. Things like raptors or screaming heads or slithering rat-snake hybrids covered in snot.

Stop. Thinking.

Max crawled along the floor. His fingers brushed against handles and blades, but the smooth, slim shape of his phone was easy enough to discern. He grabbed it, shoved it into his pocket, and stood.

He had lost track of where the tunnel was. Oh, great.

That was another thing about darkness. It killed your sense of direction. You no longer had visual markers. Well, not everybody was like that. Some people had a natural ability to sense the magnetic pole. Like a compass.

Max stood. He tried to access his inner compass. But he realized he didn't have one. Or it was temporarily out of order. But he knew it would be a good idea to move away from the tools. So he shuffled along until his toe jammed against the base of the stone tiers.

He shivered.

Stop that.

He was getting tired of telling himself not to do things. Like not to shiver. The cold made people shiver, so he just had to walk and deal with it.

Then the shivering stopped by itself, which was interesting. The air had changed. It had been a little warm and then a little colder, and then warm again. A change in temperature caused the skin to shiver. And a change in temperature only happened when an outside force caused it to.

Like a breeze.

Max stood motionless. Where had the breeze come from? A breeze meant a connection to the outside, which would be through his tunnel.

There. About two o'clock. That's how you said forty-five or so degrees to your right. Three o'clock was directly to the right, nine to the left, six behind you. Like the numbers on an analog clock.

Old clocks were useful things.

He stepped toward the tiny breeze at two o'clock and climbed onto the tier. There he was able to climb onto another and another, until he was on the highest level. He felt forward, touching his fingers repeatedly against the rock from right to left.

Wall. Wall. Wall. Wall. Wall. Wall. No wall.

Bingo.

He felt upward, leftward, downward, around the opening's circumference. It seemed smaller than he remembered it, but that was OK. It was his way out of this chamber. It would be only a matter of a minutes before he was back in the cave. Everyone would be happy except maybe Bitsy, but she would recover from her claustrophobia soon enough.

He flattened himself out and slithered forward. His backpack scraped against the top of the tunnel. That was a little weird, because it hadn't done that on the way in, but his pack was fuller now, that would explain it.

Breathe . . . breathe . . .

The air was getting cooler, and that was a good sign. But the passageway was barely big enough, as if it had shrunk while he was in there. And it was changing direction. Veering sharply to the left. And upward.

Max stiffened. This was not familiar at all. It was a different passageway. Had to be. He hadn't seen it when he was in the chamber. So now what?

Turn back and find the right one, or keep going?

If he turned back, he could retrace his path. But going back meant more time in tunnels. He could think of a million things he'd rather be doing that that. Like eating broken glass. Keeping going meant heading into the unknown. But air was flowing from the other end. That meant there was some connection to the outer world. And less tunnel.

He exhaled and inched forward again. The path continued on an upward slope, then crested. The breeze was stronger now too. And he could see faint outlines of black and gray on the walls—which could only be caused by light.

He clawed forward, moving faster. *"I'm here!"* he shouted. *"Where my voice is!"*

His voice echoed. It was the first echo he'd heard since stepping into this mess. Echoes only happened when sound had enough space to bounce around. Like in valleys and concert halls and overpasses . . . and caverns.

The light was coming from an area to his left. But it was weak. It didn't seem that it could be made by powerful lamps. Which meant he could be in another part of the cave. *"Answer me!"*

He lunged forward, toward the suggestion of light. Toward the gradations of black going to gray.

And his foot slipped.

His body was sliding now, down some kind of chute, picking up speed. Soon his arms and legs were scraping against rock, doubling his pain. He let out another scream as light began suffusing up from below.

Now he could see metal handholds in the rock above

him. People had been here. People had figured out how to negotiate the slope. All he needed to do was grab on.

He reached up with his fingers, grasping, but they closed on nothing. He was going too fast. The bottom was quickly becoming visible.

It was a hole. A hole that dropped farther than he could see. He closed his eyes and screamed as he picked up speed.

As the slide released him into the void, he wrapped his arms around his head. Hitting water elbow-first was not pleasant. But it was better than face-first, and another few inches on either side would have impaled him on a stalagmite.

He straightened out in the water, his foot striking bottom. The surface was hard and jagged and caused one ankle to buckle. With his other foot, he pushed up, thrusting downward with his arms.

He broke through with a gasp. He was hoping to see waving curtains of limestone rock and spectacular columns, but all he could see was a dull expanse of water, and stalactites from the ceiling that were way too close to his head.

What the . . . ?

This was not the Cave of Vlihada he'd left. The water was deeper, the cavern more cramped and unlit by lamps.

It was vast, extending far in all directions. But there was no way a boat could fit here.

He swam toward the light, which seemed to be coming from a spot up on the ceiling to his right. The dull *splish-splash* of his arms into the water echoed through the small cavern.

Until Max realized some of the splashes weren't echoes. They couldn't be. They had a different rhythm. He stopped swimming and squinted into the distance.

Not too far ahead, clumps of dirt and rock were falling from the roof. From the source of the light, a shovel's blade was thrusting downward.

"*Hellllp!*" Max screamed.

"Stop that confounded shovel, Kosta! I think I hear him!"

Nigel's voice. The sound startled him.

Max picked up the pace. His own labored breaths echoed against the rock.

"Max, old boy, is that you?"

"*YES!*" Max replied.

"It's Nigel! Can you see me? Can you see my arm?"

In the light, Max saw what looked like a strange stalactite with wriggling fingers. He lifted his head and cried out, "*I'm coming!*"

Nigel's arm disappeared back into the hole, and a

rope fell through, splashing into the water. Max closed the gap fast. Grabbing the end of the rope, he tied it tight around his chest, just below his shoulders. "Got it!"

Now Max was being lifted out of the water, up through a jagged column of white light that blinded him. He broke through the gap, his eyes tightly closed against brilliant sunlight. Two sets of strong arms took him by the shoulders and yanked him up into the outer world.

"Is he OK?" came Alex's voice.

"We'll soon find out," said Nigel.

Max could feel the rope being untied from around his chest. As he flopped back onto a warm patch of grass, he groaned. "I'm good. Please don't hug me."

"Oh, my heart," Bitsy said. "Oh, I think I need to sit."

Max blinked, adjusting to the brightness. Nigel and Alex were hunched over him, looking like they'd just seen a hippo spirit. "Where—what—*how did you find me*?" Max spluttered.

"Our guides figured it out," Nigel explained. "Kosta K. noticed the sign by the hole had been moved. It marked a passage that leads to an undeveloped section of the cave. Neither wanted to follow you. Apparently, the Greeks take their historical sites quite seriously, and employees are punished for transgressions. There was a bit of a row over which way you would emerge. Kosta D.

stayed by the opening in case you went back the way you came. Kosta K. brought the rest of us back through the front entrance and to this tiny opening, where he did a little work to expand it."

"Thank you," Max said to Kosta K.

"*Achhh.*" The boatman turned away in disgust, his face red and taut with disapproval.

Just beyond the boatman, a small group of tourists were taking selfies of the scene. As Kosta K. shooed them away, Alex leaned close. "Are you really OK?"

Max smiled and nodded.

"Did you do it?" Bitsy said. "Did you find the wet river horse, whatever that is?"

From behind Max came a deep cracking noise. He jumped away as the hole he'd come through opened wider.

"Oh dear, looks like some kind of sink hole," Nigel said. "Max can give us the details when we're back at the hotel. We'd best get out of here before anyone starts asking questions we don't want to have to answer."

19

"**SO . . .** you tricked me. You shouted *claustrophobia*, fully knowing what it would do to me." Bitsy paced the floor of Room 103 at the Alexander the Great Inn, which didn't exactly live up to its name. The screen door didn't close all the way, the hot water was cold, the overhead light buzzed like a flock of bees, and the air conditioner from the diner next door rattled outside the window. Max was sprawled out on a bed, Alex was sitting by his knees with the backpack, and Nigel was doing ankle stretches on the wall.

"I'm sorry, Bits," Alex said. "But we needed a distraction—"

"No, no . . . it was brilliant!" Bitsy exclaimed.

Max sat up. "It was?"

"Yes," Bitsy replied. "Finally, *something* good came of my stupid fears. Do show us the bones, Max."

Max pulled the vials out of his pack. The bones were floating in water, and everything was suffused in red that seemed deeper than Max remembered.

"This is fascinating," Nigel said, holding one of the vials up to the light. "We are off to a flying start. Perhaps this search will be easier than we thought."

"We figured out clue number one," Alex said, "and we're going to figure out the others."

"I want to text Evelyn," Max said. "But I won't. I can't get her hopes up. I'll wait till we have all five!"

"I suggest we celebrate with some Greek food," Nigel said. "I shall run next door and bring back an assortment. Any special requests?"

"Do they have Moose Tracks ice cream in Greece?" Max asked.

"Moussaka tracks, maybe," Nigel said.

"I just lost my appetite," Bitsy groaned.

As Nigel left, a silence settled over the room. Alex's eyes were drooping, and Bitsy flopped down onto the floor. Max yawned and fluffed a pillow under his head.

The last thing he saw before falling asleep was Nigel,

out the window. He was racing across the parking lot, completely missing the restaurant's entrance and heading toward the other businesses.

But Nigel was a grown man. He would figure it out.

Several hours later Max awoke with a loud gasp, into pitch darkness.

It took him a moment to remember he was not in the caves. He flicked on a lamp beside his bed. Bitsy and Alex must have gone back to their room. He spotted a handwritten sign on his dresser. He got up to read it.

> Your dinner is in the fridge.
> No moussaka tracks ice cream,
> but that's OK, b/c no freezer! ☺ —A

Grrroglll, grrrogllled Max's stomach.

He was starving, so he padded over to the fridge, which was under an old TV. As he pulled out a big white paper bag, the smell of cold souvlaki made his mouth water.

Setting the bag down on his night table, he noticed his backpack was open. The collection canister was still inside, the top off. It was filled with empty vials.

Max remembered taking out one of the vials with the hippo bones. But he'd had three. And there was nothing inside the canister.

He looked under the bed. In the bathroom.

Grabbing his key, he ran out of Room 103, and pounded on the door of 102. *"Alex, do you have them?"*

The door flew open. With a solid *thunk*, it caught itself on a short chain. Through the crack of an opening, a man with beard stubble and a white T-shirt barked something in Greek.

"Over here, Max!" whispered Alex's voice. From Room 104.

"Sorry, bad sense of direction," Max said to the guy. "Second time today."

He raced to Alex's room, and she let him in. A groggy Bitsy was just waking up from the second bed. "Is it morning yet?"

"Almost," Alex replied, then turned to Max. "Do I have *what?*"

"The three vials with the hippo bones!" Max said. "They're not in my room."

Alex shook her head. "Why would I take that?"

Bitsy was out of bed now, drawing a robe around herself and shoving her feet into slippers. "Nigel delivered the food to you, Max," she said. "You were fast asleep. Maybe he took them for safekeeping."

"He should have told me!" Max said.

Alex sighed. "Come on, let's wake him up and ask him. He's in 115."

Alex threw on a robe too, and they all headed to a room at the end of the row. Max reached 115 first and rapped on the door.

"Nigel?" Alex said quietly.

Max knocked again, calling out the name louder.

And again.

To their left, some of the lights were turning on. A voice shouted something in another language. Now the motel desk clerk appeared at the end of the row of rooms, shushing them.

"Our uncle is not answering," Alex said.

The clerk nodded, his brow furrowed with concern. "Old man, yes? Maybe something happen."

The clerk walked to the room and knocked on the door sharply, then pulled a key from a large collection on his belt. As he used it to open the door, he flicked on a light.

The room was empty. The bed was made. No one was inside.

"What the—?" Max said.

"Maybe he took a walk?" Bitsy said.

"There's no place to walk!" Alex snapped. "And all his stuff is gone."

Max, Alex, and Bitsy scoured the room. But there wasn't much room to scour. Nigel wasn't there.

Max ripped back the curtains and glanced out to the parking lot.

The car was gone too.

20

DING-DING-DING-DI-DI-DI-DI-DING!

Max couldn't stop banging his hand on the silver bell on the front desk, while Alex was checking out. Outside, the sun was peeking over the horizon.

"Will you stop that?" Alex shouted. "It's too early for noise."

"It soothes me," Max said.

"It irritates everyone else," Alex replied.

"You know what irritates me?" Max said, forcing himself to pull his arm back from the bell. "I said we shouldn't trust him. I knew it the moment we met him in the funeral home."

"He fooled us, Max," Alex said, as she waited for

the clerk to process her credit card. "It's understandable. He's our uncle."

"Fifth cousin twice removed," Max reminded her.

"Once you get past third cousin, it's barely even family," Bitsy said. "Look at the royals."

"What?" Alex and Max said at the same time.

"Never mind," Bitsy said.

"OK, let's assume he's a rat, and he's trying to get these ingredients before we do," Alex said. "But we don't know a lot of things—like why? Is he working with someone or flying solo? In what order is he going to be attacking this list? We don't know where he's getting his money. But we're the only one with the *Isis hippuris*, so I'm assuming we'll run into him again, eventually."

She pulled out her phone, tapped on her documents app, and pulled up the list of locations.

Max and Bitsy peered over her shoulder. "'Mexico . . . Kathmandu . . .'" she read aloud.

"Wait . . . what about this one?" Max said. "'Preserved with the tincture of coil dust from the Kozhim River'? Nigel said it's in Russia. That's the closest location to Greece. That would be the most efficient search method."

"That's what I was thinking too." Alex pocketed her phone and turned to the clerk. He was holding tight to the credit card, looking at the computer monitor with a furrowed brow. "I am sorry, miss . . ." he said. "It is not working."

"No prob," Alex said. "I'll pay in cash."

"I'm sorry." He pulled the card farther away. "I cannot."

"Wait . . ." Alex said. "You can't take *cash*? Money. Dollars. Euros. Whatever. Everybody takes cash."

"I cannot," he repeated, turning the monitor toward her. "Is message. Here."

"Shoot, I can't read Greek," Alex said. "Can you—?"

The wail of a siren interrupted her. Max and Bitsy ran to the front window. From a couple of blocks away, a police car was heading in their direction.

"The police?" Alex said. "Is that what the message says?"

The clerk nodded.

"We took ancient artifacts," Max said.

"Not to mention disturbing an undeveloped cave and creating a new hole in the earth," Bitsy said.

"But how would they know where we are?" Alex said.

Max was getting a headache. He began pacing. "Nigel. He's the only person who knows us."

"The creep!" Bitsy said.

Alex's eyes widened. "We are toast."

"I hate him!" Max shouted. "He doesn't have a friend who's dying! *He wants to kill Evelyn!*"

"Max . . ." Alex said.

Slowly, the clerk slipped out from behind his desk toward the front door.

Max ran after him, snatching the credit card from his hands. The guy looked afraid. Max didn't like making people feel that way. He took three deep breaths. "Sorry. *Sorry.* But it's hers. And we need to get away. Now! That guy who was in Room 115? He stole something from us. He's framing us. Is there another way out? Out? *Exo?*"

The clerk looked nervously back to the window. That was all the hint Max needed.

"Follow me!" Max called out.

Just beyond a set of restrooms was a glass door. They barreled through, emerging into the back lot of a small strip mall.

"Nice work, Max," Bitsy said.

Max broke into a jog. "I can't figure out his plan. What's he going to do with one ingredient? It makes no sense. Why not wait and use us to help him get the rest?"

"He's got a copy of the list," Alex said. "Maybe he just felt like he had his chance now to get rid of us easily, so he can go off on his own."

Max scanned the signs on the backs of the shops. He

was hoping at least one would be in English, but no such luck.

At the end of the row of shops, they circled around to the front. The strip mall followed the curvature of the road, and from their angle the motel was not visible. But just to their left was a large lot with a half-dozen cars. "A car rental place!" Alex said. "Cousin, you are brilliant."

"I saw it on the way in," Max said, handing her the credit card. "I hope it's open. One of you two can rent the car and get us to an airport. Alex, you should text Brandon now. Can he fly to meet us somewhere? The closer to here, the better. I don't want to drive over those mountains again."

"Aye, aye," Alex said, pulling out her phone.

As Bitsy ran into the rental office, Max scanned the lot. There were only a couple of cars, a four-door sedan and a minivan. Either would do.

"Max—I got Brandon," Alex said, staring at the phone. "He says we're in luck. He's able to get clearance at an airport in Kalamata, which isn't too far from here. He'll meet us there."

"We can't stop to pick up flowers."

"Not funny, Max."

Now Bitsy was emerging with a clerk, a young woman

with wide eyes and a big smile. "Guys, this is Frangitsa. She just arrived to open the shop."

"Three of you? Perfect!" Frangitsa said. "We have number two five five, two five six, two five seven. Please, let me show you."

"We only need one car," Alex said. "Not three."

Frangitsa stopped at parking space 255. She put a hand on the seat of a beat-up silver Vespa motorcycle. Two others were parked in the spaces next to it. *"Etsi!"* she exclaimed.

"Is that like *voilà*?" Max said. "Because *motorbike* is not what we said. A car. Car. *Aftokinito*. Like one of those two."

He pointed to the sedan and minivan, but Frangitsa grimaced. "One of those is mine," she said. "The other is not working."

"No cars in a car rental place?" Bitsy said. "Halfway between nowhere and nobody? How about a taxi?"

"My husband drives taxi. He can take you when he gets back. From Athens."

"Athens is hours away!" Max said.

Alex was swinging her legs around the Vespa. "Guys, I've been wanting to do this since we got to Greece."

"I haven't!" Max squeaked. "I cannot ride a motor-bike on a highway. I absolutely cannot."

"You ride a bike, no?" Frangitsa chirped. "Then you can ride motorbike!"

"No," Max said. "No no no no no no."

Bitsy was eyeing the bikes warily. "I must say, I'm with him."

"OK, no problem," Frangitsa said. "Then you have one more choice."

"Please say private helicopter," Bitsy asked.

"No," Frangitsa said with a laugh. "Walk."

21

AS the old man pulled into the parking lot of the Kalamata Airport, he noticed the gas gauge had slipped below zero.

He smiled. What timing. It had been a quiet ride, no mountains necessary, no youthful chattering. And look—it just happened to be the perfect amount of fuel! A lucky end to a lucky few days.

Stepping out of the car, he rubbed his eye. With his limited vision, too much driving was always a strain. He silently cursed the young pilot of the private plane—Brendan, Brant, whatever his name was—for having flown them all into Athens in the first place. The drive over the Peloponnesian mountains had been exhausting.

The airport in Kalamata was rather small, but it was a lot closer.

He quickly dug his phone out of his pocket, where a series of texts glared up at him:

Do you have it yet?

Where are you?

Please respond.

DO YOU HAVE IT??

Dear Nigel, are you dead?

Some people could be so impatient.

With a sigh, he quickly typed a response:

Yes. Airport. Responding. Again, yes.
No, but thank you ever so much for asking.
Will deliver ingredient to courier,
then proceed to K. River.

He sent the message, then opened the rear door. On the seat was a new backpack he had purchased at a roadside shop. Shoddy construction, really. But when you weren't in England, you had to make do. Time was of the essence, after all.

By now the police would be interrogating the children. Nothing would come of it, of course. The poor things would be set free with a scolding. They were bright. They were well funded. They'd be back on his trail in no time, seeking the ingredients. But he had one of those ingredients now. Meanwhile, he would take advantage of the distraction and the extra time. And continue the search on his own.

He recalled his instructions.

Follow them, he had been told. *Make no waves. Let them find the ingredients in their own time. We will help you take possession upon your return.*

But really. What was the excitement in making no waves? He had the list now. He had been waiting for this all his life. As had his father, and his grandmother before that, and so on. No more waiting. And no more relying on other people.

From the moment the accident cut short his dancing career, life had been a slow sink to the bottom.

Until now.

He picked up the new pack and checked inside—one, two, three vials. Such an eerie, bloodlike red they were.

He wrapped them carefully in a fistful of napkins he'd pinched from the diner. Then he zipped up the pack and slung it over his shoulder. But as he began to shut the door, he spotted a small, shining rectangle on the floor. With a sky-blue case.

"Well, well . . ." he murmured, feeling his soul instantly lighten.

It was Bitsy's phone. The girl had dropped it, poor thing. Whatever would she do for fun while in a holding cell at the police station?

He looked around for a trash can, then stopped. No, he wouldn't throw it out. The children were young. And crafty. They would play on the sympathies of the police. Claim they were double-crossed. Throw shade to the droopy-eyed old man who had chaperoned them. If their gambit worked, they'd be after him.

But he could use the girl's phone to play with them a bit.

Oh, this would be jolly fun.

He closed his eyes, recalling the movement of her fingers on the screen as she opened her phone. He had watched them all do this. It was the easiest way to pick up passwords. No one ever suspected. With proper practice, it wasn't that difficult.

Four-five-four-five. That was it. Yes.

He punched in the numbers and the phone came to life. He scrolled through her Contacts list, stopping at M. For MAX TILT.

With a giggle, he poised his thumbs over the screen. A little misdirection would be fun. Slow them down a bit. A wild goose chase to lighten the day.

He thought for a moment, until the perfect plan came to him. And he began to type:

> Helo, I am tring to find oner of ths fon . . .

"Ha!" he hooted, as he crafted a long note with many mistakes. Oh, this was going to be perfect. No one would suspect it to be him.

It took only a moment to finish, but he didn't want to send it now. The timing was off. He would do it later, when it made more sense.

He pocketed the phone and headed for the entrance. Departures and arrivals all on one level. This was the sort of airport he liked.

The next location was a bit remote. It would take time to get there. An old man needed a head start.

As he headed to the departing terminal, he leaped

over the fire hydrant. A graceful little jeté, like the old days. At the sidewalk just beyond the parking lot, a smiling young flight attendant applauded.

Nigel bowed.

At his age, he had to take what he could get.

ALEX didn't care about the dust, or the fact that her helmet was too small and kept pulling her hair. None of that mattered when you were alone on a highway roaring up the Máni peninsula.

"Woo-hooooo!" she shouted.

For the thousandth time, she checked her rearview mirror for police lights.

Nothing. She, Max, and Bitsy were lucky.

To her right, the Mediterranean was a blaze of blue. Sailboats dotted the water like paper napkins, and flocks of seagulls circled hungrily overhead. She leaned into turns, dipping just a bit farther each time. The road had been pretty empty for a while, but two trucks and a car had just approached from the opposite direction. Not too far in the distance was a small collection of white domes—Greek churches, at the edge of a beach village. A village called Gythio, according to the sign. Civilization.

Breathing in a mouthful of salty, cool air, Alex decided she could live in this kind of civilization. If she weren't dead set on catching the human slime known as Nigel Hanscombe.

She slowed a bit, checking her mirror again. Bitsy was a speck, and Max was nowhere to be seen. Also, the road was clear. She sped up and leaned hard. To the left. Into the center of the road. Making a circle. A donut. She had always wanted to do a donut.

Too wide . . .

She slammed on the brakes. The bike's wheels screeched. Her wheels dug a groove in the opposite shoulder before she zoomed back onto the road. It was a terrible attempt. The tire marks were more like an egg shape. So she did another. And another.

"Alex!" Bitsy's voice interrupted her. She was approaching quickly, perfectly upright in her seat, as if she were on a horse.

"Is this awesome or what, Bits?" Alex shouted.

"Reckless would be my word!" Bitsy yelled. "We are fugitives from the law, Alex! What if someone sees you and reports you to the authorities?"

"I think it's siesta time," Alex said. "Or whatever they call it here. Nobody's on the road but us maniacs."

Bitsy veered onto the shoulder and stopped. She took off her helmet and strapped it to her handlebar. Her voice was clipped and breathless. "I have a problem. While you were speeding on ahead like Evel Knievel's granddaughter, I had to stop to help your cousin. He's thirteen, you know, and hasn't quite got the hang of this. Anyway, I figured I'd grab my phone to call you, but . . ." She sighed heavily. "Well, call me Bitsy the klutz. It's gone."

"Oh, wow," Alex said, rolling her bike to the shoulder. "Do you want me to call the motel? They can mail it to you."

"I did call them, on Max's phone," Bitsy replied. "House cleaning had just finished, and they found nothing."

"Maybe you dropped it on the—"

"No. Listen to me, Alex. I've been thinking. Retracing my steps. I took it out of my pocket yesterday afternoon, when we were in the car. I think it's still there."

"With Nigel?" Alex said.

"Yes. And I'm pretty sure it's on. With power. If you catch my drift."

Alex nodded. "If it has power, it's sending a signal . . ."

"Exactly!" Bitsy said. "Do you have any reception in this godforsaken backwater?"

Alex quickly checked her phone. "Three bars."

"Then give it to me. I'll sign in to your locator app with my account. We may be able to find him."

As Bitsy took the phone, Alex shaded her eyes and looked up the road for Max. He wasn't far now. He also wasn't too steady on the bike. As a truck passed him, he wobbled a bit.

"You're doing great!" Alex called out.

Max picked up speed. When he finally puttered up to her on the shoulder, he had a hint of a smile. "I was scared at first," he said. "But it's not hard, if you follow the rules of the road. People are nice. And I think I've figured out exactly how much throttle pressure you need, to keep the ride smooth. Who made those tire marks in the middle of the road?"

"Never mind that," Alex said.

"What's Bitsy doing?"

"She left her phone in the car, and we're trying to track down—"

"Found him!" Bitsy screamed.

Alex and Max ran to her side and looked over her shoulder. At the center of her screen was a red dot, glowing at the Kalamata Airport.

* * *

Nigel's car was empty.

Alex had seen it first. In the small parking lot of the Kalamata Airport, it hadn't been hard to find. He had left it parked diagonally across two spaces, and he hadn't bothered to lock the doors. Bitsy and Alex were inside, rooting around for her phone, while Max checked the airport flight schedule.

"Terrible parking job," Max remarked absently, looking up from his phone.

Bitsy backed out of the car and shrugged. "Nothing."

"I didn't find anything either," Alex said. "He must have taken the phone with him. What are you finding, Max?"

Max scrolled down on his phone screen. "There's a flight leaving for Moscow in twelve minutes," he replied. "Nothing that matches any of the other destinations on our ingredients list."

He pocketed his phone, and they all ran toward the airport entrance. The lobby had only one ticket counter, with two attendants. They both eyed Max with smiles as he approached.

"Old man!" he shouted. "Eye! Droopy!"

The ticket attendant closest to him was a raven-haired woman with a severe ponytail and intelligent-looking eyes. But she clearly had no idea what he was saying, so Max yanked down on his own left eye. "Droopopoulos!"

"Am I to understand," she said, "you're attempting to describe a passenger?"

Before he could answer, Alex ran up from behind. "Sorry," she said. "We're looking for a man, maybe mid-sixties, flyaway gray hair, moves like a dancer, with an injured eye that droops. We think he may be on a plane to Moscow."

"What she said," Max added.

The woman held up a hand. "I'm sorry, there are privacy rules—"

"He's our uncle, and he's trying to kill my friend!" Max blurted.

The ticket taker to the right rose from her chair like an ancient Greek goddess, her hair falling about her shoulders like the snake tresses of Medusa. *"Vre, Soula,"* she bellowed to the younger woman, "we are here to help, no? This is small airport, we see everybody. Tell me, *paithi mou*, is thees a Breetish fellow?"

"Yes, Breetish!" Alex blurted.

"British," Bitsy said.

The woman nodded, ignoring the poisonous stare of her younger colleague. "I saw him. He bought teeket to

Moscow. Leaving in ten minutes."

"We need to talk to him!" Alex pressed.

"Gate is closed to boarding," the woman replied. "I can find seat for you on tomorrow's flight."

Max felt Alex grabbing him by the arm. "Thanks," she said, "but we have a ride."

Together they raced toward the sign that said Customs. Bitsy was still holding Alex's phone, looking at it while running. "You just got a text from Brandon," she said. "He says he's ready. But he wants to know our destination. Wants you to call him."

Alex reached for the phone and pressed Call. "Brandon? Hi! It's me! OK, the place we're going is called the Kozhim River—"

Max leaned toward her and shouted toward the phone: "Komi Republic! Near the Ural Mountains!"

Alex fell silent for a moment and then said, "Brandon's laughing. He says it's really far. He'll have to stop in Moscow to refuel. But he's here waiting for clearance to leave. The gate attendants will let us meet the plane."

"Deal," Max said.

In the nearly empty airport, customs took only a few minutes. Max, Alex, and Bitsy raced through the gate and onto the tarmac, where Brandon was waiting in front of the ladder. "Where's the old guy?" he called out.

Alex took a deep breath. "Nigel—the old guy—he betrayed us. He's trying to stop us from a search for a . . ."

"Medical breakthrough," Max said.

"Medical breakthrough," Alex repeated. "We found the first ingredient we need. And he stole it."

Brandon's eyes widened. He pulled himself to his full height. His lip curled. "Not on my watch!" he said. "Get in! We'll be there in four hours."

As he stormed up the ladder, Bitsy raised an eyebrow. "My hero."

As the plane crossed the Black Sea, Max stared at the next clue in the message: "tincture of coil dust."

Despite the spotty Wi-Fi, he'd been able to do some research on the Kozhim River. The photos were beautiful, but nothing in the descriptions helped.

It also didn't help that Bitsy was snoring in the seat next to him. "Can you kick her?" Alex asked.

"I'm a nonviolent person, except in my thoughts about Nigel," Max said. "What's your ringtone for me?"

"Some death metal band you don't know," Alex said.

"That'll do." He tapped Alex's number on his phone. A deafening scream blasted in Bitsy's pocket, and she jumped. "Dear Lord, what's that?"

"My phone," Alex said. "You still have it. Nice nap?"

"Until now, yes!" Bitsy fished the phone from her pocket and looked at the screen. "It's from . . . Max?"

"It was either that or kick you," Max said.

But Bitsy was staring at the phone intently. "Wait. I think we have his location!" she murmured.

"Of course you do. I'm right here," Max said.

"Not you," Bitsy replied. "Nigel. On the locator app."

"*What?*" Max peered over her shoulder at a pulsing red dot in the middle of a map of Moscow. He squinted to read the fine print under the dot:

"Trans-Siberian Railway station . . ." Max said.

"He's taking a train to the Kozhim River location?" Alex said. "Can you get the schedule?"

"I could fly you to the area a lot faster," Brandon said. "There's an airport in a place called Perm."

"I want to walk up to that creep, see the look of surprise on his face, and slap it," Bitsy said. "Then grab back my phone."

"While I get back the vials!" Alex said.

Brandon shrugged. "OK, I'll drop you off in Moscow and then fly to Perm and meet you, if I can get clearance. It's tough sometimes at these small airports."

Max took the phone, navigated to a browser, and searched for the Trans-Siberian Railway schedule. "There aren't that many trains, and they seem to go to the same places. Can we make it to Moscow by 13:20?"

"*Pffft,*" Brandon said with a cocky smile. "Yup. And with time enough for a steak lunch."

23

MAX pulled back on his straw hat. The red wig underneath it was slipping forward. It felt like steel wool, and Max was sweating way too much for this cold weather. "Was this necessary?" he asked.

"Nigel doesn't know that we know he's here," Bitsy said. "If we want those vials, the element of surprise is crucial. If he sees us, he may run."

Max nodded. "So we look for him, sit in the same car, wait for the door to close and the train to move, and then trap him. Like a spy movie."

"Exactly," Bitsy said.

With her fake glasses, painted-on freckles, and floppy hat with dangling tassels, she looked like a demented Pippi Longstocking. They had entered the train in the middle and were working their way to the back. Alex had gone in the opposite direction. By now, he was sure everyone in the train was staring at them and cracking up. Probably even sneaking photos of them to upload to social media. "The whole world is laughing at us," he whispered to Bitsy. "Can't we sit down?"

"We're almost at the end of the train," Bitsy replied.

Both sides of the train car were lined with open wooden booths. Each booth contained two high-backed bench seats extending from the window to the aisle. The seats were padded with worn red leather and they faced each other across a table. Just about everything else on the train was made of dark wood, worn smooth by years of handling, including the overhead compartments.

Max and Bitsy hadn't found any sign of Nigel. Max stopped at a booth where a couple in matching black leather jackets were in the midst of a long kiss. "Excuse me, sorry," he whispered, "have you seen an old man with a droopy left eye?"

They both grunted no, and Max went on to the next booth. Their answer was no too. Everyone's answer was no. At the very end of the last car, a metal stove was burning, sending its flames upward through a black metal pipe. Next to it was a basin full of split wood and chunks of coal. "Looks like something from a museum," Max said.

"And not exactly environmentally efficient," Bitsy said.

"I wonder if it will burn really bad wigs?" Max remarked. "My head feels flammable."

"Maybe Alex had better luck finding Nigel." Bitsy slid into a seat and glanced out the window, where a line of people was waiting to board. "I'm going to watch that queue. Maybe we got here too early. The old guy might have stopped at a restaurant."

"We should have gone out for that steak lunch Brandon promised us," Max said, sitting across from her, "instead of grabbing to go. That weird Pop-Tart is giving me gas."

"It was a blueberry blintz," Bitsy said, as she opened a plastic water bottle. "Not a Pop-Tart."

"Yeah, well, I'll be blintzing all over the seat," Max said.

Max could hear the clomping of heavy footsteps in the aisle. Alex peered into their booth, wearing a black-brimmed hat, checked shirt, bulky fur-lined jacket, and thick brown boots. Her chin was shaded with charcoal to look like beard stubble. "No sign of Nigel. You?"

Bitsy shook her head. She slid Alex's phone across the table toward her. "Nada. But the signal is still coming from this area. It could be at a nearby shop. Once the train starts up, we can try again."

As Alex took a seat next to Bitsy, an elderly woman in a patterned head scarf and sheepskin coat stopped in the aisle. With a smile, she said in a thick Russian accent, "Such beautiful young people. May I sit?"

Max slid closer to the window to leave room. "You didn't happen to find a phone, did you?"

"So sorry, no." The old woman slowly settled in, laying a thick pocketbook on the floor. "Eenglish?"

"I am," Bitsy said. "These two are Americans."

"Actually, I'm Canadian," Alex said. "And I'm Alex."

Max pushed back his sagging wig. "Jethro."

"Dr. Tretyakov," the old woman said as she reached into her bag. "Retired. I am going to Yekaterinburg. You call me Raisa. Do you play *huzur?*"

She slapped a set of cards on the table.

"No," Bitsy replied.

"Wonderful!" Raisa said. "I learn from Mongolian doctor. You learn too!"

Bitsy and Alex shared a wary look. As Raisa distributed the cards, she patiently explained the rules, but Max couldn't concentrate. He kept an eye out the window, at the families, young couples, and backpacking college kids in line. People were dressed in heavy clothing, and it was hard to make out faces. At least five people could have been Nigel, but it was impossible to know.

Now Raisa was shoving seven fanned-out cards into Max's hand. "We play. I help you."

A loud whistle broke the silence, and the train began to move. Max watched as Raisa put down a card, and Bitsy and Alex tentatively followed.

Max went to play an ace, but Raisa slapped his hand. "No no no, *this* one."

The midday sun glinted on the columned office buildings and the onion domes of churches as the train picked up speed. Soon the city gave way to suburban outskirts, and the outskirts became great fields dotted with houses. Max was starting to feel tense. By now Nigel would be on the train. But every time he tried to get up, Raisa urged him to play his cards.

Move by move, Max started to get the hang of the game. Soon he was hiding his hand from Raisa, so she wouldn't help. By the fifth game, he was actually winning.

"Huzur!" he shouted, slapping down all his cards.

"Smart boy!" Raisa said. "Bravo!"

"Can we take a lunch break now?" Bitsy asked. "Is there a café car?"

"Sit!" Raisa said. "Someone will come with food. This is how Trans-Siberian Railway works! Where are you going?"

"Perm," he replied. Max had memorized the route—Moscow to Perm by train, where they hoped Brandon would meet them, if he could get clearance. There he could fly them north to the Komi Republic.

"I have family in Perm!" Raisa said. "You too?"

Alex shook her head. "We're doing a wilderness exploration, up along the Kozhim River."

Raisa's face lit up. "Is beautiful in Komi! I call my nephew. He is the best wilderness guide. Living very close to Perm."

She put down her playing cards, fished a couple of business cards out of her purse, and gave one to Max:

SERGEI DIMITROVICH FORMOZOV

Tour Guide / Parkour Specialist / Outdoorsman

"Uh, thanks," Bitsy said, casting a dubious glance at Max.

As he shoved the card into his pocket, he felt his phone vibrate and nearly leaped out of his seat.

"So nervous, you Americans!" Raisa said with a laugh. "Like Sergei."

Quickly Max pulled out his phone and looked at the screen.

"Is it from Bitsy's phone?" Alex said.

Max shook his head. "No. I don't recognize the number."

He leaned forward. Alex, Bitsy, and Raisa all stared at the screen.

> Come out, come out, wherever you are. I'm feeling awfully lonely in Seat Number 2497.
> XOXOX,
> NH

The three kids jumped from their seats. Raisa gasped in surprise.

"Sorry!" Max said. He nearly fell into the aisle, quickly leaping up and breaking into a run.

As he neared the door between cars, it slid open. A twenty-something guy strode into the car, dressed in a neat red uniform and carrying a tray of food. "Nuts! Sandwiches! Juice—"

"*Watch out!*" Max shouted.

With a helpless yelp, the guy veered. Max veered in the same direction, barreling into the tray. A plateful of almonds shot upward, whizzing by Max's ears. Three plastic-wrapped pastries bounced off his face. He slipped to his knees in a rainstorm of small sandwiches, odd-looking snacks, and bottles of juice.

Alex scooped him up by the arm. *"Sorry!"* she screamed. *"We'll be right back!"*

"Where's Seat 2497?" Bitsy asked.

The guy stared at her in shock. "S-S-Second car?"

Alex, Max, and Bitsy took off, racing from car to car, narrowly avoiding two more food people, a conductor, and a little old man emerging from the restroom.

Max was the first to enter the second car. It was nearly empty, and no one looked anything like—

There.

Max could see a rumpled figure reclined across one of the bench seats. His hat covered his head, and he appeared to be fast asleep. Max had almost missed seeing him, but there was no mistaking the tweed coat and scuffed shoes.

Alex and Bitsy pulled up next to Max. Bitsy was shaking. "Wait a minute. Didn't he just write to us?" she whispered. "Then why is he . . . ?"

"Careful," Alex said. "He's got something up his sleeve."

"Nigel!" Max called out, tugging on the old man's pants.

"Rorrgmf," came the reply.

A folded note fell from the man's pants pocket onto the floor. But as Max stooped to pick it up, the old man bolted upright.

Bitsy's jaw dropped.

The cap had fallen from the man's head. He had a sharp nose, a full head of reddish hair, and a pair of bloodshot blue eyes staring through lopsided eyeglasses. When he spoke, it was in a nasal voice with a Russian accent. "Sorry. I fall asleep."

"You . . . you're not . . ." Alex stammered.

"Nigel," Max blurted.

The man's face tightened. "Nyet," he said, shimmying away from the window toward the aisle. "Take seat. Take!"

He stood, pushing Max away, and scurried down the center of the train.

"Should we follow him?" Bitsy asked.

But Max's eyes were focused on the folded-up note. He lifted it from the floor and opened it:

GREETINGS, CHILDREN,

WISH I COULD JOIN YOU,

I HOPE YOU ENJOYED MEETING MY DOPPELGÄNGER. BIT OF A NERVOUS FELLOW. I GAVE HIM THE SHIRT OFF MY BACK. ALSO PANTS, COAT, HAT, AND A TICKET. BETTER THAN WHAT HE WAS WEARING WHILE ASLEEP ON THE STATION FLOOR. HE DOES LIKE TO SLEEP. AH WELL, I NEEDED A NEW SET OF THREADS MYSELF. OH. GENEROUS SOUL THAT I AM, I ALSO GAVE HIM A BURNER PHONE. WITH INSTRUCTIONS ABOUT WHEN TO SEND A MESSAGE THAT I PRE-WROTE. IF YOU'RE HERE, THEN YOU FOUND IT!

DID I FOOL YOU? :)

ENJOY THE NEXT... OH, TWENTY HOURS.

TAG.

YOU'RE IT.

"He still has my phone," Bitsy said. "Use the locator app! Where is he?"

Alex looked up from her phone. "No signal. He shut it off."

24

"I guess if he told you he was going to Peoria, you'd follow him there too—*and lose even more time?*" Evelyn snapped.

"No-o-o!" Max moaned.

His eyes sprang open. It wasn't Evelyn—it was a dream. Maybe his fifth or sixth of the night. It had been this way since the sun set over a city called Nizhny Novgorod. Max would drift off, and a vision of Evelyn would pop into his head. She was staring at him, sitting by her windowsill in the middle of the night, wide awake, looking impatiently at her watch.

Over and over and over.

He checked his watch. 9:30 a.m. A little more than twenty hours since they'd left Moscow. He remembered falling asleep outside a city called Kazan, with gleaming white church spires. He must have gotten a few good hours, because the electronic sign showed that they were approaching their destination, Perm.

He tried to shake off his dreams as he squinted against the rising sun. It cast a wide amber belt down a river. He had looked that up too. It was called the Kama. As the train curved, a shaft of light hit Alex's eyes.

"Are we there yet?" she moaned.

"Almost," Max said.

From across the aisle, Bitsy was stretching her arms upward. "The question is, where's Nigel?"

"I think I dreamed about him," Max said. "Mostly I dreamed about Evelyn, but also about Nigel disguised as Dr. Tretyakov."

The old woman let out a couple of waking-up snorts. "If you call me Dr. Tretyakov, it makes me think I am wanted in hospital," she said, poking her head up. "Please. Raisa to you."

Alex was staring at her phone. "Oh, great. Brandon says he can't get flight clearance out of Perm until next week. So I guess we wait there, or make another plan."

"No!" Max blurted. "What happens if Nigel gets all the ingredients?"

Alex put a hand on his. "We have to stay positive. Shake off the bad dreams."

As the train curved inward to the city, the spire of a church rose above the treetops. It glowed amber and red in the morning sun, and for a moment the trip felt like a wrong turn into Disneyland.

"The cities are really pretty," Bitsy said. "We blast through all this amazing empty countryside, and it feels like we're in the middle of nowhere, then boom—a city with a million people."

"We're not here to sightsee," Max grumbled. "The only scenery I care about is the Kozhim River. And if Brandon can't get us there, we'll need someone else."

Raisa was staring out the window as the train approached the station. "That would be my handsome nephew Sergei. I know he will help! I texted him. He said he will meet me. You meet him. To meet Sergei is to love him. Trust me, I am doctor."

Max wasn't sure that made sense. In fact, he knew it didn't. But Alex and Bitsy were both giving him a look, and he shrugged. *Why not?* he mouthed.

Someone was better than no one.

As the train pulled into the station, the booths emptied. Max, Alex, Bitsy, and Raisa lined up for the exit. Max knew that the Trans-Siberian Railway continued clear across to China, and Perm was not even halfway. Still, a lot of passengers were getting off. Even more were lined up outside to board.

People exiting the train were greeted by grinning friends and families. Just beyond the small crowd, a beat-up four-door pickup roared into the parking lot. It skidded to a stop, its tires screaming, its license plate dangling from one screw. The driver's door was smashed in, so the driver slid across, emerging legs-first from the passenger side.

He didn't jump out of the car so much as unfold himself. He had to be at least 6' 4".

A shock of wavy reddish-brown hair spilled out from the sides of a red bandanna around his head. It looked like he'd forgotten to shave for a week or two, and even though it was a little chilly he wore a tank top and ripped shorts. As he ran to the train, his arm and leg muscles seemed etched like rock.

"*That's* Sergei?" Bitsy said.

"Oh my . . ." Alex mumbled.

"Looks like he spends a lot of time at the gym," Max remarked.

"*Tetushka!*" Sergei shouted.

"No, I'm Alex." Alex stepped toward him, extending her hand. "Delighted to meet—"

But the guy veered past her, where Raisa was emerging

from the train, her arms wide. Sergei lifted her off the train, swinging her in a wide circle.

"I am a dork," Alex said. "I am such a dork."

"Maybe we should interview him first," Max said.

"I think he's perfect," Bitsy shot back.

"Children, come!" Raisa said, barging through the crowd toward them with the smiling man. "Please meet my nephew Yevgeny!"

Bitsy's face fell. "Yev-who-ey?"

"Wait. He's *not* Sergei?" Alex asked.

Raisa laughed. "Ah no, he is the son of—"

"*TETUSHKA!*" The new voice was like a foghorn, blotting out everyone else.

Max spun around. Squeezing himself out of the rear door of the pickup was a squat man with bulging cheeks and shoulders like a rock outcropping. A cascade of graying hair flopped over the right side of his face, and he quickly pushed it back up and over his otherwise shiny head. He lumbered briskly toward Raisa, rocking side to side, his eyes magnified by the thick lenses of old, taped-together glasses. A paint-speckled T-shirt was stretched over the ample bulges of his stomach, and his smile revealed a sparse set of teeth like piano keys.

"Sergei!" Raisa exclaimed as the man ran to her,

lifting her off her feet and spinning her around. "So strong. Such a kind heart to offer help for my new friends! Alex, Max, Bitsy, meet Sergei!"

"Hoo boy . . ." Alex said. "I mean, greetings!"

"Charmed, I'm sure," Bitsy said, sounding anything but.

Max stared at the patterns of white droplets on the man's shirt. "You paint houses?"

"*Ha!*" Sergei honked a laugh like a broken trombone and whipped a phone from his pocket. "No house. Paintings! I show you latest! Is called *Defeated: Requiem 2*. Based on painting called *Defeated: Requiem* by Vereshchagin. You know it? Is beautiful—priest praying over field of frozen dead men. I show you."

"No, Papa," Yevgeny said, "show them painting of firing squad."

"I'll pass," Bitsy said. "On both."

"We're in a hurry," Max said. "We need to get to the Kozhim River. Fast."

Sergei scowled, putting away his phone. "Ah. Of course. What part of river?"

"We're not sure," Alex said.

Sergei narrowed his eyes. "What you want to find there?"

"We don't know yet," Max replied.

"We were hoping you'd help us," Bitsy said. "We have some clues."

"But we can pay you," Max added. "Money is no object."

"*What? You don't know what you want?*" He jammed his shoulders upward in a dismayed shrug, looking at Raisa. "*Where you find these kids?*"

Yevgeny was cracking up.

As the train's whistle sounded, Raisa planted a kiss on Sergei's cheek and spoke in a flurry of Russian.

"So far, this isn't going well," Bitsy drawled.

Raisa scurried back into the train. As it began to chug away, she blew kisses from behind a window. Without a word, Sergei and Yevgeny headed back to their car.

Watching them, Max shrugged. "Any suggestions for a Plan B?"

"What—you slow too?" Sergei called out from the open door of the pickup. His hair had fallen again, and he swept it back over his head. "You maybe waiting for written invitation? Get in!"

The second-worst part of the ride was that Sergei had to drop Yevgeny back at his house. That put Alex and Bitsy in a foul mood.

The worst part was that the pickup truck made Nigel's

rental car look like a limousine. The windshield was cracked, the glove compartment was held together with duct tape, and the engine made popping noises like gunshots. Going over small potholes felt like being hit with a baseball bat.

Sergei was whistling loudly. He stopped barely long enough to shout: *"Happeenman landskia cousin!"*

"Is that Russian for 'I know where to buy crash helmets'?" Max shouted back. "Because I really like that idea!"

"I said—I have painted many landscapes of the Kozhim!" Sergei bellowed. *"I have spent much time in area. For landscape painters, mwahh, paradise! But is big river! You need tell me—where to start?"*

They were approaching an airport now, and Max desperately wished they could get out and run for cover. He made a mental note to tell Brandon to get clearance at every airport in the world, just to be on the safe side. "OK," he said, "the only thing we know is some weird clue: 'tincture of coil dust.'"

"What?" Sergei bellowed.

Max took a deep breath. *"Tincture of—"*

"What is tincture?" Sergei asked.

"It's like *color,*" Bitsy replied.

"But we have no idea what *coil dust* means," Alex volunteered. "Sorry."

"Coil . . ." Sergei said, twirling his fingers in the air. "You say coil?"

"Yes," Max replied.

"Is curly thing, yes?" Sergei continued.

"Yup," Alex said.

"Dust is . . . poof poof poof?" Sergei waggled his fingers. The pickup veered to the left. Another car blew its horn, nearly sideswiping them.

Alex screamed. The passenger in the other car was shouting words in Russian that didn't sound too friendly. Overhead a helicopter churned into view with a noise like machine gun fire.

"Can you take us back into town now?" Bitsy cried out. *"I am really having second thoughts!"*

Sergei yanked the steering wheel to the right. The pickup screeched into a large open area with a parking lot, a security booth, and a cement section marked off with white paint like a dodgeball court. He pulled to a stop, then jumped from the car. "Get out!"

Max didn't need a written invitation for that. He opened the door, stepped onto the pavement, and took a deep breath. Bitsy and Alex scrambled out after him, looking bewildered. The helicopter hovered directly over-head now, and the noise was deafening.

"Sergei!" a smiling woman shouted from inside the security booth.

"Tinatchka!" Sergei ran to hug her.

"Is he going to do this to everyone he knows along the way?" Max said.

"That does it," Alex said fumbling for her phone. "I'm getting a taxi."

"Shto? What taxi?" bellowed Sergei, who was march-ing toward them. "You say money no object, right?"

"Uh, I guess we did . . ." Max said.

Sergei gestured to the chopper, which was making a smooth landing in the center of the circular area. "Then we get to Kozhim very, very fast."

MAX squinted out the window. Directly below them was a range of mountains that thrust up from the earth like a tsunami of white-capped rock. "Is that snow?" he shouted, his face pressed to the glass.

For the first time during the whole trip, he was sitting in the copilot seat, and he liked it. A lot.

"You like the Urals?" Sergei yelled back. "We take detour and see them!"

As he yanked the throttle to the left, the helicopter banked sharply. Detours were not on Max's wish list these days. But Bitsy and Alex were totally into it, busy taking photos with Alex's phone. The chopper scaled the side of the mountain range, lurching left and right. "Too much wind!" Sergei yelled. "I go higher!"

Now the helicopter was rising over the peaks. Across a vast, flat plain, Max could see the silver glow of a body of water. "So that's the Barents Sea, right?"

"Very good!" Sergei replied. "Goes into Arctic Sea— straight to North Pole! Santa Claus!"

"I can't see the workshop," Bitsy said.

"Probably underwater by now," Alex replied.

"Can we get back on track now?" Max asked.

The chopper banked, rose, and dropped. It dipped into valleys where the streams looped and twisted like some secret script handwriting. It buzzed over villages ringed with mud huts and cattle. Sheep moved like earth-borne clouds among vast grassy fields, and a mysterious cloud of dust rose just above the horizon. Out of it emerged a herd of horses galloping fiercely toward nothing in particular, their manes snapping like flags.

Soon the mountains and sea were far behind them, and Sergei descended. Not far from another village, a river cut through the landscape like a blue knife wound, bruised on either side with rock cliffs and thick vegetation.

"Welcome to Kozhim River!" Sergei said, maneuvering the chopper over a scrubby clearing.

"Wait, we're here already?" Max said, feeling a jolt of excitement.

"I took shortcut!" Sergei said with a laugh. As they descended to the top of a cliff, the expanse of river disappeared below them. "I lead tours here many times! Steep! Most important to be careful! Very sacred place."

In minutes the helicopter was on land, the rotors slowing. The ground was parched and flat, and a ramshackle shed stood off to the side. Max grabbed his pack and jumped to the ground. It was much colder here than in Perm. He ran from the helicopter with Alex beside him. She was crouching superlow under the still-moving blades.

"You don't have to duck," Max said. "Those blades are nowhere near your head."

"It's the way people do it in movies," Alex said, shivering.

The thrum of the helicopter rotors slowed and stopped, replaced by the wind's hollow *whoosh* and the soft crackle of swaying branches. Sergei had a huge backpack of his own, and from it he pulled out three lined anoraks. "Here," he said. "You need."

The jackets were all too big, but at least they cut the chill. Together they walked to the point where the land ended.

Max gasped. Below them, the river was tiny and distant, gashed into the earth between two grayish-white cliffs. The drop-off was a nearly vertical wall of rock, grooved into chutes that seemed to beckon a slide straight downward to death. "Limestone?" Max asked.

Sergei smiled. "How you know?"

"Long story," Max replied.

"Isn't there a place where it's less steep?" Alex asked.

Sergei took a deep breath. He was still in just his paint-spattered T-shirt but didn't seem to be feeling any cold. "This . . . *coil*," he said. "This is same as . . . what is word . . . *screw*?"

"Not exactly," Max said. "A screw has spiral threads. A coil itself is a helix. Basically, a three-dimensional spiral with a constant diameter."

"What he means to say is, very similar," Alex cut in. "Why do you ask?"

Sergei took a deep breath. "This part of Kozhim River is very special place. Much, much gold here, but hard to find. Many years ago—1990, 1991, I think—international scientists travel along river looking for gold. They stop to rest here." He pointed downward. Max squinted and saw a small group of wooden shacks dotting the rocky banks of the Kozhim.

"One great scientist, Regina Donner, she cannot

sleep," Sergei went on. "She feel something. Like electricity. Like headache that will rip open skull. She runs out of tent. Something is glowing in bushes. She picks up. Looks like gold coil . . . or screw. But she knows is very, very old—so . . . maybe great discovery of tool from ancient times? Right then she hear noises, like animals. Shadows moving along shore. Creatures, picking these coils out of bushes. Their faces are covered with hair, like wolves! Donner puts gold coil in pocket, but now entire body is growing hot, like fever. She runs back in tent, grabs rifle to scare away monsters. *Bang!* Soon other scientists are running out of tents!" Sergei removed his glasses and rubbed his eyes. He reached into his pack for a water bottle. "Sorry. Dry."

"Keep going!" Alex shouted. "What did they find?"

Sergei took a swig and continued. "Creatures gone. But Donner—she is lying on rocks. Groaning. She tells them what happened—monsters, coils, everything. How can such a thing be from this earth? The scientists, they don't know how to think. Delusions, maybe? Then . . . *cccchhhh* . . . she dies. No bullet, no knife. Only bruise is where she fell. They take body home and empty Donner's pocket. All they find is . . . dust. Which scientists determine is thousands of years old."

"So . . . *coil dust*!" Max blurted. "Like in the hint. Which is why you brought us here!"

Sergei nodded.

"Wait, this story is true?" Alex asked.

"This is Russia," Sergei replied with a shrug. "Could be. Could be no."

Max looked over the edge. "There's no way we can get down there without dying."

Sergei smiled. "Sergei will take care of you. This is my job."

He walked to the small shed, spun the combination on a lock, and pushed the door open. Disappearing inside for a few moments, he came out with three huge harnesses connected to wings that were folded like bats. "We use these."

Bitsy looked like she was going to faint. "G-G-Gliders?"

"I show you," Sergei said. "Not as dangerous as you think, if you do it right. Wind currents along river are perfect."

"This is soooo cool!" Alex said. "I have been wanting to do this all my life. My parents? They're like, 'over my dead body'—"

"You have very good parents," Bitsy said.

Sergei was already strapping one on. "Sorry. Only three gliders in shed."

"No problem," Bitsy blurted out. "I'll wait."

"Maybe you won't need to," Max said. He set down his pack and unzipped it. Jammed against the side was the cylindrical container he'd been neglecting the whole trip. With a proud grin, he opened it and pulled out the lightweight hang glider he and Evelyn had made. "We designed this for Charles the robot. But I can try using it."

"*What?*" Bitsy said.

"No," Alex said. "Just . . . no."

"You just said it was so cool!" Max protested.

"Yeah, I meant using real, outdoor-tour-tested, tried-and-true gliders," Alex said. "You've never tested your contraption, Max! Do you even know how to work it?"

"Ms. Williams, our robotics teacher, gave Evelyn and me an *A* plus on the project." Max slipped on the harness and fastened the belt. "Not just an *A*. No one else has ever received a plus. It passed every aerodynamic test we put it through. We even made a report. And Sergei can give me tips."

"I don't believe this is happening . . ." Bitsy said.

"Is beautiful!" Sergei exclaimed. "So light. I give you tips if you let me try later?"

"Maybe." Max pulled his phone out of his pocket and thrust it toward Alex. "Will you video me, so I can send it to Evelyn?"

"No, I won't video you!" Alex protested. "And just so you understand where I'm coming from—no. Just abso-totally-lutely *no!*"

Max stepped toward the edge of the cliff. "Then I'll have to take a selfie."

26

HIS wings snapped open. The wind buffeted his ears with a harsh, high-pitched wail. It took Max a few minutes to realize the wail was coming from above. From Bitsy and Alex.

They were scared. But Max wasn't. He didn't need help from Sergei. It was a matter of weight distribution. And flexibility. With the breeze brushing back his hair and the river racing over the rocks below, he let the wings carry him close enough to the cliffs that he could see tiny caves in the limestone. He wished Evelyn were here. She would have loved this more than anyone else.

"Haaaaaa-hahahaha!" He wasn't sure why he was laughing. Nothing about this was funny, really. But he couldn't help himself. He wanted to stay up for hours. It was working. He knew it would. He just hadn't realized how awesome it would be.

As the cliffs came closer, his voice caught in his throat.

He was *too* close.

He leaned his body back toward the other bank, his left hand gripping one lightweight crossbar and his feet resting on a lower one. Theoretically, he should be able to use the bars to steer. He concentrated on shifting his weight.

Lean left . . . lean right . . .

He needed both hands to control this thing. Taking a video wasn't going to work. He would have to memorize every detail to tell Evelyn later. He glanced upward toward the top of the cliff. Alex was stepping off now, in a much bulkier glider . . . then Sergei . . .

A scream echoed through the canyon, and Max smiled. Bitsy was stepping off too.

Max turned his focus downward. The winds were tossing him, the cold air piercing his jacket and making his teeth chatter. He held tight as a shadow passed across eye level—a gliding hawk, its black-and-white-striped tail spread like a shovel blade. He wondered what it was thinking, and he gave it a big wave.

The glider lurched, but the hawk didn't seem to

notice. Max gripped the handle and felt himself slowing, sinking closer to the gravelly bank. He took care to stay over the solid bank, not the river. And far enough away from the shacks.

His feet hit the rocks with a solid crunch. A jolt of pain traveled up his leg. He tried to break into a run but instead stumbled, falling to the bank and tumbling head over heels. When he stopped, the wings were wrapped around him, their support rods bent but intact.

He lay there, catching his breath. The river was swollen, the water lapping loudly against the rocks. Farther back, he saw Sergei land on his feet, pumping his fists triumphantly. Alex and Bitsy landed near him, their legs buckling just like Max's had.

He took a deep breath and stood, quickly unbuckling his glider and folding it tight. Time to get to work.

"That was awesome!" he shouted. As he walked toward the others, he stuffed the glider back into its container and nested it in his backpack.

Alex was sitting on the rocks, shaking her head. "Did that just happen?"

With a laugh, Sergei threw Max a thumbs-up. "He did not even need Sergei! Someday, Max, when you need job as tour guide—you call, eh? And you bring some gliders!"

"I think the crossbars could stand to be stronger," Max said.

Bitsy was shaking all over. She'd been on the ground for ten minutes but was still trying to undo her harness. "Would you . . . ?" she said.

Alex rushed over and helped her out of the glider. "That took a lot of courage, Bits."

"Or stupidity," Bitsy said. "Although I admit, aside from the fact that I nearly had a heart attack, it was glorious."

As Alex threw the harnesses aside, she glanced up the river. "I'm more concerned about the other direction. We can't fly up. How are we going to get back?"

Max glanced up the sheer rock face. "Maybe Sergei has climbing gear?"

But the guide was backing toward them with a loud "Sshhhhh!" His smile had tightened into a look of concern, and he reached into his own pack for a set of binoculars.

Bitsy and Alex fell silent. Squinting against the low evening sun, Max could see a figure approaching from upriver.

It seemed to have emerged from a distant shack. It moved along the rocks with surprising speed. Sergei shouted something in Russian but got no response.

"Friend of yours?" Max said.

"Old Fyodor . . ." Sergei said. "Must be hundred years old. Met him when I was boy. Hiking. I was very sick. He had a medicine that made me better. Other hikers, they have met Fyodor too. Is very private man. But he can help us, if he wants to."

They walked closer until they met in the middle. The old man was tiny and whiskered, at least five inches shorter than Max. He was bent at the waist, his tattered coat wrapped around him like a cape. The rocks did not move under the weight of his feet, and Max could swear he was floating. He stopped, nodding imperceptibly. Then he muttered something to Sergei, who laughed and answered in Russian.

After a brief exchange, Sergei turned to the kids. "He remembers me! He says he knew I would return. So . . . chit chat chit chat, thank you, nice to see you . . . then I ask him about legend of Donner. And coils."

"And . . . ?" Alex asked.

Sergei shrugged. "He say nothing."

The old man turned and walked away from them. Max, Sergei, Bitsy, and Alex shared a confused look. As if in response, old Fyodor crooked a bony finger to the sky.

"I guess that means follow," Bitsy said.

Together they walked down the rocky shore. Max

squinted against the sun and wished he'd brought sunglasses. After about fifty yards, even with shoes on, the soles of his feet began to ache against the sharp stones. After about a hundred, he thought he was going to scream.

That was when Fyodor stopped.

He was standing just before a deep pit in the ground, near the base of the limestone cliff. The angle of the sun cast the opening in deep shadow. Turning toward Sergei, Fyodor muttered in Russian. His speech was slow, soft, and droning, and it seemed to be taking a long time to make his point.

The area just around the pit was smooth, more like gravel than rocks. For the sake of his aching feet, Max decided to walk closer. He wasn't far from Fyodor now, but the old man didn't seem to mind. Or didn't notice him. He was intent on Sergei.

"Max, what are you doing?" Alex hissed, but he ignored her.

Taking out his phone, Max flipped on the video. He turned the lens downward, facing the hole, and moved as close as he could. The screen captured nothing but blackness. He knelt, playing with the brightness controls until a constellation of shapes appeared, like a grave site full of bones. Max activated the phone's flashlight and shone it down again. He glanced over to his friends. Bitsy and Alex were looking at him nervously, and Sergei was keeping up the chatter, distracting the old man.

As he leaned over the pit, he could clearly make out the shapes now. They weren't bones at all. They were golden cylinders, some as big as fists or even forearms. Each shape was a thick shaft surrounded by a coil, like a screw with the caps and pointed tips shaved off.

Max shut off the phone, jammed it into his pocket, and reached down into the pit. His fingers closed around one of the odd objects. It was warm. As he lifted it upward, it seemed to glow with his touch, but that might have been the reflection of the sun. Quickly he shoved it into his pocket.

A moment later, Sergei was pulling him back by the shoulders. "We have problem," he said.

"The coils, Sergei—they're at the bottom of the pit!" Max said.

Over Sergei's shoulder, Max could see that neither Fyodor nor Alex nor Bitsy was paying him a scrap of attention. They were all looking forward, over his shoulder.

"Bravo," Sergei said. "But we have to go."

Max spun around. Looming out of the dusk, as if arising from the stones themselves, was a group of men and women dressed in ragged gray robes. All Max could see of their faces were eyes staring out of blackness. He assumed they were wearing face masks or had covered their faces with tar, until they drew closer.

That was when he realized the covering was hair—hair across cheeks, hair tufting on noses and foreheads.

In their arms were wooden clubs embedded with sharp, jutting stones.

27

MAX leaped to his feet. "We come in peace!" he cried out.

Alex pulled him back from the rim of the pit. "Let's assume they don't understand English!"

The robed gang approached the other side of the hole and stopped, looking like hairy Druid priests. Fyodor was talking to them in Russian now, his arms extended to the sides, palms up.

"What's he doing?" Bitsy asked.

"I don't know, but at least it's not fists," Max said. "Fists would be bad. Let's just go."

"Go where?" Alex said, glancing up the cliff wall. "We're trapped."

"Wolf people . . ." Sergei called over his shoulder. "Amazing, no? Like Donner said!"

When Fyodor finished speaking, one of the gang answered him in a sharp, high-pitched voice.

Sergei let out a loud snort. "Haaaa! Oh. Sorry. Sorry." He turned away, with his hand over his mouth. "Woman with beard! Is just funny."

Alex stared at him, aghast. "Are you serious?" Alex said. "Did you just diss her to her face?"

"Guys . . . maybe we can slip away?" Max said. "Walk down the banks . . . ?"

"OK . . . OK . . . I'm sorry." Sergei swallowed back another laugh as he stared at Fyodor, listening hard to the old man's conversation. "Fyodor says these people very primitive, living here in caves for many generations. These coils . . . they all fall from sky one day, like holy rain. They do things—make people sick, punish for bad hunting season, blah blah blah, the usual local superstitions. Before this, the tribe looked like everyone else. After, they changed." Sergei turned to Max. "Aha. Probably radioactive, no? Giving mutations! So what do these people do? Destroy coils like normal people would? No! They think coils are sacred. They believe they must protect holy coils from intruders. They are angry. Because someone else come here yesterday. English man. Very nice. Ate food, learned how to do sacred dance, and so on. Then boom, he stole from this pit."

"Sacred dance?" Bitsy repeated.

"Sounds like Nigel," Alex said.

"Ni . . . gel," one of the wolf people grumbled. A couple of others nodded.

Max's jaw dropped. "I don't believe this. He got here first . . ."

"Friend of yours?" Sergei asked.

Max took a deep breath and choked on the acrid smell of ammonia. Ammonia came from betrayal. Nigel had tricked them. "He stole from us," Max said. "Now he stole from these people, and he's probably on to the next place, and our mission just blew up in our faces . . ."

"Max, we still have a chance," Alex said. "Nigel hasn't taken it all, and we can find him." She turned to Sergei. "Look, Fyodor knows these people. They trust him. Talk to him. Maybe *he* can convince them we're friendly, non-flying humans. There are so many of these coils. They can spare one or two."

"But—" Max protested.

"Shhh," Alex said.

"I will negotiate directly." Sergei took a deep breath and sucked in his ample gut. "I have best words. I am best negotiator. It is what I do."

He stepped toward the pit and yelled something in Russian that was more a bark than a sentence. Fyodor let out a gasp. Across the pit, the wolf people glared back in stony silence. Now several of them were speaking at once. Some were waving their arms in a way that did not seem friendly.

"Sergei, what did you say?" Bitsy asked.

"A joke about hairy monster, just to lighten things," Sergei said. "Humor is important step in negotiating."

"Let's just go!" Max said, digging into his pocket.

"Will you stop it, Max?" Bitsy said. "We still need—"

Before she could finish, Max held out the golden coil he'd swiped.

Alex and Bitsy fell silent. Max glanced at Sergei. The guide was training his phone on the group now, taking a video. "What is he doing?" Max said.

"Getting the wolf people angry, it looks like," Bitsy said.

"Tell him what we have!" Bitsy said.

"What if one of them understands English?" Alex said. "They'll come after us."

"If they don't go after him first!" Max cupped his hands over his mouth and yelled, "Sergei, stop negotiating! Let's go! I have a you-know-what!"

Sergei spun around. "You took coil? *Now* you tell me?"

He shoved his phone back in his pocket. But the

people were moving around the pit, coming closer. Fyodor's face was ashen, his eyes darting from the gang to Sergei. With a tight smile, Sergei threw them a salute and called out, *"Do svidaniya!"* As he turned to run away, someone from the back of the crowd threw a fist-size rock. It rose and fell across the orange disk of the sun, in a straight path for Sergei.

"Duck, Sergei!" Max shouted.

With a soft thud, the rock hit the back of Sergei's head, and he dropped to the ground. The wolf people were surrounding him now. Max, Alex, and Bitsy rushed in, but they hadn't gotten more than a few feet when Sergei sprang to his feet. He turned to his attackers and bellowed a honking cry. With a leap, he decked one of the wolf people with a solid martial-arts kick to the jaw. He spun through the air, grunting and kicking like an overweight kung fu film star. The wolf people backed away, looking more baffled than scared.

"Some negotiator," Alex remarked.

Max leaped at Sergei, trying to grab his arm. But the guide was spinning again, and he landed a kick that sent one of the robed people staggering toward the hole. It was a kid whose face was only lightly tufted with fine hair, who was now windmilling arms, panicking.

As the kid fell in backward with a scream, Max knew by the sound that it was a girl. He sprinted toward the hole as Sergei continued his whirling display. Leaping over a fallen man, Max dropped to the ground as a splintered wooden club flew by his face.

"Max, what are you up to, are you crazy?" came Alex's voice.

Max ignored the plea, crawling the last few feet to the rim. The pit wasn't very deep, but the young woman had fallen badly. She writhed on a bed of golden coils, crying in pain.

Max leaned over the edge and reached down. "Grab on! Take my hand!"

Tentatively, the girl rose to her feet. With a grimace, she lifted her arm, but the other one dangled by her side. Max stretched until he was able to clasp her hand. "I've got you! You don't need the other hand. Just dig in to the wall with your legs!"

She just stared back blankly, so he tightened his grip and yanked hard. Letting out a shriek, she planted the soles of her feet on the side of the hole.

Max rocked back to a sitting position. Leaning backward, he pulled as hard as he could. "Heave . . . ho!"

The girl scrambled over the top. But she wasn't looking at Max now. Her eyes were the size of saucers, staring at something over Max's head. She yanked her hand free and then used it to swat Max aside. He yowled in surprise, tumbling away.

From behind him, a club thudded to the earth, sending up a cloud of dust. The girl leaped at the attacker, yelling at him, smacking him with her good arm. Max had no doubts about her toughness now. He bolted through the mob—and ran smack into Bitsy and Alex.

"What did you just do?" Bitsy shouted.

Max kept running. "What I had to do. Hurry!"

Now Sergei was lumbering toward them, moving faster than Max imagined he could. *"We go now!"* he commanded.

"Excellent idea!" Alex yelled.

They sped along the rocky bank, their panting breath sending up clouds of white into the darkening sky. Max looked over his shoulder. The sun was almost to the horizon now, and the scene was still chaotic and confused near the pit. Some of the wolf people were tending to the injured girl, some arguing with Fyodor, others fighting among themselves.

"There is place to climb—not far away!" Sergei shouted. "Is not cliff there. Just rock scramble!"

The bank was narrowing now, and Max had to veer to avoid stepping in water.

Water.

He stopped short, feeling the cold wetness seeping into his shoes. The words of their original mission shot through his brain: *Add the salubrious and catalytically marvelous effects upon this substance, derived from the following water sources . . . Preserved with the tincture of coil dust from the Kozhim River . . .* "Wait!" he said. "We're not done. It's not just the coil. We need the water source. Like we had with the hippo bones."

He unhooked his pack and removed one of the empty vials. Kneeling, he scooped up water from the river, then dropped the coil inside.

It began to glow.

"My cousin is a genius," Alex said.

With a smile, Max tightened the top and put it back into his pack. "How much farther?" he asked Sergei.

The guide thought for a moment. "In kilometers?" he asked. "Or hours?"

"I'm already in pain," Alex groaned.

With a leap and a whoop, Sergei began running along the edge of the cliff. Alex, Bitsy, and Max trudged behind, as the color began to drain from the sky.

28

IT felt like someone had snuck inside Max's legs and was twanging each muscle as if it were a guitar string.

Sergei's route included a two-hour hike to a break in the wall, followed by a rock climb in the dark. By the time the sun was dropping below the horizon, they'd all banged their knees and elbows and ankles, and by the end of it Bitsy nearly had to be carried aboard the helicopter.

Now, on the chopper flight over the night-blackened landscape, Max struggled to sleep. But the pain in his body wasn't allowing it. And his brain reeled.

The vial in his backpack was glowing. There was no doubt about that. Max opened the pack every few seconds to check. The coil had sunk to the bottom, and it was now a dull gray. But the water around it pulsed and churned orange, as if there were some life force inside. There had to be an explanation for this. Some kind of chemical reaction. The wolf people thought it was magical, but Max didn't believe in magic. In life, magic was just facts in disguise.

In the cockpit, Sergei was muttering in rapid-fire Russian through his headset. Bitsy was looking over the list of locations, and Alex was deep in thought. "You awake, Max?" she said.

"Yeah," Max answered.

"I'm feeling guilty," Alex said.

"I'm smelling garlic," Max said. "So, yeah, me too. I mean, I'm really happy we got this. I keep thinking about Evelyn in the hospital. And now we're a step closer. So that's good. But those wolf people . . . this stuff was so important to them. And we just wrecked their world."

"Whatever is in those coils, it's affecting them in a strange way, Max. Changing their hormonal balances, *something*. I don't think they're healthy, not really. I'm thinking that if we succeed, if we get all the ingredients to this serum, we can return and bring it to them. We owe them that."

"Yeah, good idea. Maybe you can use my glider." Max thought a moment. "The garlic is fading."

"That's the spirit," Alex said.

Bitsy looked up from the list. "I won't even begin to try to understand that last bit of conversation. But are we agreed that our next stop should be the closest one as the crow flies?"

"Kathmandu," Max said. "Just south of the Himalaya. Most people say 'Himalayas,' but *himal* means 'mountain' and *aya* means 'range.' So *Himalaya* means 'mountain range' and you don't have to add an *s*. Kathmandu is in one of the three major valleys of Nepal. Also, you know someone there. You said so when we first translated this message."

"You amaze me," Bitsy said.

"God is in the factoids," Max replied.

Bitsy took a deep breath. "I have been educated in international schools. Many I.S. teachers migrate from one country to another, so my former teachers are now all over the world—and one of them runs a British school in Kathmandu. If you let me use one of your phones, I will contact her. Have you reached Brandon? Can he meet us in Perm with the jet?"

"I texted him," Alex said. "He says the Perm airport is very tight about scheduling outside private craft. We'd have to meet him back in Moscow."

Bitsy blanched. "No. Absolutely not. I refuse to take

that tedious Trans-Siberian Railway ride all the way back!"

Alex called to the front of the chopper: "Sergei, are there direct commercial flights from Perm to Kathmandu?"

Sergei snorted. "Big passenger planes? Not Perm. You would have to go through Moscow. Although there is faster way—charter flight yourself. If you have money."

"We have a jet," Alex said with a sigh. "But our pilot is in Moscow too. And they won't let in private craft from the outside."

From the side, Max could see a smile sprouting on Sergei's face. "Well," he said, "he is not only pilot in world . . ."

They were on the ground in a half hour. In another half hour, Sergei had negotiated a small private jet. And a half hour later, they were high above Siberia, heading south. The plane had two seats up front. The copilot seat was empty, Bitsy and Alex shared the bench seat behind Sergei, and Max was alone on the rear bench. The seats were made of slightly worn plastic, and the cabin had the faint smell of old underwear.

"Comfy?" Sergei said.

"Nothing that a little Febreze couldn't improve," Bitsy said.

"Or a nice bed, maybe with lacy curtains," Alex replied. "It's been a long day."

It wasn't until Bitsy and Alex were fast asleep, pretzeled together on the long seat, that Max began to feel the tiniest bit tired. As he stretched out, yawning, he caught a glimpse of Sergei's old-fashioned TV-screen navigation system. And he saw something familiar on the screen.

His own face.

Max's eyes sprang open. It wasn't just him. Bitsy's and Alex's faces were there too. A voice was speaking very urgent-sounding Russian. Max had no idea what it was saying, but a large phone number was flashing at the bottom of the screen.

And somewhere in there he heard another familiar name—"Pirgos Dirou."

Max tapped Alex on the shoulder. Before she could react, he put his finger to her lips, shushing her. Quietly Max pointed to the screen. Alex's eyes widened.

While the image played, Sergei was on his walkie-talkie, droning in Russian. Max could hear the words "Kozhim" and "Kathmandu." He was telling someone where he'd been and where he was going.

Alex nimbly extracted herself from her seat and

squeezed around it to join Max. "That looks like a wanted poster!" she whispered.

"I guess we're criminals," Max said.

"But why?"

Max checked if Sergei could see them, but the pilot was still busy talking. "The voice on that broadcast said something about *Pirgos Dirou* . . . the caves," Max whispered.

"The police were after us, and we escaped," Alex whispered back. "Stealing the artifacts is one crime. Evading the law is a whole other one. Someone must have tipped them off that we went to an airport—"

"Frangitsa, at the rental place! Or Nigel." Max shook his head in confusion. "So we're international fugitives? Because of a hippo bone that we don't even have anymore?"

Alex glanced again toward Sergei. "We can't trust him. I'll wake up Bitsy. She needs to know. We have to make a plan to ditch him."

"There are parachutes in the back," Max said.

"Ha-ha, Max," Alex said, glaring at him. "Just ha-ha-ha."

29

THE Hotel Himalaya had a grand breakfast, with a spectacular view of a courtyard filled with palms. Outside it was hot, polluted, and crowded, as always in Kathmandu. But how refreshing to be in a place where the climate was cool and the impeccably dressed staff greeted you by name.

"Good morning, Mr. Hanscombe," said the maître d' with a courteous bow. "The gentleman from Interpol is waiting. Follow me and watch your step."

Nigel was a sucker for a big entrance. He took the steps at a leap and finished with a little pirouette. A man at the table by the window looked up from a folded newspaper, startled by the move. Despite being indoors, he was wearing a trench coat and a brimmed hat.

"Hrrm," he said.

The nice maître d' pulled out the opposite seat, and Nigel handed him a crisp ten-dollar bill. It was always good, he thought, to be generous with the help. Turning to the rumpled man, he said, "Are we expected to have a password of some sort?"

"Ha," the man in the coat grunted, slapping his newspaper on the table. "Lyle."

"I will assume that's your name." Nigel held out his hand. "I am Hanscombe. I'm feeling a bit peckish, Mr. Lyle, can I get us, perhaps, some custom omelets—?"

"Facts first," Lyle growled. "Greek authorities. Theft of antiquities."

"Do you speak in sentences or have you given up verbs for religious reasons?" Nigel asked.

Lyle's face flinched. "Wise guy. I don't like being pulled into little jobs like this. Could take you in too."

"Garçon? Coffee?" Nigel called out to a passing waiter as he pulled a sky-blue-cased phone from his pocket and pressed the Power button.

It was safe to do this now.

"As you no doubt know," Nigel said, placing the phone on the table, "two of the children have been in the news regarding a rather spectacular recovery of a treasure left by Jules Verne."

"Noted."

"It would seem that they would have everything a child could need," Nigel said. "But you know what they say about children, give them an inch and they take a mile."

Lyle snickered. "Got two kids myself."

"I'm sure the conversation at home sparkles." The waiter filled both coffee cups, and Nigel leaned across the table. "To answer your question, I befriended these children in Greece. As an amateur archaeologist, I am appalled at their crime. Far be it for me to recommend tactics, but it wouldn't be unwise to have a few eyes at the Kathmandu airport."

"Do you have proof?" the man barked.

The phone was powered up now. Nigel entered the password, accessed Bitsy's contacts list, and scrolled until he reached MAX TILT. Then he pushed the phone across the table toward Lyle.

"You recognize this name, no?" Nigel said. "The phone belongs to a friend of his. She dropped it. And according to common international law dating back to the Code of Hammurabi . . . loosely translated, finders keepers."

"So?"

"So, let's say Max receives a message from this phone

asking 'Where are you?' He will answer truthfully, as he thinks he is texting a trusted friend. Simple, no?"

Sometimes you had to spell things out to these people.

Lyle nodded, his eyebrows tented way up. "Text him."

"Brilliant idea indeed." Nigel raised his index finger over the phone, then stopped. "Oh, by the way, you don't happen to know anyone here with the name Armando?"

30

MAX plopped a gray-and-red Nepali hat on his head, and it promptly drooped over his face. Which wasn't the disguise he'd intended.

He lifted it quickly, keeping sight of the airport concourse through the shop window.

"You flatten the top and crimp the two ends," said the clerk with a patient smile, skillfully removing Max's hat. "Like this."

He held out the traditional hat to Max. Looking in the mirror, Max placed it on his head again. The hat surrounded his scalp above the ears, rising to form a front-to-back peak above his head.

"I'll take it, and a scarf." As the clerk moved to the cash register, Alex and Bitsy ran in. They were wearing patterned floor-length dresses, and colorful scarves around their heads. "And also whatever they bought."

"Very stylish," the man said as he rang them up.

Max wrapped his own scarf around his neck, covering the bottom of his face. In a moment, he, Alex, and Bitsy were out the shop door and walking fast through the airport concourse. By the gate entrance, Sergei was talking to two towering men dressed in blue blazers. He was gesturing like crazy.

"Who are they?" Alex asked.

"I don't want to know," Bitsy said, picking up the pace.

"Don't run!" Max said. "It will attract attention."

Together they walked swiftly to the ground transportation area. Alex glanced over her shoulder back into the terminal. "They're still talking."

"Good," Max said. "We'll have to lose them."

Outside, cars were lined up, their grills to the curb, as drivers-for-hire beckoned to the departing passengers. Several of them were shouting to them: "You American? British?"

"So much for the convincing disguise," Alex drawled.

"There she is!" Bitsy blurted, and she began running toward the end of the line of cars. *"Ms. Munson! Hi!"*

A petite woman in a cowboy hat stepped onto the

sidewalk. At the sight of Bitsy she whooped and lifted off her hat, unleashing a cotton-candy spillage of straw-blonde curls. "*Yeeeee-haw*, well, ain't you a sight for sore eyes, sweet sister!"

"I'm betting she's American, not British," Max said.

By the time he and Alex reached the car, Bitsy and her friend were already inside. The moment Max and Alex closed the door, the car took off.

"Look at y'all with your beautiful outfits!" Ms. Munson said, turning toward them from the front passenger seat. "Bitsy calls me Ms. Munson, but I prefer Sal. Sal from Nepal! Our driver is a fine gentleman I've known since I got here. Still can't pronounce his name so I call him by his initials, KB." The driver flashed an easy smile in the rearview mirror as they sped to the airport exit.

"This is Max from Ohio and Alex from Quebec," Bitsy said. "Ms. Munson was a teacher at my high school in London before moving to Kathmandu. From the States, you know."

"Military brat. Mostly raised in Texas." Sal gave Bitsy a probing look. "From your last message, I gather you're not here to sightsee."

Bitsy leaned forward. "We're in a pickle, Ms. Munson, and you were the only one I knew to call. Please forgive me if I sound vague, but we need help solving a kind of mystery."

"Honey, I was the one who taught you Sherlock Holmes and Agatha Christie," Sal replied. "I'm all over mysteries. And I'm all ears for you."

Bitsy handed her Alex's phone, which showed an image of the list. "What if I told you that we needed to find something 'derived from the black smear of eternity from Armando of Kathmandu'?"

Sal stared at her a second. "I'd say, give it up and let's go have lunch! Haa! Just kiddin', darlin'. I will confer with KB, who knows this place like the back of his hand."

She took the phone and began speaking to the driver in Nepali, slowly reading the list from the screen.

KB the driver was now rolling up to the entrance of a jam-packed highway, where he stopped. There were no street lights, just a mass of cars, motorcycles, and crowded buses moving at insane speeds. People were weaving in and out, cutting each other off. It was the kind of driving that would make people scream and curse in Ohio. But all Max heard were the beeps of a few half-hearted horns.

Sal and KB kept up a steady conversation as he edged the car into the street, inch by inch. No one slowed down, no one moved aside, and there was no break in traffic. Max cringed. Another inch and they'd all be dead.

Finally, as two motorbikes approached at top speed, KB jammed the accelerator.

Alex screamed. Bitsy hid her head in her hands. Max's stomach jumped. A horn beeped so loud and close, Max thought it was in his hair.

Sal turned toward them with a sweet smile, as if they'd glided onto a sleepy suburban street. "So, y'all, KB and I have a good idea."

"Passenger-side air bags?" Max squeaked.

"Is this how everyone drives?" Alex asked.

Sal waved a dismissive hand. "Honey, you get used to it. Now, KB has never heard of Armando of Kathmandu. I haven't either. But it sounds like a company, right? Maybe fashion . . . makeup . . . hairstyling? I mean, I'm just imagining an advertisement—you know, 'The finest shoppers I ever knew go to Armando of Kathmandu'! Something like that?"

"That sounds really dumb," Max said.

Alex elbowed him.

"Yeah, it does," Sal said with a sigh, "but we have to start somewhere. So KB's going to take us to the Thamel district," Sal said. "Very famous for shopping and restaurants. If we don't find anything, at least we'll get something to eat."

They sped down the main drag, passing columned

buildings, warrens of small shops, gas stations, and billboards. It was crowded, drab, congested, and dirty. But in a park to the left, Max spotted monkeys climbing in a palm tree. And on the horizon to the right were the towering, snow-capped Himalaya mountains, peeking in and out of the smog and clouds like a trick of light.

KB maneuvered the car into the left lane and made a turn, nearly wiping out a bus, a motorbike, and two backpackers. He drove into a narrow, winding side road, where the din of traffic instantly dwindled. Shops and restaurants lined either side, and tourists meandered among tables neatly stacked with fabric, clothing, and trinkets. KB let them all out by the entrance to a parking lot.

As he drove in to find a spot, they walked up the street. Through the windows of different storefronts, Max could see jewelry counters, fast-food places, and shops selling artwork and shelves of fancy paper. "Welcome to Thamel," Sal said. "If you have a minute, between you and me, the handmade paper here is to die for. Like nothing else in the world. But I know you're after this Armando of Kathmandu. So I'm thinking maybe we start our search here."

She gestured past the handmade-paper shop toward a

small storefront, where three elegant women were applying makeup to tourists sitting on stools.

"A *cosmetics* store?" Max said in horror.

"Suck it up, old boy," Bitsy said.

Max backed away. "I hear the handmade paper is to die for. I'll meet you in the paper shop."

Without waiting for a reply, he ducked next door. There, a wizened old man was laying piles of thick paper on a long counter. All it took was one touch, and Max knew why it was special. He loved the feel of the soft fibers. It was like fabric, with delicate designs that seemed to have been baked in rather than painted.

Behind him, a voice whispered, "I like this one best."

He turned to see Alex holding up a sheet of paper with an intricately colored design around the edges. "What are you doing here?" Max asked.

Alex grinned. "I hate makeup."

"Ah, young lady, that one is my prize creation!" the old man said, nodding with admiration to the sheet Alex was holding. He sounded creaky and fragile, as if his voice itself was filtered through paper. He walked with a stoop, and what was left of his hair formed two identical Nike swooshes on either side. "I mix the colors personally—Tyrian purples from shellfish and lichen, the reds from brazilwood and insect-derived cochineal, the amber-yellow from safflower, and this gorgeous color—" He ran his fingers along a thick strip of bluish black. "This is from a special black turmeric, only grown locally."

"Cool," Max said. "Can we get some? Evelyn would love these."

As Alex paid up, Max heard the door open behind him. "Good news!" Bitsy's voice cried out, as she ran into the shop. "We solved the riddle!"

Alex whirled around, the paper wrapped into a tube and tucked under her arm. As Sal led them outside, her face beamed. She held open a plastic bag and lifted out a small white tube labeled ETERNITY. Whisking off the top, she revealed a small black brush. "Ta-da!"

"What is that?" Max asked.

"Mascara, silly!" Sal replied. With a dramatic flourish, she stroked upward on her eyelashes with the brush. "'Black smear of eternity'! Get it? What do you think? Do I make Agatha Christie proud?"

Max shook his head. This wasn't it. It couldn't be.

"No," he said.

"No?" Sal's smile drooped.

"It's too easy," Max said. "What's the name of the

manufacturer? Is it Armando? That's a pretty important piece of the clue."

Sal squinted at the fine print. "Um . . . Schweitzer Industries."

"Well, it's a start," Bitsy said with a sigh. "OK, I don't mean to be rude, but you mentioned—"

"Lunch," Alex quickly added.

"Can we discuss this over a meal?" Bitsy said. "I'm absolutely famished."

Sal thought for a moment. "I know just the place."

She walked briskly out and down the block, her heels clacking loudly on the pavement. Just around the next corner, she stopped in front of a big yellow neon sign.

Max took one look at the sign and stopped in his tracks: The Yak Restaurant.

As the others walked in, he stood frozen on the sidewalk. Max loved yaks. They were hairy and awkward. They were like the unloved child of a moose, a camel, and a water buffalo. They had horns and grunted. They were odd. Ignored. Looked down upon compared to more classic beasts.

They were the Max Tilts of the animal world.

But . . . *a yak restaurant*? What was on the menu? Max's mind danced with the possibilities. Yak burgers garnished with yak hair. Yak eyes floating in steamy brown yak soup. Yak salad with grated yak horn.

"I can't do this . . ." he murmured, closing his eyes.

"Are you coming?" Alex shouted from the front door.

Max shook his head. "I don't eat yak."

"Max, it's just a *name*," Alex said. "I looked at the menu. It's regular meat. They even have vegan options."

She took Max's hand and led him through the door. Behind the counter was a painting of a massive yak, its belly hair nearly touching the ground. *"Gllrrp,"* Max said.

"What?" Alex said.

"Nothing, just a little puke. But I swallowed it."

The room was crammed with families laughing, chatting, celebrating. But Max's eyes were fixed on a plate of ropy meat that a little boy was shredding with his bare hands.

In his mind, he heard a yak in pain.

"I need to use the restroom, be right back!"

Sprinting to the back of the restaurant, Max pushed open the door of the men's room. He took a deep breath. And another. The place was empty, spacious, cool, and nice smelling. There were big, artsy black-and-white photos on the wall. He locked the door from the inside, put his back against the wall for support, and raised his head.

He needed to think of something else. Anything but yaks. He glanced at the photos to stabilize himself—a line of hikers summiting Mount Everest . . . the outline of the Himalaya looming over a farm . . . Nepali women carrying enormous baskets of farm crops on their backs . . . a food merchant with a groaning cart full of canvas sacks . . .

Max's breath caught in his throat. But not because of nausea.

He moved closer to the last photo and squinted closely at the sacks. Some were labeled in Nepali script, others in English . . .

He zeroed in on one name. A small sack in the background, its print clear and sharp.

Whirling to the door, he yanked it open and hurried through the restaurant. In a table in the back, Sal was talking to a waiter while the others scanned the menu.

Max grabbed Alex's arm. "Come."

"I can't. We're ordering," Alex said.

"It can wait. Come!"

He pulled her from her seat. Together they ran back through the house to the restroom. Max yanked open the door. "Max, this is not a gender-neutral bathroom!"

But Max was already inside, pointing to the photo.

Alex walked in slowly, taking in the black-and-white image . . . the cart . . . the big burlap sacks . . .

She gasped. "Oh. My. Beating. Heart."

There, printed on the fabric of one of the sacks, was a label they both recognized.

ARMANDO

31

AS KB sped down the highway, the lights of Kathmandu faded into the distance. Traffic had thinned out, but occasionally Max saw buses so crowded that people sat on the roofs. The car drove past marshy fields, small villages, and entire mountainsides carved into long horizontal tiers. "Terrace farming," Sal explained. "In hilly places like Nepal, they grow crops in those furrows along the mountains. When you don't have flat land, you improvise!"

Soon the terrace farms became dull gray shadows, and the back seat was feeling more and more cramped. "I thought he was Armando of Kathmandu," Alex finally said. "Not Armando of Halfway-to-China."

Sal and KB exchanged a flurry of words in Nepali,

and Sal turned. "Apparently this fellow Armando's original farm was on the outskirts of the city. But as he expanded and got more successful, he moved to the countryside near a mountain stream. We're getting close. KB says the owner lives on the place. Ought to be someone there to talk to."

By the time KB turned off the highway onto a smaller road, a full moon hung swollen and heavy in the sky. In its silvery light, Max could see the silhouettes of grazing cattle. As some began to lope closer to the car, Max narrowed his eyes at their slope-blacked profiles. "Wait. Are those yaks?"

"You betcha," Sal said. "Are you going to feel sick?"

"I love looking at yaks!" Max replied. "They're so beautiful!"

"To each his own, I guess," Sal said. "Heck, I'm partial to iguanas."

This new road was solid-packed dirt, and KB drove carefully, avoiding potholes. The yaks stared at them with blasé expressions. Soon the road slanted upward, and the car seemed to go slower and slower.

Until finally it stopped.

KB shook his head. He muttered something in Nepali and let out a small nervous laugh.

"Does he have to pee?" Max asked.

"No," Sal said. "We're out of gas."

"*What?*" Alex placed a hand over her face. "How much farther do we have to go?"

"That's Armando's farm on the horizon," Sal said.

Max didn't see any farm, just a tiny distant speck at the crest of a vast, sloping field. It looked miles away. "Great. What do we do now?"

KB jerked a thumb backward. Max, Bitsy, and Alex all turned to look through the rear window. Another set of headlights had appeared in the dusk, bouncing toward them along the rutted road. "I'll be darned, what are the chances?" Sal said. "Well, now, don't fret, we'll just ask this person to fetch us some gas."

As the other car slowed and stopped, Max had his eye on the yaks, which were now wandering toward them. Their eyes were enormous orbs of black, their faces whiskered and narrow.

One of them grunted. "Hey to you too," Max said, leaving the car. "Do you guys belong to Armando?"

Now someone was emerging from the second car, calling out to KB. In the night's silence, the voices seemed crisp and close. The two men spoke for a moment, and then the second driver called back toward his passenger in clear English: "This driver needs petrol! I will help him, all right, sir?"

But no one answered. The second car looked empty.

"Sir?" the driver repeated, walking warily back.

From inside the car, Max heard a voice hiss, "Yes! Yes, of course!"

It was a man's voice. With a British accent.

"Bye, nice to meet you," Max said to the yak. He walked toward the second car. As he neared it, he could see movement in the shadows of the back seat.

This was weird.

Flounder-in-the-nostrils weird.

He glanced back toward KB's car. Alex and Bitsy were climbing out the rear door. Max put his finger to his lips and waved them over toward the other car and mouthed, "Someone is in there."

The two girls froze for a moment, then walked toward Max. KB, Sal, and the other driver were leaning over the open trunk, searching for something. As Bitsy passed them, she reached in and extracted a flashlight.

She and Alex tiptoed wordlessly to the other car and stopped by the rear door. There, Bitsy shone the flashlight through the rear window.

"That's awfully bright," came a voice.

"Nigel?" Alex said.

The old man, who had been lying in the back seat, sat up. "Well, hello! Isn't this a glorious evening?"

Max instinctively leaped away. "Not with you in it!"

"No need to be harsh, old boy," Nigel replied, climbing out the opposite side of the car.

"I don't believe this . . ." Bitsy said.

"You want to know what harsh is?" Alex snapped. "You, at the Kozhim River, all by yourself. You misled us with texts from a burner phone on the Trans-Siberian Railway. You dressed up another person in your clothes. And now you're sneaking after us. Oh, and did I mention? You are a class-A creepo."

"Where's my phone?" Bitsy demanded.

"Where's the stuff you stole from us?" Max added.

"Oh, dear . . ." As Nigel spoke, he stayed behind his car, keeping it between him and the kids. "I know—I know what this looks like, but please hear me out. I was forced to do this for your own safety."

"And the world is flat, asparagus tastes like candy, and your nose has grown about five inches," Bitsy said.

"We want the hippo bone, now," Max demanded.

He made a quick run for Nigel at the front of the car, with Alex and Bitsy behind him.

The old man bolted, leaping into the field with the speed and grace of someone half his age. Alex and Bitsy took chase, but Max veered toward the yaks. "Attack him!" he yelled. "Bite!"

Nigel ran directly to the yak in front. He placed his hand firmly on the beast's spine and leaped onto it. *"Choo! Choo!"*

The yak grunted. Then it let out a deep fart, turned toward the hill, and began to trot toward the farmhouse of Armando.

The trio ran after him.

"What in the world are y'all doing?" Sal shouted.

"He stole from us!" Alex replied. "And now he's trying to steal again!"

Bitsy had already climbed aboard one yak. Max felt Alex lifting him onto another. She then ran to another and swung her legs over it.

Nigel was already way ahead of them. Max's yak seemed more interested in eating grass than racing. Its spine was hard and sharp underneath him, and its hair made Max's legs itch. He hated long pants, but this would have been a good time for them. Max was slipping from side to side, so to keep himself from falling off, he leaned forward, hugging the yak's neck. "So, what's your name?"

The yak grunted again.

"Hi, Snort, I'm Max. Tell me if I'm wrong, but if I want you to go, do I say *'Choo! Choo!'*?"

The yak lurched forward. Max nearly slid off. With a slow, lumbering gait, it marched toward the car.

"Other way!" Max shouted. "Go after your friend!"

"Grab his mane, Max!" Sal yelled. "Pull it in the direction you want to go, and give the yak a little kick!"

"I'll hurt it!" Max replied.

"A *little* kick!" Sal urged. "They're built for it!"

Max took two handfuls of mane. He dug his heels into the yak's right flank, and it veered that way. *"Choo!"* Max shouted.

Sal shook her head. "Lord, I believe this is shaping up to be the slowest race I have ever seen."

Max was well behind Alex and Bitsy. About fifty yards ahead of them, Nigel's yak had stopped.

"Go, blast it, go!" Nigel shouted.

Bitsy and Alex were gaining. But as they reached Nigel, their yaks stopped too. Both of them sniffed the grass and began to eat.

There was something in that grass. The yak equivalent of chocolate.

Max yanked way to the right. "Sorry, Snort. No time for you to be Ferdinand. Gotta get to that farmhouse. Last one there is a rotten egg."

The yak veered around. As it picked up speed, Max felt his body jamming down into the spine with every clop of the yak's hooves. But he was in the clear now. He urged Snort on, keeping his eye on the farmhouse in the distance, which was growing ever-so-slowly nearer.

For a few minutes the hooves were the only sound in the night, until Snort lost interest and began to slow down. Another set of hooves was pounding the soil behind them. Max turned quickly. Nigel was bearing down, holding on for dear life.

Max kicked harder. Snort snorted.

And stopped.

"This isn't a rest stop!" Max shouted. *"Choo! Choo!"*

Snort turned, but he was too late. Max felt a hand on his back. *"See here, lad,"* Nigel yelled. *"Now who's the rotten egg?"*

Max felt himself slipping. He grasped the mane as hard as he could, but Nigel's push was too much and he fell.

As Max hit the ground hard, the pain shot up his spine. He let out a yell and lay facing the sky. The pain came in waves. He took deep breaths. Snort gave him a deep, appraising gaze, like Max was some mildly interesting weed.

And Nigel receded from view, up the hill toward the farmhouse of Armando.

"Max!" Alex's voice. Her yak was galumphing up behind him, and she jumped off. "Are you OK?"

"No! But I *will* be, if you beat Nigel," Max said.

She knelt by his side, helping him into a sitting position on the ground. The pain was sharp. He saw a sky full of imaginary bright colors, and he heard a shriek to his left.

Except the shriek wasn't imaginary.

Max blinked. A shadow was moving by them. Fast. Bitsy's legs pumped out and in, kicking the flank of her yak. The animal moved its bandy legs in a rough imitation of a gallop.

Her silhouette passed them and drew closer and closer to Nigel's, until the two beasts rammed into one another at the sides. Both yaks seemed surprised by this. With a grunt, the old man's yak went down on its hind legs. Nigel slid down the beast's back and onto the dirt.

Alex let out a loud hoot. Max scrabbled to his feet. Nigel's backpack had been flung aside in the fall, just out of his reach. He moaned, writhing in agony.

"Be right back," Max said.

"What? Where are you—?"

Max raced up the field, ignoring his own pain. He scooped the backpack off the ground and hooked it over his own shoulder.

"No!" Nigel protested. *"You can't do this to an old man,*

Max! Would you really leave me here?"

Max stopped. A great big *yes* burned in his brain.

But the old man was lying in a cold, dark field in the middle of nowhere, and soon he would be alone. There wasn't anyone around for miles. "Do you have a phone?" Max called out.

"In my pack," Nigel said. "But don't leave me here. Please, Max."

"You lied to us," Max replied. "And stole!"

"I did not want to leave you in Greece." The old man grimaced. "I was told to leave. I was to take the bones, and then to follow you. I was to find out where you were going and try to beat you to the punch. I was even given a story to tell you in case I was caught. My hands were tied, lad."

"You were *told*? Who was bossing you around?"

Nigel moaned again. "Someone I met years ago, when I went to Niemand Enterprises. You have to understand, only two people in my life were ever kind to me. One was the fellow who died, Basile. Unfortunately he didn't call the shots."

"Stinky did," Max said.

"Right you are. But someone else even closer to Niemand took the time to listen to my story about Gaston," Nigel said. "I wanted very badly to redeem his name in the historical record. And before I knew it, this person involved me in this plan to sabotage your mission."

Max cocked his head. "Who was this?"

"You wouldn't believe me if I told you," Nigel said softly. "Open my pack. My phone!"

Max yanked open the pack, took out Nigel's phone, and handed it to him. In a moment Nigel was turning the screen back to him. "My list of texts over the last few days . . ."

Narrowing his eyes, Max stared at the scroll of names. Every single one was the same.

BENTHAM, GLORIA.

32

BITSY Bentham's face was pale in the moonlight as she read some of the messages from her mom to Nigel. "'Have you found them yet?' . . . 'They will reach the Kozhim River before you. We must stall for time' . . . 'Darling, you were not to go rogue in Russia. Be sure to stay with them in Kathmandu.'" She handed the phone back to Nigel. "Wow . . ."

Alex put her hand on Bitsy's shoulder. "I'm sure it's complicated," she said without much conviction.

"I'm so sorry," Nigel said. "She was good to me for many years."

"She hated how Spencer Niemand dismissed you," Bitsy said, her voice choked and distant. "That's all I

knew. I had no idea you and she were working together."
Her eyes were moist as she looked at Nigel. "After Uncle
Basile died, Mummy became . . . oh, I don't know, cut off.
Angry. Impatient."

"When she found out Max and Alex would be coming to London, everything changed," Nigel said. "The
genius sleuths who had discovered a secret treasure—
decoding hints no one else could! She got it in her head
that you'd be the ones who could solve the mystery of
Gaston's missing work."

"She never asked us," Max said.

"She wanted to," Nigel replied. "The idea was, she
and I would entice you—little by little. I would show
you the code . . . we would get to know one another.
She didn't want to overwhelm you after your ordeal. But
things didn't go quite as planned at the funeral home.
You went off with . . ."

He looked at Bitsy.

"They went off with me," she said. "And I was worried Mummy would be upset. So I kept our whereabouts
a secret."

"I contacted her when you found me," Nigel said.
"She began imagining herself as a silent partner. An
overseer. At first I was to be her eyes and ears. Then the

keeper of the artifacts." Nigel sighed. "After things went bad in Greece, I'm afraid she rather snapped. Her assignments to me became more bizarre. I believe she lost track of the mission. She thought that I could find the ingredients myself."

"Did she make you rat us out to the police?" Max said.

Nigel chuckled ruefully. "I'm afraid not. I was being followed too, you know. A fellow from Interpol tracked me to my hotel. I had to give him back an artifact so he would leave me alone."

"He didn't lock you up?" Alex asked.

"Darling, they're hippo bones, not Rembrandts." Nigel smiled. "He doesn't know that I kept a couple hidden in my skivvies."

Bitsy squeezed her eyes shut. "Did you have to tell us that?"

"I still don't trust you," Max said.

Nigel sighed. "I don't blame you."

"We're trying to save someone's life," Max went on. "My friend has a few weeks to live. This could save her. For us, it's not about some dead ancestor. So give us what you have and leave us alone."

Nigel rose from the ground, struggling to stand upright. He reached into his backpack, pulled out a small sack, and handed it to Max. "I had a daughter once. And a wife. I lost my girl to sickness and my wife to grief. Take these, please. They're yours."

Max took the sack and opened it. He pulled out four water-filled vials, two containing hippo bones and two containing coils. "Thank you."

"I'm . . . so sorry about your family," Alex said. "I didn't know . . ."

Nigel nodded. "Save your friend. You have two of five ingredients. I am old and tired. I am more than willing to go back home and fade quietly into history. But if you would have me, I'd help you heart and soul, to my last breath."

Alex and Bitsy stood silent. Both of them looked at Max.

"What do you think?" Alex finally said.

Max's eyes were fixed on Nigel. He wasn't smelling fish. Or ham. Or cat pee.

No fear, no confusion, no anger.

Just yak manure. But that was real.

"One for all, and all for Jules Verne," Max said softly.

Nigel nodded. Max saw his shoulders shaking. Alex put her arms around him first. And then Bitsy.

Max didn't bother. He moved toward Snort, who nodded his head and grunted.

"I like your attitude," Max said.

Out by the road, two sets of headlights approached. Bitsy tore away from Nigel, running toward the lights, waving her arms. A moment later, Sal's voice called out from the first car, "Who won?"

Nigel laughed, wiping his eyes. "Children, it looks like our chariots have arrived."

"It was a tie!" Max shouted to Sal. He and Alex each took one of Nigel's shoulders and led him out to the second car.

As Bitsy climbed into KB's car, Max remarked, "She looks sick."

"I don't blame her, given the rather shocking news," Nigel said, as both vehicles snaked up the hill toward the farmhouse.

"I can't even imagine what that must have felt like for her," Alex said. "Her own mother . . ."

"Between you and me," Nigel said, "I never thought those two were very close. Gloria always regretted marrying Niemand. The way she told it, he influenced Bitsy. Turned her into a mini-him."

"Bitsy isn't at all like that guy," Max said.

Nigel shrugged. "I don't see it either. I suppose Gloria was lying to me about that too."

The cars were approaching the top of the hill. Max

could see the farmhouse behind a wrought iron gate. The building was made of stone, with large front windows and an ornately carved wooden front door. Furrowed fields stretched out on either side, extending back to the foot of a terraced mountain. A stream wound its way downward through the crops. Closer to the house, at the edge of the field, crates and sacks were piled high, waiting to be picked up. Two white domes loomed overhead—one belonging to a nearby silo and the other to a Buddhist temple visible over the tree line in the distance.

They stopped before the gate, where a sign in many languages was embedded into the stones. Max's eyes immediately went to the English part:

WELCOME TO
ARMANDO OF KATHMANDU
PRODUCE FOR RESTAURANTS AND HOMES

The gate opened with a loud metallic groan, and they drove up a winding gravel driveway to the front door. A thin man with salt-and-pepper hair emerged. Shielding his eyes against the headlights, he called out to KB in Nepali.

"He doesn't look too happy," Alex said.

"Wait a second . . ." In the front car, Sal rolled down her window and called out to the man. "Aren't you the father of little Milan Karkhi?"

The man's annoyed expression vanished. *"Ms. Munson?"*

"You know him?" Max called out.

"I had his daughter in fourth grade! This happens to me all the time." With a laugh, Sal bolted from the car and gave the man a hug. "Mr. Karkhi! I didn't know you lived here!"

"Of course," the man said. "Armando was my wife's great-great-grandfather."

As Max, Bitsy, and Alex got out of the cars, Sal quickly introduced them and took a deep breath. "Mr. Karkhi, I'm dying to catch up, but first I have a favor to ask. My friends here are on a search for something important that you may be able to give them."

Max quickly explained the basics and showed him the list, pointing to the entry "Derived from the black smear of eternity from Armando of Kathmandu."

Mr. Karkhi scratched his head. "Well, we're Armando of Kathmandu all right. But I don't know what the black smear could be."

"Sherlock Holmes would ask to see the grounds," Bitsy said. "He'd come up with ideas by observing."

"I'm happy to show you around, if you think it would

help," Mr. Karkhi said. "Come."

He led them around the house, gesturing toward the silo. "We built that to echo the dome of the stupa, just beyond—the Buddhist worship site. Although much of Nepal is Hindu, Buddha himself was born in this country. His name was Siddhartha Gautama, and Armando believed that his spirit blessed the soil."

Max dug his hand into one of the furrows. "What's this stuff?"

"Mustard," Mr. Karkhi said. "The blossoms cover the fields with yellow in the winter. Up ahead we grow many squashes. Some of the harvest is already packed into the crates and sacks, which we'll bring to market in the morning. The soil is perfect for okra and spinach and potatoes, and up there in the hills we also grow cauliflower and rice." He stopped. "Any of this ringing a bell for you?"

"Not yet," Alex said. "Let's keep going."

"We're proud of our terrace farming," he said. "Many people in Nepal grow their own family crops this way...."

As he led them up a pathway, pointing out features of the farm, Max peered into the crates. They were full of berries, plants, beans, and twisty, odd-looking root vegetables. The mountain stream burbled just beyond them. He dug his hand into a crate and pulled out a green bean.

It smelled amazing. His stomach let out a growl, and he realized he hadn't eaten in hours.

Max spat on the bean, washed it in the stream, and wiped it on his pants to clean it. Then he bit into it, releasing a tangy, sweet burst of flavor into his mouth. He finished it in four big bites, and then ate another. The next crate was full of berries. He grabbed a small handful and tossed it in his mouth.

But after the second bite, he gagged. "Yyyyeeewww!"

Alex was the first to come running. "Max, are you all right?"

"B—berrible terries—pkaacch!" he said, coughing and spitting. "Terrible berries!"

Mr. Karkhi helped Max to his feet. "Come into the house. What did you eat?"

"I don't know!" Max moaned.

As they ran in, Max choked and coughed into his hand. Mr. Karkhi gave him a water bottle from his counter, then gestured to a room tucked behind a door under a set of stairs. "Fill your mouth to dilute the taste, then spit it into the sink."

By the time Max got there, his palm and forearm were speckled with dark spots. He swallowed some water, spat, and looked in the mirror. His tongue was coated black.

He lifted the bottle to his lips again.

Then he stopped.

Putting the bottle down, he looked in the mirror again, sticking his tongue out.

"*Moo-huh-ha-keh!*" he yelled.

He raced back into the kitchen, where Alex and Bitsy stared at him in dismay. "Put your tongue back in your mouth, it's disgusting," Alex said.

"Mr. Karkhi, do you sell stuff to anyone besides restaurants?" Max asked.

"We have clients in many industries," Mr. Karkhi said.

Max dug around in his backpack and pulled out the paper he'd bought in Thamel. Ripping off the wrapping, he unfurled a sheet on the kitchen counter. "Like the paper industry?"

"Such gorgeous colors," Mr. Karkhi said, running his fingers along the paper. "Yes, I sell to this designer. Why—?"

"What does he buy from you?" Max asked.

"Black turmeric," the farmer replied. "He uses it as a base for his permanent black ink."

"*Black turmeric, grown locally*—that's what the old guy said! Does that stuff come in the form of berries—and is it this color?" Max opened his mouth and pointed to his tongue.

"Oh, dear," the farmer said. "That will take a long time to fade."

"The black smear," Max said, "of eternity . . ."

33

"**WHAT** did you do, stick your tongue in ink?" Brandon asked as Max climbed into the Tilt family jet.

"You said something a little smart," Max replied.

"Ignore him," Alex said. She buckled herself into the copilot seat, then reached into Max's backpack to hold up a vial of black liquid. "It was black turmeric. Which is the thing we needed to find. We put it in some water from a mountain stream that ran nearby."

Brandon looked confused. "Uh, awesome. Where to now?"

"The fat mountains of Mexico?" Nigel piped up, as he and Bitsy slipped into their seats. "I believe that is the closest of the remaining sites."

"Fat mountains?" Brandon scratched his head. "Never heard of those."

"Yes, I thought that sounded odd too," Bitsy said.

"If it's in Mexico, it means we have to think in Spanish," Max said, already tapping away on his phone. "So if we translate *fat mountains* . . ."

With a triumphant smile, he held up the phone. Brandon, Nigel, Bitsy, and Alex all craned to see the screen:

"So where is this place?" Alex asked.

"There's a 'Montaña Gorda,' but it's in Spain," Max said, doing a quick search.

"Wait, isn't *sierra* the way you say 'mountain' in Spanish?" Alex asked. "Like the Sierra Nevada in California?"

"On it," Max said, his thumbs flying. "OK . . . *sierra* equals 'mountain range'!"

Brandon nodded. "Sierra Gorda . . . I've taken hikers to that place. It's in the middle of Mexico. I'm thinking Querétaro Airport."

"You're a genius!" Alex blurted.

"Let's not go overboard," Max remarked. "Know anything about golf balls?"

"Nope," Brandon said, pressing his phone to his ear. "But you'll have plenty of time to figure that one out, once I get permission to land. Because the flight's about twenty-three hours."

When Max was a little boy, he once tried to break open his mom's iPad. He was worried about the characters inside it. He thought they were trapped and needed to escape.

Flying from Nepal to Mexico, he knew what that felt like.

As the Tilt family jet made its way over the Atlantic, he looked at his watch. Twenty-two hours and counting. Twenty-two out of twenty-three, including a refueling stop in Germany.

The incessant buzz of the engine clashed with the snore stylings of Alex, Bitsy, and Nigel. Max hadn't been able to sleep. Insomnia wasn't fun, but it was great for research. Now, as they neared the end of the flight, he stared at an image on his phone screen.

And he was not happy about it.

"Everybody, wake up!" he called out.

Nigel snuffled awake from the back of the plane. "How much longer?"

"Two minutes less than the last time you asked," said Brandon the Pilot from the cockpit.

"Fewer," Max said. "Two minutes fewer."

"OK. Well, we're close," Brandon said.

Bitsy yawned and rubbed her eyes. "Tell me I dreamed yesterday."

"That was some bad news about your mom," Alex said, her voice deepened by sleep.

"So sorry to be the bearer of it, dear girl," Nigel said.

Bitsy stared out the window. "Well, I'm glad we're not going home just yet. I'm too angry."

"I have some other bad news," Max said. "I found out what we're looking for."

"Max, that's awesome news!" Alex said.

Bitsy peered at his phone. "When I tried searching, all I got were images of golf tournaments."

"It helped to know the location," Max said. "There's a weird cactus that grows in the Sierra Gorda. It likes the high desert and steep rocky formations. Its technical name is *Echinomastus mariposensis,* but it looks exactly like a golf ball. People call it the 'golf ball cactus.'"

"What's so bad about that?" Nigel asked.

"Well, there's one problem." Max turned the phone to them. The image was clear and beautiful—a pure white, round cactus with tiny, golf ball–like segments. But he pointed to the heading at the top of the webpage.

CRITICALLY ENDANGERED PLANTS OF MEXICO

"Uh-oh," Bitsy said.

"It's against the law to pick them," Max said.

"Really, lad, you scared me," Nigel said. "I thought it was something serious. Surely this won't stop us. The hippo bones . . . the coils . . . they're rare too!"

"It says *critically*," Max replied. "If a person is in critical condition, it means close to death. If a plant is in critical condition, it means close to extinction."

"How many are left, Max?" Alex said. "One? Twelve? Three hundred? Taking one or two is probably fine!"

"I made Evelyn a promise!" Max palmed the phone and shoved it back into his pocket. "I said I would never torment or kill an endangered animal or plant."

"Are you serious?" Alex said. "We need to do this or *she'll* be extinct! Is that what you want?"

"Uh . . . make up your mind because we picked up some tailwinds and we're landing!" Brandon said.

"Please fasten your belts and return seats to their upright positions."

Max's brain was swimming with confusion. A promise was a promise. Betraying Evelyn was the worst thing he could do.

Everyone was buckling up silently. And Max nearly choked on the smell of ham.

As the taxi sped from the Querétaro Intercontinental Airport, Max rocked in his seat. The heat was blistering, the desert landscape was parched and bleak, and they were nearing a group of jagged mountains that marked the beginning of the Sierra Gorda reserve. Which meant he, Nigel, Alex, and Bitsy might be minutes away from finding ingredient number four.

Max knew he should be excited. He tried to feel it. But thoughts were banging around in his brain like frightened bats. "I was looking at Evelyn's Pinterest page," he said. "There are some amazing images of dodo birds. Also passenger pigeons, Balinese tigers, moas, tarpans, great auks. Quaggas, too. That's a zebra-like animal. She has a stuffed version in her hospital room. Anyway, those are all animals that don't exist anymore."

"Thank you, Max," Bitsy said.

"Do you know about the sixth extinction?" Max barreled on, his words coming faster and faster. "The first five were natural. Caused by comets, volcanoes, whatever. The sixth is caused by people. It goes on every day, and that's a fact. It's bad of us to do that. It's wrong. That's a fact too. We shouldn't be causing these—"

"Max, stop!" Alex said.

"Animal extinctions, plant extinctions, these things never, ever come back—"

Alex took his arm, held tight, and looked him in the eye. "Once upon a time there was a man who controlled a drawbridge."

"Wait, what?" Max said.

The car fell silent. Alex cleared her throat and continued: "Now, his job was to close the gates to traffic and raise the bridge whenever a tall boat approached. If he failed at his job, what would happen?"

Max swallowed. "People would be killed in a crash?"

"Lots of people," Alex said. "Anyway, one day the man sees a big boat speeding toward the bridge during rush hour. Hundreds of people are heading for the bridge in their cars. As he puts his hand on the lever to stop traffic and raise the bridge, he stops. His little puppy has wandered into the gears of the machinery. He loves the puppy more than anything in the world, and if he raises the bridge, the puppy will be crushed. But if he doesn't, masses of people will die. What should he do?"

"Alex, that's horrible and unfair," Bitsy said. "Why are you even mentioning this?"

"Honestly, I'm not sure," Alex said. "My teacher told this story in ethics class. We argued about it for two days. And I'm thinking about it now. This guy had two choices. Neither was good. Either breaks the commandment 'Thou shalt not kill.' But he had to make a calculation. Drawbridge dudes, world leaders, doctors—they're faced with life-and-death decisions all the time. They have to make a commitment and stick with it."

"But . . . but . . . this decision isn't like that at all!" Max protested.

"That's exactly my point!" Alex shot back. "Put that into your extremely gifted mind, Max. And let's just do this."

"Children, let's stop," Nigel suggested. "We'll get something to eat. I think we're all tired and punchy."

"We stop at Bernal?" The driver cocked his head, then pointed to a cluster of buildings just ahead. "Very nice."

As the car pulled off the highway, Max sank back into his seat. Bitsy and Nigel were giving Alex the classic LSS look—Long, Silent, Stupefied. As if she'd temporarily lost her mind.

But for Max, the smell of ham was gone. The choice didn't seem so difficult after all.

"I get it," he said softly, glancing toward Alex. "The golf ball is the puppy. But it's not a puppy, it's a plant. So the right thing is to save human lives. Thanks."

Alex smiled. "Who knows you better than anyone, dude?"

The driver cruised onto the small city's main road, lined with colorful shops painted in white and pastels. He parked in front of a restaurant with a sign that said Tamales. Towering over the city was a steep rock mountain, maybe a mile away.

"Awesome tower," Alex remarked.

Max nodded. "An exposed volcanic core. Like Devil's Tower in Wyoming. It began as molten lava at the center of a volcano. The lava cooled and hardened into rock. Then, over the years, the dirt eroded, leaving just that core. So what you're seeing is just a big plug of lava. And that's why it's so weirdly steep."

"Now you're sounding like you," Bitsy said.

Another group was heading into the restaurant, and a young woman held the door open for them. She was extremely tanned and wore a khaki shirt, cut-off shorts, and a red bandanna that barely contained her thick, black hair. "You know a lot for a young guy," she said. "A future geologist?"

"I just like facts," Max said.

She let them in and then offered a hand to him. "Me too. I am Rosalena Garza. My group is doing research on the formations in Sierra Gorda. We have a compound up the road."

"I'm Max. Are you a conservationist?" Max asked.

"No, a geology professor," Rosalena replied.

"What do you think of endangered species?" Max said. "Like cacti? Would you trade the last of an entire species for the chance to maybe save one person? Have you heard the story about the guy, the puppy, and the drawbridge?"

"Max, no . . ." Bitsy moaned.

Nigel laughed and gestured toward a table. "Erm, let's sit, shall we? Let this nice young lady have her lunch. Very good to meet you, Professor Garza. And best of luck in your studies."

But as they settled at a table by the window, Rosalena pulled up a chair with them. "Go on, Max. It's an interesting question you asked about the cacti. Botany is not my specialty, but I do know the area."

"It's shaped like a golf ball," Max said.

"Ah . . ." Rosalena turned and pointed to a small sign by the door. "Like that?"

Max's eyes widened. He and Alex stood, walking to the door with Rosalena. On the sign was a photo of a basket full of little white spheres. Beneath it was a message in angry-looking red and black print, all in Spanish. "What's it say?"

"It is telling hikers not to pick the cacti on the Peña de Bernal—the Bernal Mountain," Rosalena said. "Apparently there are only a handful of those cacti left in the world."

"A *handful*?" Max said.

"It also says there will be fines for locals who pick them and sell them to tourists in roadside stands. And penalties for internet sales."

"If we needed a chemical in one of those cacti," Max blurted, "how could we get a sample? Is there a way, without making it go extinct?"

Rosalena thought for a moment. "Would you like to come to our research site after lunch? It's a short drive out of town. My colleagues will help us. We have a very good botanist. He'll answer your question. And you might enjoy seeing what we do. We are the only team that conducts studies from the air, you know."

"I'm down for that," Alex said.

Max whirled around toward Nigel and Bitsy. "Guys, can we skip lunch? We're going to get professional advice before going to the mountain, so we don't get into trouble for this."

"Now?" Rosalena laughed. "You are not hungry?"

Bitsy's hands were in a basket full of chips. "Max, sorry, I'm famished."

"As am I," Nigel said. "You two go ahead with Rosalena. Elizabeth and I will take the drive to the mountain and meet you there. I adore botanists as much as anyone, but for the next few minutes, no one comes between me and my guacamole."

34

THE jeep jounced off the road onto a dirt path. About a quarter mile ahead was a fenced-in compound of trailers and stucco buildings. Rosalena drove in, waving to some of the other workers. She headed toward a set of stucco buildings in the rear and stopped in front of the largest one. "Come. We will talk to Dieter Auerbach. He is our botanist."

They ran inside and down a hallway, to a steamy greenhouse in back of the building. There, a small owlish man with black glasses and curly red hair glanced up. He looked startled and horrified. After Rosalena quickly explained their problem, he still looked startled and horrified, so Max figured that was just his resting face.

"Hooo . . ." he said, exhaling. "Hoo hoo hoo . . . Your friends are heading up there? For reconnaissance, you say?"

"That's what they said," Alex replied.

"Well, they are in for a surprise, I'm afraid. Hooo . . ." With a startled, horrified glance, he pointed to the mountain outside the expanse of glass. "Do you see the tiny, ancient chapel on the side of the Peña de Bernal?"

"No."

"Take my word. Very famous. Very sacred. Also, very popular this week. Someone reported a patch of the precious little golf balls behind the building."

"That's awesome!" Max said.

"Awesome indeed!" Auerbach exclaimed. "Exciting news in ecological circles. So, to protect it, the authorities constructed a fence. An alarm with the sound of fake dogs—*arf! arf!*—and many signs explaining the importance. But the tourists yesterday, what did they do?"

"Uh . . . I'm guessing they ripped the fence down?" Max said.

"*Ripped the fence down!*" Auerbach pushed the glasses up his nose. "We are working with an environmental group to protect these cacti. Just a few left, you know. But if we can reach a crucial number, then we will regrow some of them in a more controlled setting. For now, the group has set up a trap for poachers with the help of a local news station. Anyone who tries to steal will be exposed on video. National TV—ta-da! Shamed! Caught red-handed! Seen by millions!"

"Is this guy serious?" Max asked softly.

Rosalena nodded. "He is always serious."

Alex plopped her face in her palms. "Hello, Interpol, my old friend . . ."

"We need a sample of that cactus," Max said. "Is there any way to get some? I mean, in a nice way, without destroying the ecosystem?"

Auerbach stroked his startled and horrified face. "Well . . . we are trying to establish a relationship with universities in the southwestern United States," he said. "In New Mexico and Arizona, for example, these cacti could grow with proper care. I suppose we could make an arrangement in that case."

"I could do that!" Max said. "My mom teaches everywhere. My dad's a lawyer who represents universities."

"Promising. Well then, put me in touch," Auerbach said. "If it seems feasible, I can write a grant to the proper government funders. And if they approved it, we could carefully remove a sample for transportation."

"How long would that take?" Max asked.

"Maybe two weeks, maybe six months." Auerbach shrugged.

"That's too long," Max said. "We have a friend who's got about three months to live!"

"Can't you just grant us one or two cacti from the mountain?" Alex asked.

"Ohhhh, that would be improper indeed!" Auerbach said.

"Meaning no?" Max asked.

"No." Auerbach shrugged. "Welcome to academia. Well then, lunch? I'm starving."

As he turned to Rosalena, Alex leaned in to Max. "I am hoping you have a Plan B, because I'm empty."

But Max was staring out the greenhouse window, to a distant, basketlike contraption in a scrubby field out back. He was pretty sure he recognized the shape.

We are the only team that conducts studies from the air. That's what Rosalena had said.

Taking Alex's arm, he blurted to Auerbach, "We have to pee!"

"First and second doors on the left," the botanist said with an impatient sneer.

Max pulled Alex down the corridor. They veered out a side door. The field was to their left, behind the building. "That way," he said.

"Where are we going?" Alex asked.

"Hurry," Max said. "Let's get out of their line of vision."

They raced across the scrubby desert soil, to the basketlike object Max had seen. It was shoulder high. On all sides, it was attached to a steel frame that rose over the top to a small platform, which housed a contraption that looked a little like a gun and a little like a barbecue grill. Attached to that housing was a huge piece of tough fabric, like a giant's blanket. The fabric drooped from the metal housing to the ground, where someone had neatly folded it.

The whole thing was moored to stakes in the ground by four thick ropes. Max began untying the closest one. "Help me," he said. "And then climb in. We're going to help Nigel and Bitsy."

"*What?*" Alex said. "Is this your idea of a joke, Max Tilt? Or did someone tell you *Plan B* stands for 'Bonehead'?"

"These guys are not going to let us up that mountain. Nigel and Bitsy are probably on their way. If I know them, they're going to head straight up to the chapel and look for those cacti, right? OK, if they get caught in that trap with the cameras, our whole mission dies. So we come in at a different angle. We distract the authorities. This gives Bitsy and Nigel a chance to sneak in and take a couple, then sneak away." Max quickly untied the knots by himself, then pulled open a little door in the side of the basket and stepped in. He reached for the handle of the contraption and squeezed it hard. A flame shot up into a hole formed where the fabric was attached to the frame.

"That is the most crackpot plan I've ever heard," Alex said. *"And this is a hot-air balloon!"*

"I know," Max said. "I've worked one."

Alex cocked her head. "Seriously?"

"Yup. Back home." The fabric was moving now. Expanding. This would take some time. Max glanced over his shoulder. They were pretty far from the greenhouse. Even farther from the rest of the compound. No one was expecting any activity out here. They'd be OK.

For a while.

"Tell me something," Alex said. "That morning, a few weeks ago, when you broke into the state fair? They said you fell off a trampoline. That wasn't true, was it?"

"No."

"The fair had a balloon . . ."

"Yup. They lied. They didn't want to be embarrassed

that I got in under their noses. It was our little secret."

Alex shook her head. "That was a bad move, in so many ways."

"But . . ." Max said.

"Yeah." Alex climbed in and latched the little door behind her. "Hurry before I change my mind."

"You're not scared anymore?"

Alex arched an eyebrow. "Dude, I'm *me*."

The fabric was unfolding. Rising. This balloon seemed smaller than the one at the state fair. Newer. It was inflating way faster. Alex let out a squeal. "It's just like the movie. David Niven. *Around the World in 80 Days*!"

"Cool, I haven't read that part yet," Max said.

"It's not in the book. The movie people put it in. They took the idea from *Five Weeks in a Balloon*. Another awesome JV story." Alex was bending down now, opening a canvas sack at the bottom of the basket. "Hey, there's some equipment. Sunglasses, sunscreen, binoculars."

Now the basket was starting to shake. The fabric was expanding like a microwave popcorn bag. It crackled and rose upward, shaking off dirt as it separated from the ground.

"*Eeeeeee!*" shouted Alex.

"Awesome!" shouted Max.

"Heeeeeyyyyy!" shouted a voice from the direction of the greenhouse.

Max glanced over his shoulder. Auerbach was running across the field, his white lab coat flapping behind him. Rosalena followed at his heels.

"Come on, balloon . . ." Max shouted. *"Up . . . up . . ."*

The basket juddered. Max felt a sharp movement to the left that forced him to grab the railing. They were rising. Swinging from side to side and rising.

"And . . . awaaaaay!" Alex shouted.

Max was scared. Petrified. His knees felt brittle.

For about thirty-nine seconds.

That was about the time it took to pull in the last of the four anchor ropes. The one that Auerbach's fingertips just barely grazed.

They were floating now. Auerbach was shaking his fist and yelling, *"You ca-a-a-n't!"* Rosalena stared up at them in total shock.

Alex held onto the railing. With a big smile, she closed her eyes and raised her head. Her hair blew back, the sun dappling her brown skin to a hundred beautiful shades. Below them, the desert was a gray-green board that seemed to roll out to the edges of the world. *"Oh yes we ca-a-a-n!"*

"This," Max said, "is everything."

"That morning you first did this, I don't know how you could have returned!" Alex shouted. "I don't ever want to come down!"

Max shrugged. "I had no choice. Someone tried to pull me back."

"After we get Nigel and Bitsy, can we just keep flying . . . all the way to our next stop?"

"To Antarctica?"

"It was a joke. I think."

Max manipulated the swing bar on the overhead mechanism to the right. The balloon moved toward the mountain, picking up speed. From a distance, the peak looked almost sheer. But now Max could see a steep footpath winding up the side.

"Max—there they are!" Alex shouted.

She handed him a pair of binoculars. He glanced through, following the footpath up to a building tucked into the side of the mountain. It didn't look like much, a squat, square stone cube on a ledge.

A flash of white caught his attention. Nigel's shirt.

He adjusted his focus. Bitsy was ahead of Nigel. They were almost to the chapel.

"He's complaining," Alex said.

"How can you tell?" Max asked.

"Body language," Alex said. "And besides, it's Nigel."

"There are two people sitting by the chapel door."

"Guards?"

"Or those authorities, waiting to catch them." Max put down the binoculars and held tight to the steering mechanism. "Hang on. We're going in."

35

NIGEL had had his share of bad ideas in his life. Hiking the Peña de Bernal was right up there with leaping over a fire during a performance of *Petrushka*, in flammable tights. "Darling Bitsy, slow down," he whispered. "It's awfully hot, and I'm awfully old."

"We're almost there," Bitsy said. "I see the chapel."

"Would you scurry ahead and say a prayer for my knees?" With each footstep, Nigel felt every pebble like a tiny knife point through his soles. He had wrapped a handkerchief around his head, but by now it felt like he'd soaked it in warm soup.

Bitsy had crested a ridge and had turned to Nigel, her finger to her mouth. "Sssshhh."

"You would deprive me of the pleasure of groaning?"

Nigel whispered. As he stepped into a small clearing behind Bitsy, he saw the cause for her concern. Two men were asleep on webbed chairs in front of the chapel entrance.

The building, like everything else about Peña de Bernal, was a disappointment to Nigel. It was squat and square, made of old, mismatched stones that had shifted with time. Bitsy was walking silently by the men toward the back of the chapel. Nigel tried to tiptoe quietly, but the rocks were like snare drums beneath his feet.

Still, the men snored obliviously as he and Bitsy neared a metal cyclone fence. It encircled a small area that seemed at first glance to be a patch of snow. As Nigel moved closer he could make out tiny, perfect white spheres. He couldn't help but giggle. It looked like some nefarious trap for wayward balls on a golf course. "Surely we can take a few," he whispered.

Bitsy stood before a sign with an angry-looking message in several languages, the English stating Ecological Preservation Site: Keep Out! Grabbing onto the fence, she dug in her feet and began to climb.

In a moment she was over the top, dropping to the ground below.

Nigel swallowed hard. "My girl, you do not expect me to do that."

"I'll pick a few and stuff them into the vials," Bitsy whispered. "If those guys wake up, you bat your eyelashes and look fetching."

"I beg your pard—"

Wahh . . . Wahh . . . Wahh . . .

As an alarm rang out, Nigel screamed and whirled around.

The chapel's old wooden door was opening. Three uniformed officers ran out, holsters flapping ominously on their belts. The two sleeping men were wide awake now. One of them was talking in very urgent-sounding Spanish into a handheld microphone, while the other had somehow unearthed a large and very professional-looking video camera.

"Good Lord, it's a cactus sting operation," Nigel murmured. He thrust his hands in the air and shouted, *"I am a British citizen! I demand to see the ambassador!"*

"Nigel, that makes no sense!" Bitsy yelled from behind him. *"Come with me!"*

The men were arguing. The fellow with the camera shouted instructions to the officials, who looked to Nigel as if they would prefer to eat him for lunch. Spinning around, he saw Bitsy running to the rear of the cactus patch, where she climbed the fence and dropped to the other side.

Nigel edged along the outside of the fence. There wasn't much room. It had been built nearly to the perimeter of the ledge, and the drop-off was sheer. Bitsy was around the back, standing stock still, looking down.

As Nigel reached her side, he gasped. They were at the top of a curved stone chute, which led at a very steep angle and a very great distance to another ledge below, about the circumference of a rather large tutu. "This is doable," Bitsy said. "We'll use the chute."

"*Doable*?" Nigel said. "Absolutely not! It is easily four stories down. And what you call a chute appears to be a torture mechanism from the Spanish Inquisition."

"It's either that or a Mexican jail," Bitsy said. "I'll go first."

To Nigel's horror, she swung her legs around and slid. He screamed, fully expecting the girl to bounce off the ledge and tumble to an untimely death. But she landed with a thud and immediately gazed upward. "Come on!"

Now the authorities were edging their way around the fence, followed by the cameraman. Their shoes were heavy and wide, and Nigel could tell by their cloddish movements that they clearly had not had ballet training.

Shaking, he sat on the ledge and tossed the men a kiss. "Catch us if you can, fellows!"

With a shriek, he slid down the chute and landed in a heap beside the girl. A scream ripped upward from his toes. His legs felt as if they'd been put through a trash compactor, and he was quite certain he'd shed most of his backside by about halfway down.

But the girl was silent, staring down over the ledge of *this* clearing.

There were no chutes here. It was a sheer drop to the bottom and no other way to get there.

"No . . ." she said. "This can't be happening."

"But it is," Nigel said, "and you and I have just made the biggest mistakes of our lives." Panicked, he raised his face to the landing above. There, the uniformed men were shouting to them all at once.

"What are they saying?" Bitsy asked. "I thought you knew Spanish."

"They're too far away," Nigel said. "I'm assuming it is *'You are dead'*!"

But the men had fallen oddly silent. One by one, they were turning toward the sky.

A round white disk emerged overhead like a giant errant soccer ball. As Nigel watched in utter bafflement, it grew and swung out over the top of the mountain, trailing a square brown basket beneath it. "Elizabeth," Nigel said. "Tell me about those cacti. Does proximity to them have some sort of hallucinatory effect?"

"What on earth . . . ?" Bitsy murmured.

A face was peering out over the edge of the basket now. Two faces.

Nigel began cackling. "Great Scott, I am dreaming that Max and his cousin are up there . . . above us . . ."

As he turned to Bitsy, he felt a rap on his head. He shrieked, nearly falling off the ledge.

"Nigel," Bitsy said, standing unsteadily. "It *is* them. Turn around."

Nigel stood. Two thick ropes dangled just beyond Nigel's shoulder. He followed them upward with his eyes to a massive hot-air balloon swinging high above them. Both Max and Alex were leaning over the basket, gesturing to Nigel as if his life depended on it.

Which, he realized, it did.

"Hurry!" Alex's voice carried downward on a gust of wind.

The old man did not need any further urging. As he grabbed the rope, Bitsy looped the very bottom of it around both thighs, forming a kind of harness. Then she tugged twice on the rope.

Nigel began to rise. He gripped the rope tightly, swinging left and right like an acrobat, the wind buffeting his ears.

"Stop screaming!" Max shouted from above him.

"Am I screaming?" Nigel screamed.

"You're not as heavy when you're quiet!"

Nigel was mum as the two children hoisted him into the basket. Trembling, he turned and helped them lift Bitsy. As the girl swung below them, her legs akimbo, the balloon moved away from the mountain. Nigel could see the authorities near the chapel, staring up like open-mouthed zombies. *"Ta-ta, you cheeky amateurs!"* he cried out.

"Nigel, did you get the cacti?" Alex said, gritting her teeth against Bitsy's weight.

"She did, the blessed girl," Nigel said. "We are four for five."

"Hallelujah," Max said.

Bitsy's fingers clutched the edge of the basket, and all three hauled her in. She fell to the floor with a gasp, her face deep red. "Did that just happen? Tell me I am not in a hot-air balloon like *Around the World in 80 Days.*"

"Just the movie, not the book," Max said. He grabbed tight to the steering bar and pointed the balloon back the way they'd come. "Next stop, somewhere near the airport. Call Brandon, Alex. Tell him to fuel up, because we are heading toward the bottom of the world."

36

Nigel? Nigel, I received your email. Thank you for sending it, I was worried about you.

But why are you not using texts?

Is there a security concern?

I was able to trace the IP address of the email message, Nigel. It seems to be coming from Mexico.

Is this correct?

Nigel?

It must be very late there.
Pls contact me asap!!!!!!!!

37

MAX was tired and cranky. Normally he wouldn't have been. Tierra del Fuego had crisp, cold, blue skies; dark snowy mountains; a harbor that opened to an unending sea; and a restaurant with amazing steaks. Hugo, the guide Brandon hired, was friendly and very excited to talk about the battle between Chile and Argentina for the control of the islands at the tip of South America.

But Max didn't care about any of that.

He was a fact guy. The balloon landing had not been smooth. They'd nearly flown into the flight path of a small Cessna. Brandon had had to make excuses to the airport people, and when they finally took off, he announced the flight time would be fifteen hours.

Fifteen.

Max hadn't prepared for that, and Max didn't like not being prepared. In his mind the flight from Mexico to South America would be like Ohio to Florida. But Tierra del Fuego was literally half a world away, at the southern tip of the continent.

At least the flight from Tierra del Fuego to Antarctica would be short. If they could get one. Which they apparently couldn't.

And that was the other thing making Max cranky.

"When you say 'no flights to Antarctica,' do you mean, like, *ever*?" Alex said.

"September is late winter in Antarctica, and flights are limited," Hugo said. His office had a plateglass window overlooking the frigid bay, but Max was sweating as if it were a steam bath. "You can't just call the airport and tell them you're on your way. Military transports get quick clearance, but commercial and personal flights? It's a strict process. You must apply and wait your turn."

"Cat pee!" Max screamed.

"Pardon?" Hugo said.

"He's angry," Bitsy explained.

"Ah, I understand," Hugo said. "Tierra del Fuego is lovely, and ordinarily I would invite you to stay awhile. But if you are truly in a rush, I suppose I can contact my friend, Captain Oswaldo Perez, who is leaving tomorrow on a cutter to bring medical supplies."

Max sat forward, hopeful. "How long will that take?"

"Two days," Hugo said.

"Two days is good," Max said. "We can do that."

"Thank you!" Alex blurted.

Hugo raised his eyebrows. "Save the thanks until after the trip. To get from Tierra del Fuego to Antarctica, one must cross the Drake Passage. Do you understand?"

"Yes," Max said. "The only part of the ocean that circles the entire world uninterrupted by land."

"Smart boy," Hugo said. "Six hundred times the water flow of the Amazon River. With no constraints to the water's movement, everything is bigger—waves, wind, rain. In good weather, it's the 'Drake Lake.' But in bad . . . well, it is not for the fainthearted. Waves can be as high as forty feet." He laughed. "Then we call it the Drake Shake."

"Lovely . . ." Nigel drawled.

"So," Hugo said, "I strongly suggest you wait for a plane."

Before Max could answer, he felt a buzzing in his pocket and looked at his screen. A call from his dad, not a text. Nigel and Bitsy were arguing with Alex, who was looking at Max for support. But he ducked out of the office and into a waiting room. "Hello?"

"Max? It's Dad!"

He loved hearing his dad's voice. It had been so long. Every incident, every weird moment of his adventure bubbled up inside his brain and crowded just inside his mouth. Before he could think of what to say, it all began spilling out at once: "We're fine. We found four of the ingredients. One of them was a hippo bone! We were in Greece, where I rode a motorbike, and then we took a trip on the Trans-Siberian—"

"Max, I can't wait to hear more," his dad interrupted. "But I'm afraid I have some news. Nothing to panic about right now. But your mom . . ."

His voice trailed off. That was not good. That didn't sound like a nothing-to-panic-about thing.

Max sat down. "My mom what?"

"Her cancer has returned, Max. Apparently the treatments didn't quite knock it out."

"But that can't be true," Max said. "We got the best doctors in the world."

"Absolutely. We did. But . . . the human body is unpredictable, Max. Even with the best care—"

"Is she going to die?"

"We're taking her for more examinations. There's a good chance we may have to return to the Mayo Clinic. The doctors don't know much yet—just that it's back.

But she's a fighter, Max. You know that."

"Yes, she is," Max said, because it was a fact.

"Sorry to call with bad news, but I'll work out your return with her and the pilot. Mom will love to see you."

"Yes."

"In the meantime, stay safe. Listen to what Alex tells you, OK?"

Max didn't know where to begin with that one. So he just said, "Yes," and hung up the phone.

He sat. He looked out the window to the sea. The silence was growing around him now. It was so loud he had to put his hands to his ears and scream.

"Max!" Alex barged into the waiting room, but Max ran out the door. *Max, where are you going? It's freezing!*

He wasn't feeling the temperature. Or the snow that was just beginning to fall. He wasn't seeing the sea lions on the shore reacting to his screams, slinking into the ocean. He wasn't looking at the patch of ice he stepped on as he ran toward the shore.

But he felt the sharp pain up his spine as he fell. And the warmth of a thick parka Alex was wrapping around him as he sat on the ground. "What happened?" she said.

Max tried to swat away the skunk smell. It was suffocating him.

"Did something happen to your dad?"

"No no no no no no no no no no."

"Your mom? Is that it, Max?"

Max was rocking now. "It didn't matter. The submarine. The money. Everything we did. It didn't work. She's sick. She's sick again."

"Oh no . . . no . . . I'm so sorry." Alex wrapped her arms around Max, and he didn't fight it. Bitsy, Nigel, and Hugo were by his side now. Alex must have mouthed something to them, because they were all saying how sorry they felt.

"Do you want to go home?" Alex said.

Max looked out to sea. Five brownish-gray whiskered seal faces stared at him, bobbing on the water. It looked like they were waiting for his answer. He wanted to tell them it was none of their business. But he knew Alex would take it the wrong way. So he took a deep breath and answered her question with the only facts he knew. "I wouldn't be going home," he said. "Dad's probably taking her back to Minneapolis."

"I meant, to be with your mom wherever she is."

"That's what he said," Max replied. "He wants me to come back."

Alex turned him around and forced him to look into her face. Max hated looking into people's eyes. It creeped him out. When he was a kid, he thought other people's eyes were like the black holes in outer space that could suck you in. But he didn't feel that now. In Alex's eyes he saw two little mirrors, two images of himself staring back. He wondered if that meant a part of him was actually living inside her. And vice versa. He had never thought of that before.

Max shook his head. "We need one more ingredient. One more and we have the cure that saved Jules Verne. We have been doing this for Evelyn. That's enough reason to keep going. But now Mom's sick again. We can't go back, Alex. What if we can save Mom too? We're so close . . ."

"Why? Because it might not work," Alex said. "We have to face the fact that this mission could be hopeless and crazy."

"Maybe," Max said with a deep sigh, "but stopping it would be crazier."

38

CAPTAIN Perez was about a hundred feet tall and shaped like a question mark. At least it seemed that way to Max. He moved fast and laughed a lot, his body stooped forward and his eyes constantly darting around.

"Tell me again why you are traveling to the Frozen Continent?" he asked Max.

They were sitting in the ship's mess cabin. *Mess* was a good name for it. The crew members ate a lot of fast food and left a lot of wrappers. But Perez had treated Max, Alex, Nigel, and Bitsy to a breakfast of whole wheat toast, jam, and tea. Which was fine with Max. He hadn't slept much the previous night, and he was not all that hungry. "All we know," Max said, "is that we have to get water from a hot cave."

"Really?" Perez said. "Someone asked you to do *that*?"

"A hot cave in Antarctica seems like an oxymoron," Bitsy said.

Nigel's stomach growled. "Breakfast without scrambled eggs seems like an oxymoron," he muttered.

"I caution against scrambled eggs if you've never experienced the 'Drake Shake,'" Perez said. "But you're welcome to help yourself, if you must."

As Nigel went for the stove, Perez stood from the table and began walking toward the stairs to the upper deck. "Well, good luck to you, kids. And do let me know if you find a three-headed seal."

"Is there such a thing?" Max asked.

"About as likely as finding a hot cave." Perez threw his head back and let out a sharp, barking laugh. "I will radio my buddy, Dr. Blomdahl, at the base. She knows the island better than anyone. See you in a minute. And stay put. Looks like we had a recent drop in barometric pressure."

As he walked away, Max turned to the others. "That wasn't funny. About the cave."

"Or the drop in barometric pressure," Bitsy said. "What does that mean exactly?"

Nigel shrugged. "Sounds like a good thing to me. The lower the pressure the better, yes?"

The ship moved, and Alex's plate slid across the table. Bitsy caught it before it fell. Max heard voices outside and went to the window. In the distance, a wall of gray clouds had settled over the sea.

They were moving in, fast.

"Looks like London," Nigel said, scarfing down a pile of scrambled eggs. "I feel right at home."

Max shook his head. The sky was darkening now, the voices on deck getting louder.

Alex and Bitsy joined him at the window. In the distance, it was hard to tell the sea from the sky now. But just outside the ship's hull, the water seemed to be boiling. Max grabbed on to a guardrail. The ship tilted slowly upward. "Hang on!" he warned.

In a moment their side of the ship slapped back down. Water cascaded over the rail and onto the deck. Behind Max, Nigel's plate crashed to the floor, and he let out a scream.

"What on earth is happening?" The old man staggered up to the window, a few flecks of yellow egg on his scraggly beard.

"High air pressure pushes the humidity away," Max explained. "When the barometer is low, it means low air pressure. All the clouds and yucky weather can rush in. High barometer is good weather, low barometer is bad."

"Now you tell me," Nigel said.

Captain Perez opened the hatch and peeked in. *"Batten down everything,"* he shouted, *"and stay where you are, for your own safety!"*

"Is this the 'Drake Shake'?" Bitsy called up.

Perez smiled. "Something you can tell your grand-kids about."

Now the water was churning against the sides. It exploded into violent sprays and flooded over the decks like a river. It smashed against the windows of the mess hall and seeped under the door. "It feels like we're in a bloody washing machine!" Nigel cried out.

Max stared at the sea, his jaw dropping. The boat was rising again. The expanse of water before them seemed unbroken to the horizon. But something was wrong. The surface was no longer flat and choppy. It was swollen and slanted upward, like an endless skateboard ramp or the climb to the peak of a roller coaster. "I don't like this. . . ." Bitsy said.

"We're going up," Alex said. "And what goes up must come—"

"Hhhrrrlp," gulped Nigel, pressing his hand to his mouth.

Max slipped to his knees but held on tight. Alex and Bitsy screamed. The boat couldn't have been vertical, but it felt that way. Abovedecks, Perez and his crew were yelling.

Max smelled fish.

And in a moment, as the boat slammed down with a *thhoooom* onto the sea, he also smelled why Captain Perez had warned Nigel against scrambled eggs.

39

"**PEREZ** calls me Dr. Blomdahl, but I prefer Ingrid," said the apple-cheeked woman who greeted them at the base medical center—which was kind of a grand name for a group of modest trailers and huts on one of Antarctica's outer islands. Max's legs were wobbly from two days on the rocking boat. It was mid-morning but the sun was barely over the horizon. Even though the temperature felt close to zero, and they were all in down coats, the doctor stood at the open front door in a loose white shirt and jeans. "He tells me you're searching for some scientific mystery? I warn you, a trip to Antarctica can be addictive."

"Pardon me," Nigel said, "but if you can conjure up anything less addictive than that atrocious trip across the sea, do let me know. I would prefer to do it in a balloon. And I detest balloon travel."

"What is your time frame on this quest?" Ingrid asked.

"ASAP," Max said. "Or people will die."

"Oh, dear," Ingrid said.

"It's a long story," Alex said. "We can pay for lodging. We'll need some help. We can pay for that too."

"Well, there is plenty of room," Ingrid said. "And in this remote place, everyone loves company. Especially in the darkness of the winter. And even more especially from budding young polar scientists. I suppose I can arrange things."

"Awesome," Max said.

As they all introduced themselves, Captain Perez backed away. "Ciao, everyone. I'll be back when you need me."

Ingrid led Max, Alex, Bitsy, and Nigel into a solid, one-story building sheathed in metal. "As you can see, everything is a little bare-bones here. There is no permanent habitation on the continent. No ancient humans had any way to migrate here and settle. No villages or towns. Until the nineteenth century, this was basically a twenty-seven-billion-ton hunk of ice. It's heavy enough have a flattening effect on the Earth. There are parts of the year when the sun barely rises at all, and the winds can reach two hundred miles an hour. It's brutal. No one would want to live here."

"*You* live here," Max said.

"I work here. Just several weeks a year." Ingrid brought them into a room that looked like a laboratory struggling to be a lounge. A couple of ragged sofas had been pushed against the wall and covered with books and stacks of paper. A sink and a drying rack were full of test tubes, and boxes of cereal and noodles shared the shelves with textbooks and discarded lab coats. "I study ice," she went on, throwing some of the books off the sofa and onto the floor. "Down here, that's a form of time travel. What froze millions of years ago stayed frozen. The farther you drill down, the deeper into the past you go. You find secrets about the early atmosphere, prehistoric marine life—"

"How about hot caves?" Max asked. "Are there any of those?"

"We have a sauna, if that's what you mean." Ingrid looked at her watch, then quickly began pulling the blinds. "Ach, so much to talk about! Sit. Please. Make yourselves at home and help yourselves to food. I have some work to do before I join you. Put your stuff on the table. I will take it to our mud room after I do this."

"Why are you pulling the blinds down?" Max asked. "It's nearly dark."

"Ah, but this is the rare time of day when the sun on the horizon will blind you through those windows at this angle."

As she bustled over to the window, Alex shot Max a disappointed look and shrugged. She, Max, Bitsy, and Nigel peeled off their coats and packs and laid them on the table. "Be back soon!" Ingrid said, scooping them up and disappearing into the hallway.

Alex watched her duck into a room near a rear exit. "Max, are you sure you want to let that pack out of your sight?"

"This is an island," Bitsy pointed out. "There's no place to go with it."

Max sat at the table, tapping with his hand. "We have to talk to more people. Someone must know about the cave."

"No doubt," Nigel said. "But I shall be no help without a nap. I understand the urgency, but this has been a taxing voyage."

As Nigel flopped down on the couch, Max heard the sound of barking outside the window. He stood and peeked through the slats of the closed blinds. There, behind the hut, he saw the movement of gray-and-white fur and the black, eager eyes of excited dogs.

He slipped behind the blinds and pressed his face to the window. The dogs were huskies—maybe two dozen. In their midst were a man and woman dressed in thick down coats. They were working on a couple of sturdy-looking sleds. Each sled had a wood platform maybe two feet by eight. Underneath, the runners extended backward from the rear by a couple of feet, like skis. The dogs were lining up in front like soldiers, wagging their tails in excitement. Working quickly, the two people swapped out some of the sled's ropes and shouted to each other about guy lines, tug lines, and gang lines.

Now Bitsy was joining him. "Awww, they are so cute!"

"The people?" Max asked.

Alex sidled in beside them. "The dogs."

The man slid one of the two sleds off to the side of a nearby shed. Then he helped the woman hook up six dogs to the other sled. When she was finished, she stood with each foot on one of the two rear runners. She clutched a curved handrail in the form of an upside-down **U** bolted to the sled below. Then, with a deep voice, she yelled, *"Hike!"*

The dogs began to pull, slowly at first and then with greater strength. Max watched them take off and pick up speed. They had gone about thirty yards when she shouted, *"Gee!"*

The dogs veered right. After a few seconds she shouted, *"Haw!"* and they veered left. As they circled back around to the starting point, the other worker kept busy hooking up more dogs to the second sled.

"Some kind of training exercise?" Nigel asked from the sofa.

Max nodded. "They sure are more obedient than yaks."

"Who-o-o-oa!" yelled the woman, a big grin on her face, which had grown red in the wind. As the dogs stopped, she leaped off the runners and went to hug the dogs.

"That looks so fun," Alex exclaimed.

"I prefer snowmobiles," Bitsy piped up.

"Alex and I haven't had good experiences with those," Max said.

"A nice newspaper and a roaring fireplace for me," Nigel said. "And by the way, my poor tummy is quite angry at me for that wretched boat trip. Do you happen to see any Tums here?"

"We are doing nothing," Max said. "I can't stand doing nothing. Also, Ingrid was wrong about the blinding sun. You can't even see it."

Max lifted the blinds, turned back into the room, and began pacing. But out of the corner of his eye, he caught the shape of another person joining the first two outside.

Someone in a hurry.

This person was wearing a thick winter coat but also thick pants. The two backed away, nodding in response to something Max couldn't hear. The newcomer stood on the sled runners and tossed a backpack into a storage basket.

Max's backpack.

"What the—?" he murmured, moving closer to the window.

"*Hike!*" a voice snapped.

Max felt his blood drain to his toes. He couldn't see the face through the fur, but he recognized the sound.

"Max?" Alex said. "Is that . . . *Ingrid?*"

But Max didn't answer. He was sprinting into the hallway.

40

"HELP us, please!" Pulling on his coat, Max shouted to the dog trainers as he raced outside. "That person— Ingrid—we have to follow her! She stole from us!"

The young woman stared at him through her furry hood. "Excuse me, who are you?" she said, her voice making thick white puffs in the air.

Behind her, the guy was hooking up about a dozen dogs for another training session. He looked up at the commotion. "Stole? Is this some kind of joke?"

Now Nigel was strutting out of the building, with Bitsy and Alex on either side. "My good man," Nigel said, holding out a business card. "Does this look like a joking face?"

"Wait, who are *you*?"

"Dr. Cesar Untermeyer," Nigel said. "Perhaps I may have a word with you both . . ."

At the sound of that name, the two young workers snapped to attention. Nigel walked them back to the building, blabbering on about inspections and proper behavior.

"What was that about?" Bitsy mouthed.

Alex shrugged.

But Max's eyes were trained off into the field. Ingrid was heading across the flat, icy plain toward the horizon. There wouldn't be much time before she was out of sight. "We have to get her, now!"

He eyed the sled. One foot on each runner. That was how it was done. He had seen it.

Max ran to it and got himself in position, gripping the wooden crossbar.

"Whoa—are you kidding, Max?" Alex hissed. "You think you're going to operate this thing?"

"It's easier than a balloon," Max said. "I saw them. Get on! She's getting away."

Bitsy sat on the sled, and Alex reluctantly followed. The dogs seemed to sense something, and they began whining and wagging their tails.

A door slammed to Max's right, and Nigel came bolting out of the building, giggling. He was carrying a small rucksack. "The game is afoot!"

He leaped across the snow, did a turn in midair, and scampered onto the sled. "No seat belts?"

"Who's Dr. Cesar Untermeyer?" Bitsy asked.

Nigel shrugged. "I saw the name at the top of the plaque as we walked in. I figured he was important. I sent those two off on an errand so we would have freedom to steal this sled. I brought goggles for us all. Under the circumstances, I thought them prudent."

As Max took a pair and slipped them on, Nigel slipped in behind Alex and Bitsy. *"Hike!"* he shouted to the dogs. *"Hike like crazy and follow her!"*

The dogs dug in hard, and the sled lurched forward. Max nearly fell off, and Nigel let out a little scream.

Max's legs were stiff. He bent them. He had to stay loose. The dogs were doing their job, pulling with a smooth forward motion. *"Hi-i-i-i-ke!"*

The wind bit against his cheeks. Flecks of ice flew up from the runners onto his goggles. From where he stood, the rise and fall of the huskies' backs was like one churning mass of fur. It felt like they would take off into the sky. He thought about the sounds of their trip—the jet's whine, the echo of the Greek cave, the chug of the railroad, and churn of the Kozhim, the grunting of Nepali yaks, and the balloon's buffeting winds—but nothing compared to this. The ropes' rhythmic slap, the footfalls and chuffing breaths of each dog, the steady *ssss* of the runners were like a song of whispers.

The dogs didn't seem to be seeing Ingrid anymore, but Max could make out a trace of her shadow in the distance. He steered them as best he could. "*Gee!* No, not that much *gee!* A little to the *haw!* That's it!"

They were picking up speed now. Ingrid seemed to have stopped. Behind her, a wall of white was rising like a curtain. What little was left of the sun had dimmed, as if someone had flicked a switch. She was turning toward him, Max could tell. He wished he had his binoculars because she seemed to be gesturing.

In a moment, a wash of whiteness wiped her out of sight like an eraser. In the sudden blast of wind, it seemed to be snowing upward. "*Hike!*" Max shouted. "*Hike!*"

"*Did anyone look at a weather forecast?*" Nigel called from the sled.

Max could barely even see him. He gripped tighter to the bar. Either Bitsy or Alex screamed. Or maybe it was Nigel.

The dogs were barking now. A not-too-distant barking answered them. Max could see a shadow up ahead, flickering in and out of the whiteness. Maybe twenty feet away. "*Good work!*" he yelled. "*Whoa!*"

As the sled came to a stop, Max jumped off. *"Hold hands!"* he shouted. *"Or we'll lose each other!"*

He gripped Alex's hand, she gripped Bitsy's, and she gripped Nigel's. Max trudged forward, guessing as best he could where Ingrid was standing.

"Ingrid!" Max shouted. *"Ingrid, where are you?"*

From behind, Ingrid's voice said, "Whoops, passed you right by. I recommend you turn. Slowly."

Max felt Alex's hand tighten, then let go. They all did as she said and clasped hands again. Ingrid stood facing them, finally visible at only six feet away. The backpack was hooked around her shoulders.

In her right hand she held a gun.

"By the ghost of Gaston . . ." Nigel said.

Ingrid flashed a smile. "Do you know what leopard seals do? They swim in channels under the ice, coming up for air in strategic blowholes. When they see a shadow moving overhead, they follow it from underneath. If the prey approaches the hole—surprise! They leap up at the last moment, jaws wide, ready for dinner."

"So . . . you're the leopard seal in this story," Nigel said, "and we're—"

She moved the gun toward him. Nigel swallowed the rest of his sentence in a choked *yeep*. "I brought this gun for protection against predators like the leopard seal, not you! This continent is brutal and unforgiving, full of traps and fissures and murderous tricks of nature. Just as it was at the turn of the twentieth century for those who first set foot here—Shackleton, Scott, Amundsen, Mawson. Imagine their surprise to find that someone had been here before them. A man who had not only lived to return home, but who had never taken any credit for the discovery. Not a hardy explorer but a science fiction writer, a French ex–stock broker named Verne! The embarrassment was overwhelming. These men agreed to suppress the secret, and after they died it was forgotten—but for a small, secret group of researchers employed by a powerful private company."

"Don't tell me," Max said. "Niemand Enterprises?"

"Oh, dear Lord," Nigel said. "You've been in touch with Gloria Bentham, haven't you? This was a trap."

A noisy rush of frigid wind blasted, but Ingrid stood solid. "Most rational people scoffed that an amateur explorer like Jules Verne could have reached this impossible place. But some, like Gloria, persisted. You see, Verne left clues, if you knew how to look for them. Clues in the ice." Ingrid smiled. "She is a visionary woman, Mr. Hanscombe, wouldn't you say? And you, Bitsy, she always wished you had followed in her footsteps. Have you discussed this with these friends of yours? Have you told them who you really are?"

"Just give us the pack, you blowhard!" Bitsy said.

She flew at Ingrid. They both fell to the snow and rolled. In the blowing snow, the two women flashed in and out of sight.

"Get the gun!" Alex said, jumping on top of them. Max moved closer, looking for signs of the weapon, afraid it might go off in his direction.

There. A flash of steel.

As he reached down, Bitsy bit hard into Ingrid's wrist. With a scream, Ingrid let go of the gun. It sailed into the whiteness. Max dove after it, flailing in the snow to find it, but it was buried. Lost.

Now Ingrid was jumping to her feet, backing away. "I came here to do some good in this world. To find secrets from a time when the world had no disease. This has been my life, and you greedy little thieves are not about to—"

Her sentence ended there, and so did she.

Max had to blink. She was gone.

"Ingrid?" he called out, stepping forward.

He tried to pull his foot back. But there was nothing under it. As his body fell forward, Max stared down into a bottomless black crevasse.

41

HE was panting. Sweating. Achy. He could hear his own ragged breaths. Dreams faded in and out. He was home, early in the morning, and it was time to wake up. His mattress was lumpy and uncomfortable, and it made him twist and turn.

The sound of his name, soft and faraway, made his eyes flutter open.

"Morning," he drawled. "It is time for school?"

"Hrm," his mattress responded.

Max jumped. It was so the wrong move. Every muscle in his body screamed in protest. He felt like a head-to-toe bruise. He stood, letting the pain wash over him and his eyes adjust to the surrounding brightness. Then he looked down.

His mattress was Ingrid.

"Whoa," he said, jostling her with his foot. "Hey, sorry I landed on you. Are you OK?"

She rolled to her back without a reaction, but he could see her chest heaving. His backpack lay on the ice about a foot away. He scooped it up and yanked open the zipper. Pulling out the container, he reached inside and carefully pulled out the vials.

They were all there, unbroken.

"Maaaaax!" came Alex's voice from above. And then Bitsy's and Nigel's.

He looked up into the falling snow. His goggles had snapped off in the fall, so he shielded his eyes, but he saw nothing but white. *"I'm down here!"* he yelled. *"But I guess you know that!"*

As his voice boomed and echoed against the ice, he caught a glimpse of the goggles on the ground. He went toward them but had to stop in his tracks. Now, looking straight in front of him, he saw the entrance to a deep cavern, like the open mouth of an ice ogre. The chamber beyond it stretched into darkness, but the immediate area glowed. Ice formations like white teeth hung in endless rows from the ceiling and jutted upward from the floor, flashing pinpricks of green, blue, silver, and white. He walked slowly, stepping high over fresh snow that drifted to his knees, passing pillars of ice, daggers of ice, and webs that seemed spun from sugar. It was as if the Cave of Vlihada had been transported here and then flash frozen.

As he made his way around a bend in the cave, the surface became flatter, harder. Sweat dripped down his torso. The jacket was too warm, so he unzipped it. And that fact made him stop in his tracks.

He had felt too cold in Greece. Here in the Frozen Continent, encased in ice, he was sweating.

Here, in a hot cave.

"It's hot!" he yelled. *"It's really hot! Woooo! Guys, I found it!"*

He didn't know if they heard him. He was far from the crevasse now, but he didn't want to go back. Not just yet. On the other side of a thick ice column, wisps of steam fogged the air. They curled toward him like beckoning fingers.

He walked toward a quiet bubbling sound. A tiny brook, sliding silently over a deep groove in the icy surface, led him deeper into the cave. There, embedded in a giant fist of ice, was the water's source. It was a hole about a foot wide and ringed in solid greenish blue.

Greenish blue meant algae. Algae was life. Life meant heat. He took off his glove, dipped a finger, and yanked it back. It was hot to the touch.

A water source rescued from a hot cave in the world's coldest land mass. That was Jules Verne's last clue.

Max swung his pack around. His hands were shaking with excitement. This was Verne's fifth stop, his final ingredient. Max didn't know how Verne had gotten here. Was it on Captain Nemo's submarine, the *Nautilus*? The novel *Twenty Thousand Leagues Under the Sea* described a stop in Antarctica. Everything in that novel seemed too far ahead of its time. But it had happened. Verne had lived it. Maybe this too. Maybe he actually had reached Antarctica before the great explorers.

"I love my family. . . ." Max said.

Max opened the last, empty vial and filled it with the water from the brook. His face felt hot and wet, and as he wiped it dry, he realized he was crying. The ice seemed to wink back at him, forming shapes before his eyes.

For a brief second, he could swear he saw his mom's face. It was a trick of the mind, he knew. It was wishful thinking. But when he stood, he couldn't feel a single bruise.

He wanted to run back but he stopped himself. One bad fall on the ice, one broken bone, and he'd have no chance of getting back. Getting back *without* an injury was going to take a lot of creative thinking. Hooking the pack over his shoulder again, he headed out of the cavern and into the crevasse. Ingrid was lying exactly as he'd left her. From this angle he could see that one of her legs was twisted into an unnatural position. That, he knew, was going to hurt.

"Max, can you hear me?" echoed Alex's voice from above.

"Yes!" he shouted.

"Nigel and Bitsy are trying to figure out how to work the sled! They're going to get you some help!"

"Bass . . ." Ingrid was writhing on the ice, trying to speak. Her face was twisted with pain. "Bass . . . ket."

"Hey, Ingrid, it's me, Max. I fell on you." Max knelt beside her. "Did you say 'basket'? What do you mean?"

She nodded, her eyes squeezed shut and her teeth gritted. "On . . . sled . . ."

"Basket on sled. Got it." He looked up and shouted: *"Alex, get the basket from Ingrid's sled!"*

"OK!"

"Yes . . . good . . ." Ingrid said.

"What's in it?" Max asked.

But Ingrid was gazing toward the cave with the vaulted ceiling. *"Refugio . . ."* she whispered.

"Ref-*who*-hio?" Max replied.

"It means . . . 'refuge.' These places . . . refuges for

forms of life . . . for biodiversity . . . in the ice." She grimaced and took a deep breath.

"You said 'places,'" Max said. "There's more than one?"

Her eyes flickered as she faded in and out of consciousness. "Under the continent . . . active volcanoes. Heat rises. Through miles of ice . . . through seams, crevasses . . . It carves out openings. Caves. *Refugia.* There's a whole system . . . like a big . . . ice subway."

Max heard a thump behind him and turned around. A rope ladder had smacked against the wall and dropped to the ice floor.

Ingrid smiled. "That rope," she said softly, "is what's in my basket."

The wind screeched like a thousand wounded animals as Max pushed Ingrid up the rungs of the ladder. Her right leg hung at a grotesque, broken-doll angle, and she choked back cries of pain as she hoisted herself with the power of her arms and one good leg.

"*I got you!*" Alex shouted, reaching down to clasp Ingrid's arms and pull her the rest of the way.

The scientist rolled onto the snow, groaning. Alex's face was deeply red, and Bitsy and Nigel were grayish shadows in the raging white storm, lit dimly by a sun that seemed stuck on the horizon. *"The weather's gotten worse!"* Max shouted.

"Worse than you think!" Alex shouted back. *"The dogs are gone!"*

"What?" Ingrid cried out.

"I said the dogs are gone!" Alex said.

"Mine too?" Ingrid asked.

"Nigel spooked them!" Alex shouted. *"He wanted to go back, to get you help! But he forgot the words! He just started shouting random stuff! When he got to 'Hike!' the sleds took off without him! Both of them."*

"Fool!" Ingrid shouted.

Now Bitsy was rushing toward them. "He's awfully upset. Why don't we climb down the ladder and wait down there until the storm blows over?"

"No way! Can't . . . in my condition." Ingrid struggled to sit up. "Please tell me you have the pack from my basket."

"We do," Alex said.

"I have flares in there," Ingrid said. "Set some off. Back at base they'll be looking for us."

Alex disappeared into the storm. Moments later a line of red light flashed briefly. Max could hear it whistling overhead, but it was invisible in the whiteness.

"Help me up," Ingrid said. "The dogs must be nearby. We just can't see them. I know my babies. They wouldn't just bolt, no matter what you tell them."

As Max and Alex hooked her arms around their shoulders, she called out: *"Roald! Ernest! Robert Falcon!"*

"Those are dogs' names?" Max said.

"After polar explorers," Ingrid explained. "Come on. Let's move. Grab the GPS from my coat pocket and show it to me. I'll get us back to base if you keep me upright."

As they stepped forward, she let out a scream. "Your leg!" Max said.

"I can do this," she said through clenched teeth. "We'll die if we stay here. *Douglas! Frederica! Where are you?*"

Max struggled to keep his balance while Ingrid leaned on him to keep the weight off her bad leg. The snow was caking on his goggles, the ice clinging to his hood. Nigel was with them now, apologizing like crazy. But Ingrid ignored him, summoning up all her strength, calling out names.

They walked for what felt like hours, Ingrid constantly checking the GPS, until finally she shouted, *"Stop!"*

She was pulling Max downward, sinking to her knees. "A minute . . . give me a minute. . . . My dogs abandoned me. . . . I was sure they wouldn't go far. . . ."

"Lift her up, Max!" Alex shouted.

"I can't!" Max said. "She's too heavy!"

Bitsy ran to his side and tried to lift Ingrid, but she was pretty much dead weight now, muttering to herself.

"I don't know what to do!" Nigel was yelling.

Max let go of Ingrid and ran to his side. He yanked open the pack and looked inside. "There are packs of flares, Nigel! Let's get to work! Activate and toss!"

He glanced at Ingrid, whose face was now the same color as the snow. With a silent prayer for help, he began launching the last of the flares.

42

AFTER Max's near-death experience by snowmobile in Greenland, even the sound of a lawn mower had made him scream. But now, wrapped in a blanket like a human burrito, he thought the snowmobile's deafening whine beneath him was the sweetest ugly noise in the world. He couldn't see a thing as it flew through the snow, but that was fine with him. Being rescued felt awesome.

It seemed like it had taken them hours to reach the *refugio*, but the trip back was quick. He, Alex, and Bitsy were squeezed onto one snowmobile, Ingrid and Nigel, the other.

As they stopped at the base, the driver helped Max unwrap himself. His name was Pablo, and his thick beard looked like a hedgehog clinging to his face. "Thanks," Max said.

"You were smart to bring those flares along, dude," Pablo said. "Once those dogs came back alone, we began looking with infrareds."

"The flares were Ingrid's idea," Max replied.

"Are the dogs OK?" Alex asked.

Pablo grinned. "Totally. They're built for this."

Max stood and removed his goggles. The storm had let up as suddenly as it had started. A team of lab workers had been mobilized. Two of them were lifting Ingrid onto a stretcher while two more waited to carry her inside. Her body was limp, her face the color of ash. The sun had completely set, and everything around the building was pitch-black. "Is she . . . ?" Bitsy asked.

"She's breathing," said one of the stretcher bearers, a red-haired woman at least six feet tall. "But we'll need to fix that leg."

As the bearers rushed into the building, Max, Alex, and Bitsy followed. Max passed Nigel, standing against the side of the other snowmobile. "Are you coming?" Max asked.

The old man seemed lost in thought. "You know, lad, my mum got me a Lhasa apso when I was five, and it ran away. A year later Dad brought home a cocker spaniel, but it bit my arm and they had to give it away. Basset hound, pug, poodle . . . no matter what I did, things never worked out between dogs and me. I thought maybe this time . . ."

Max put his arm around Nigel's shoulder. That was what people did to make other people feel better.

"Well," he said, "we all suck at something."

Nigel smiled. "Thanks for the thought. I may put it on my tombstone. So. All's well that ends well, I suppose. You got all your ingredients, lad!"

Max reached around for his backpack, but it wasn't there. He whirled around to the snowmobile, where Pablo was checking the engine. "My pack!" Max blurted.

"Pardon?" Pablo asked.

"I had a backpack!"

Pablo thought for a moment. "Right. Yeah. Blue one. It fell off your shoulder when we put Dr. Blomdahl on the sled. Not to worry, I put it in that sack. Sorry."

He gestured toward a big canvas sack on the floor of the snowmobile, jammed against the curved front wall where he'd stood while driving.

Max yanked it open and pulled out his backpack. It was partly unzipped. He reached in and pulled out the big canister. The top had fallen open.

Three of the vials were inside—the golf-ball cactus,

the glowing coil, and the water from the *refugio*. Max peered into the pack and spotted the black water from the Nepali turmeric.

Three of them. Nothing else.

"The bones . . ." he said.

He ripped the bag open. He felt around. The bottom was cold to the touch. Something had spilled and frozen. He felt a sharp pinch on his finger and pulled it back. It was bleeding from a tiny shard of glass.

"The bones!" he repeated. "It's missing the hippo bones!"

"Well, it was unzipped," Pablo said, "and you had quite a rough ride there—"

"We have to go back and find it!"

Pablo gestured out toward the expanse of black. "There's a lot of territory out there, my friend. And it's all been covered with blowing snow since we've been through it. Plus, the sun won't be up for a very long time. You have a better chance of finding a hair in all the haystacks of the world."

"No! No-o-o-o-o!"

Alex was running out of the building now. "Max?"

"I dropped the hippo bone," he said.

"You're kidding."

"Is this my kidding face?" Max said.

Nigel tapped his shoulder. "Max, old boy—"

"We only had one of them!" Max snapped, spinning to face him. "If you hadn't taken the others, we might still have one or two."

"Yes," Nigel said, "but—"

"OK. OK. Calm down," Alex said. "I got through to Captain Perez. He will pick us up first thing in the morning. And Brandon will be waiting for us at the airport in Tierra del Fuego. We'll just have to make a detour. We'll go back to Greece and get more bones—"

"We can't go back, remember?" Max said. "They know who we are! We're wanted—"

"We'll think of a Plan B," Alex said. "There's always a Plan B."

"May I suggest one?" Nigel said.

Max and Alex both turned to him.

"You're right, Max," the old man said. "I did take them. As you know, in my delusion of grandeur, I saved one of them for myself. And in Nepal I gave that to you. But the others still exist. They were sent to London in very secure packaging. To Gloria Bentham."

Nigel's words floated in the biting-cold air. Max's heart did an agonized dance, one minute happy for the extra chance and the other dreading what it might take to get it. "We have to go to London," he said.

"Unless . . ." Nigel said, tapping his chin. "We can get her to the United States."

"How?" Max asked.

"She still thinks I work for her," Nigel said. "And she believes I have the ingredients. I shall tell her you stole them, and I was forced to chase you back to the States. She's aware that Interpol was following me. This scares her. She just may be willing to come to where I am."

"Do you think that will work?" Max asked.

"Did we ever think any of this crazy scheme would work?" Nigel said.

"I'll get Bitsy," Alex replied. "Let's get out of here."

Max felt his phone vibrate and pulled his own phone from his pocket. He noticed about a dozen unopened text messages from his dad. But he looked at the last one first. It was only three words:

Come home. Now.

43

MAX didn't recognize the gray Toyota Corolla parked in front of his house. As his limo rolled closer, a priest emerged from the smaller car. He was a kind-looking man with wire-rim glasses and dark-brown skin. The sight of him made Max panic.

When someone was dying, a priest came. Max knew that from movies. It was a sign. He squeezed the door handle and jumped out while the car was till in motion. He could hear Alex shouting his name as he fell onto the grassy patch by the curb. The priest glanced toward him, startled, and called out a greeting. But Max ignored him and bolted straight for the front door.

His dad was in the living room, talking to a woman over a stack of papers piled on the coffee table. "Max!"

he cried out, bolting up from the couch and knocking his cup of coffee onto the floor. "Welcome home! We missed you!"

Max knew he was supposed to say "thank you" and "I missed you too," but the smell of fish blotted out every thought. "Where is she?"

Dad nodded. "I'll take you. Come. Smriti's here too."

Leaving a very bewildered-looking visitor in the living room, Max walked with his father through the house to the sunroom out behind the kitchen. The Tilts had added the room to the house as a study, but now there was a bed in it. Mom was fast asleep under a down comforter. Her face was paler and thinner, and the gray roots of her hair were growing out.

Smriti and her dad were sitting on folding chairs next to her, and Smriti nearly flew across the room to Max. "I know you hate hugs and I'm sorry, but I was so worried about you, and I'm glad you're home!" she said, throwing her arms around him.

"I'm glad to be home too," Max said.

He shook loose from the hug and sat at the edge of the bed. "Hi, Mom, it's Max."

Her eyes fluttered open. She reached up to touch his face. He didn't flinch. Under the circumstances, it felt kind of nice. "I missed you so much," she said. "I lost the Hulk, you know. Your protection charm. He was in my purse when I had a little fainting spell in the card store. Stuff scattered, and he must have slid away."

"I'll make a new one for you, Mom," Max said. "How are you feeling?"

"A little tired, that's all," she said with a rueful smile. "It all happened so fast, didn't it? Did you find what you needed?"

Max struggled for the right words. Alex was slipping silently into the room, and now he felt five pairs of eyes drilling into him from all sides. "We—we tried," he said. "We got all five. Everybody was awesome. We visited a cave and we fought wolf people. But after that we had a yak race and flew a balloon and visited a volcanic vent in the ice. And oh yeah, the hang glider works. Anyway, I'll tell you more facts about the trip later. But I have work to do, Mom. I—I lost one of the ingredients."

"Oh, wow . . ." Smriti said. "Hey, it's OK, Max. You tried, that's what counts."

Max shook his head. "Trying isn't enough. Mom, you have to hang in there. OK? Will you? I have to take another trip. We're going to save you."

His dad's voice called from the doorway. "Max?"

Dad was standing there with Nigel and Bitsy, and behind them was the priest.

Max stiffened. "Get him out of here."

"Dear boy, we've had our differences," Nigel said, "but—"

"Not you," Max said. "The other guy!"

"It's just a pastoral visit, Max," Dad replied. "The church has a new pastor, and he's getting to know—"

"Get him out of here!"

As the priest stood, looking baffled, Nigel pointed to the screen of his phone. "May I speak to you, lad?" he asked softly. "It's important."

Max nodded and kissed his mom's forehead. "Sorry. I just saw his collar and—"

"I know, Max, it's fine," she said. "And to answer your question—yes. I will hang in. I promise. Now go see what your friend wants."

"Love you, Mom. Be right back." Max got up and followed Nigel into the kitchen, with Alex close behind.

Nigel was stuffing chips into his mouth, but a lot of them had spilled and he was crunching them underfoot. He seemed agitated. "I heard from Gloria," he said. "She is here. In Savile. Our plan worked. But I wish I'd thought it out more. She would like to meet with me, alone. At an old, abandoned train station. I am to bring the remaining ingredients, and the *Isis hippuris*."

"Does she have the hippo bones?" Alex asked.

"Yes," Nigel said. "Gloria is diabetic. And greedy. She is eager to combine the ingredients and test the serum by using it herself."

"But you can't just bring everything with you," Max said. "She'll take it all!"

"Exactly!" Nigel said.

Max began pacing. He thought about the four ingredients in his pack. The *Isis hippuris* in his room. They were safe for now. And he didn't want to let go of them.

His mom let out a groan, and he looked inside. The priest was kneeling by her bed, which made him want to scream. Just beyond him, Max could see the windowsill where Hulk used to be.

His homemade 3D-printer Hulk.

An idea was barging its way into Max's head.

"Tell her you'll do it," he blurted. "You'll bring everything. Alone."

Nigel nearly spat out his chips. "Pardon me. I just imagined you asked me to tell her I'd do it."

"Text Gloria. Tell her you will meet her with everything she needs. But you'll only do it if she brings the hippo bones. And shows them to you."

As Max headed for the stairs, Nigel said, "What if she says no?"

"Then the deal is off," Max said with a shrug.

And he ran up to his room.

MAX tightened his harness and crouched low. A pair of binoculars, hanging from his neck, clanked softly against the roof of the old grain elevator. The ladder had been wobbly, but the structure itself felt sturdy beneath his feet. In the setting sun, the abandoned train station looked on the verge of collapse. Its tile roof sagged, weeds snaked up its graffitied walls, and the light from the only working streetlamp didn't quite reach it. One of the station's side windows was bricked over, and a dim light flickered in the other.

Gloria Bentham was inside, waiting.

The rusted gate in the cyclone fence had a sign that said Trespassers Will Be Prosecuted, but the lock had broken off years ago, and no one had bothered to replace it. As planned, Nigel walked through it at precisely 7:15.

Max waved. As planned, Nigel didn't wave back.

Draw her out, Max thought, hoping Nigel would somehow pick up his mental message. *Let me hear her voice.*

Max saw a movement from within the station house, and a moment later Gloria Bentham emerged. She wore a plain black waist-length jacket and jeans, with a plain black canvas bag slung over her shoulder.

"Where is the boy?" she asked.

"With his mother," Nigel replied. "She is very ill, and he would not leave her side."

"Would that all children show such love to their mothers," Gloria said. "It is good you won their trust, Nigel. I do have your payment. Are you certain you weren't followed?"

"Of course not." Nigel was sweating.

Don't sweat, Max thought. *You look so guilty.*

"Let me see the bones," Nigel said. "I worked very hard to get them, and I want to know you did not lose them."

Reaching into her shoulder bag, Gloria took out a vial. Max lifted the binoculars and looked through. His pulse quickened. He could see at least one bony shape inside the liquid.

Gloria dangled the vial in Nigel's face, and then put it back into her purse. "You did good work, my friend. How do feel about finally lifting the curse on your family? Righting the wrong of your vile ancestor?"

"Gaston was in great pain, Gloria," Nigel said.

"Yes, enough pain to take every bit of the serum that Jules Verne concocted," she said. "My ex-husband, Spencer, was not a good man, but he knew many very valuable secrets. He knew that Verne had produced a tiny amount of serum, Nigel. He knew that Jules was in contact with the best scientists of the day, to analyze the compound in order to mass produce it. But when they asked him to provide a sample, there was none left."

Nigel nodded. "And now there will be."

"Thanks to you, for keeping it out of the hands of those children, who were influenced by my daughter!"

The comment about Bitsy shook Max. It didn't sound like the way a mom would talk about a daughter. Max was so intent on listening, he almost missed the slight movement at the side of the building. Another figure was moving closer, pressed against the wall. It was a man dressed in black clothes and a black mask, clutching something in his hand.

Max tensed. Nigel was reaching into his backpack

now. "The children were the ones who found these. I know you don't trust them, Gloria, but if you contacted them—"

"It's not them, you fool!" Gloria said. "It's Bitsy I don't trust. Now give me everything. Now."

The man in black inched along the wall, toward the front. Max could see he was holding a gun. *A gun?*

Max tensed again. He checked the harness, reaching back to make sure the wings were not tangled. He bent his knees. Up here on the grain elevator, he was maybe three stories off the ground, tops. To float with a glider, you needed good elevation. He didn't know exactly how much, but at this point, not trying wasn't an option. He closed his eyes and pictured the Kozhim River. Even though the distance had been way farther down, it had seemed less scary.

As Nigel held out the *Isis hippuris*, Max opened his eyes and jumped.

45

HE was moving fast. Too fast. He felt his wings snapping into place behind him. His body jerked back. It squeezed the air from his lungs and he gasped.

The man whirled around. But that was about all he had time to do before Max smashed into him. With a cry, they both fell to the ground. The gun flew out of the man's hand and slid away.

Max rolled off. He tried to scramble to his feet. Behind him, the attacker was lifting him by the glider. Max could feel the metal bending. *"You're ruining it!"* he yelled.

He planted his feet on the ground, bent his knees, and jumped backward. He must have hit the guy in the jaw because he heard the smacking of teeth. They both flew back, hitting the wall of the old station house.

The guy grabbed Max by the front of his shirt and spun him around. He was wearing a black knit cap, his lip was bleeding, and his eyes were wide and angry. "You're a kid," he spat. "A little punk."

He lifted Max off the ground. Max struggled against the man's grip, but his fists were like stone. As Max rose, he could see Nigel sneaking up behind the attacker. In Nigel's hands was the *Isis hippuris*.

"Nigel, you fool, don't!" Gloria shouted.

The man turned. He let go of Max. As Max crashed to the ground, he saw Nigel bring the *Isis hippuris* down hard on the guy's head with a shout: "Take that!"

The attacker had no time to react. He fell to the ground, limp.

Max jumped to his feet. Nigel was staring downward. But not at the unconscious man.

The *Isis hippuris* was now a scattered pile of dust on the ground.

Gloria's bottom lip was quivering. "You . . . you . . . destroyed it. You imbecile."

The attacker let out a muffled groan. Max spotted the gun lying on the ground about ten feet away. He ran over and scooped it up. It was heavier than he expected it to be, and he hadn't the faintest idea what to do with it.

As he turned toward the others, Gloria sprang back, hands in the air. "You wouldn't . . ."

You're right, I wouldn't! Max wanted to say, but he just held steady. He had to admit he liked seeing Gloria lose confidence.

"He doesn't know how to use that properly," Nigel said to Gloria. "Which makes him more dangerous than you know. Now back into the building."

Gloria looked from Max to Nigel. "This is preposterous. Why are you doing this, Nigel? Everything is lost. This makes no sense."

"Get in!" Nigel said.

As Max waved the gun uncertainly, Gloria lifted her hands and backed into the old station house. Nigel knelt over the unconscious gunman and dragged him in too. As Max yanked the station door shut, Nigel pulled a thick lock out of his pack. He slapped it through a hasp on the door and clamped it shut.

"You can't do this to me!" The door was shaking now. Gloria was trying to get out. The mechanism was ancient and rusted, but it seemed to hold tight.

Max took out his phone and called 911. "I want to report a break-in at the old train station in Savile. A man and woman vandalizing the station house. Looks like they got themselves locked inside!"

As Max pocketed the phone, Nigel held out his palm. "One last thing, old boy, if you don't mind."

Taking the gun from Max's hand, Nigel emptied it of its bullets and then reared back and tossed it deep into the woods behind the train station. They heard it splash into the nearby creek, and Nigel smiled. "I believe American custom dictates a triumphant collision of fists."

Max gave him a fist bump, and they both ran down the street.

"Yes? Yes?" Alex cried out.

She, Bitsy, and Smriti were gathered on the Tilts' porch as Max and Nigel ran up. The old man was out of breath, and his drooping eye seemed lower than usual. "The lad . . . was brilliant!" he said. "Like Batman."

"We have all the ingredients!" Max shouted.

He did not want to stop. Not for a second. Racing into the house, he ran straight up to his room. His 3D printer had completed a perfect plastic Hulk. Next to it were three crude replicas of *Isis hippuris.*

As he put down the backpack, the others rushed into the room behind him. "I was so worried Gloria would see through the fake coral, Max," Alex said, fingering one of the replicas.

"I took the best replica," Max said. "They're all pretty

low-res. I had to do it for time's sake. In the dark, it looked pretty real."

"Oh, the way the plaster shattered—such drama!" Nigel exclaimed. "I nearly had a heart attack myself!"

"Be right back. Nigel will tell you everything." Max ran downstairs with the Hulk and placed it on his mom's windowsill. She was fast asleep, holding hands with his dad, who dozed on a chair next to her. He kissed them both on the forehead. Hers felt hot. And wet. Her hair was stringy with sweat, plastered to her head, and her mouth was set in a grimace.

"Did everything work out?" his dad asked hopefully.

Max nodded. He turned and ran back upstairs.

It was time.

As he opened his bedroom door, Alex, Bitsy, and Nigel were laying out all the vials on his desk, along with a big empty mayonnaise jar someone had brought up from the pantry. It was the first time he'd seen all the ingredients together, like the travelogue to an adventure that now seemed like a dream.

The ancient hippo bones from Pirgos Dirou.

The strange glowing coils from the Kozhim River in Russia.

The black turmeric from Kathmandu.

The golf-ball cactus from the Sierra Gorda.

The stream water from the volcanic Antarctic *refugio*.

"Jet, car, rowboat, motorbike, train, hang glider, yak, balloon, ship, dogsled . . ." Bitsy murmured. "Did all of that actually happen? Our own *Around the World* adventure?"

"As far as transportation went, we *owned* Jules Verne and Passepartout!" Alex said. "Except they rode an elephant. We didn't do that. And I'm kind of glad."

Max looked at his watch. "We beat eighty days," he said, "by a long shot."

"Adjusted for inflation," Nigel said, "it's probably about the same."

Max reached into his closet. He entered the combination on his safe and pulled out the chunk of *Isis hippuris*. The real one.

He smelled fish, but that was because it smelled like fish.

"I like the name 'sea fan' better than *Isis hippuris*," Alex said, examining its bulbous but delicate fingerlike tendrils. "Although 'mutant many-fingered hand' might be better."

Max set it on the table. His hands were shaking. "Mom is not looking good. Whatever we're going to do, let's do it in a hurry."

"Keep in mind too, Mummy will be on the loose,"

Bitsy said. "She's no doubt browbeating the police about now. Depending on how much she alienates them, they'll either be hauling her off for investigation or pulling up here, to question us." She leaned close to the sea fan. "I propose we break it in half."

"Why?" Alex asked.

"If we use half of everything," Bitsy explained, "we'll have some left over in case anything goes wrong."

"But what if half isn't enough?" Max asked. "What if we need twice as much? Or three times as much? How can we be sure?"

"Now we know how my great-great-grandfather Gaston felt," Nigel said with a sigh.

Max closed his eyes and took a deep breath. *Sometimes you can't be ready to do the things you really need to do. You just do them. And that makes you ready.*

He looked closely at the coral until he found a small fault line. Carefully he gripped it on either side and snapped it in two.

It wasn't exactly half, more like sixty-forty. Max held up the bigger part. "I'll use this," he said.

Alex unstoppered the vials, one by one. Max poured out the Greek cave water. Only half. Then half the coil dust–filled Kozhim River water, which was still glowing. After he poured in some of the turmeric water, the solution turned black and began to bubble.

Alex, Bitsy, and Nigel flinched and stepped back.

Max held the golf-ball cactus in his hand. He felt bad about this one. But of all the ingredients, this is the one they had the most of. Some of the specimens still had roots. As soon as this was over, he would get Dad to contact his friends out west. He was determined to help preserve these. Nothing should go extinct because of him.

But for now, he had first to figure out how to add it in.

"Do you just throw one in?" Bitsy asked. "I mean, this was supposed to be all about the water. There was no water on that Mexican mountain. We looked."

Max shook his head, thinking. Cacti grew where water wasn't. Because they held their own moisture.

He smiled.

Holding the cactus over the glass jar, he split it open with his fingernails and carefully squeezed. A thin substance dripped in with a soft, repeated *sssss*.

Last, he poured in the water from the volcanic ice cave.

Alex handed him the *Isis hippuris*. He held it over the rim of the jar. "This better be good, Grandpa Jules," he whispered, "or I'm never reading another one of your books again."

He lowered the coral into the jar. The bubbling and hissing softened, then stopped. The swirling colors, which had become inky black with the Nepali turmeric, now dulled to a gunmetal gray.

"What's happened?" Alex asked.

Max shook his head. "Nothing."

"It's like the sea fan *stopped* any reaction from happening," Nigel said. "We don't have enough information, lad. I believe we are going to have to find the entire manuscript—if such a thing exists!"

Max's nose was filling with smells, but they were things he didn't recognize. He didn't know how to feel. He wanted to stop time, to freeze Mom in exactly the condition she was. Because time was the enemy now. If you let it run away, it would take her and he'd never see her again.

And then it would come back for Evelyn.

He banged on the desk, letting out a cry so low and strange it scared him to hear himself. *"Do something!"* he shouted. *"Do something do something do something do something do somethiiiiiing!"*

"Max . . ." Alex said. "Maybe we should break off some more . . ."

But the jar was moving now. Juddering from side to side. From within the opaque gray liquid, the tendrils of the *Isis hippuris* pulsed. It was slow and subtle at first, like a snow-covered blinking light, but as they watched, it sped up until it was flashing brightly.

"Do you hear something?" Alex said.

Max nodded. It was a soft, high-pitched *eeee*, like the whistling of a kettle. The jar began to spin clockwise. The liquid inside churned and spat, and Max quickly jammed the metal top on it to keep the liquid from shooting out.

When it came to a stop, the entire mixture had turned a deep amber color. Max took off the lid, and a sharp, acrid smell blasted upward into the room, like the fart of some toxic alien beast.

It caught in Max's throat, which instantly closed up. He turned away, coughing violently. Nigel darted into the hallway, and Alex began throwing open windows. "Someone is supposed to *drink* that?" Bitsy said.

Max fought the feeling that this was all wrong. That the whole thing was one big, evil joke concocted by the members of the Reform Club. Or by Gloria Bentham.

Alex touched the glass and drew her hand back. "It's boiling hot."

"An exothermic reaction," Max said with a nod. "I was expecting that."

"But what exactly are you expecting to do with it?" Nigel asked.

From downstairs, Max heard his mother moan.

"Max?" his dad called up. "What's that smell?"

"It's the healing potion, Dad!" Max said.

"*What?* I think every pet in the neighborhood just dropped dead from that stink."

Max raced down to the kitchen, took two pot holders from a drawer, and brought them back, taking two stairs at a time. Cautiously he pressed the pot holders against the sides of the jar and lifted.

Alex, Bitsy, and Nigel proceeded to the stairs, backward and single file, ready to catch Max if he lurched forward and fell. He made it safely to the bottom and veered into the back room.

Dad was holding Mom's hand. She was still asleep, and tears were running down his cheek. "You know, I never liked exploring, and I nearly flunked chemistry and biology," he said. "I'm just a lawyer. And a husband and a dad. Those are the only things I know how to do. I love those things. And I don't want to lose what I love. So I have to tell you, I don't really care how it smells. Do you have faith that it will work? Because I don't know that we have a lot of other options at this point."

"I don't have faith it'll work," Max said. "But I have less faith it won't."

Dad smiled for the first time since Max got home.

He leaned over and whispered into his wife's ear, "Michele . . . Max is back."

Her eyelids slowly lifted. "Max? Hi!"

"He and Alex and their friends found what they were looking for," Dad said. "They would like you to try some."

She struggled to rise from the bed, then sank back. "Try again . . ." Dad said. "Come on, Michele, sit up."

He turned her on her back and tried to lift her into a sitting position, but it wasn't working.

Max set the jar on the table. It had cooled off. He didn't know whether that was good or bad. It still smelled, but not nearly as strong. He didn't know whether *that* was good or bad either.

Or how much to give her.

Dad was shaking. He held out a clean paper cup but had to balance the bottom on the night table. Carefully Max poured some of the amber liquid into the cup. It was completely uniform—no fragments, no pieces of *Isis hippuris*, no swirls of black. Nigel, Alex, and Bitsy stared at it in utter shock.

Dad's face was wet with tears now, and Max tried not to look. He needed his own vision to be clear and his hands to be steady. "Mom," he said, "remember when

I was little and didn't want to eat? You would hold up my spoon and say, 'Heeeere comes a rocket ship!' And I loved rockets so much I would open up even if I hated the food?"

No response.

"Well, OK then, here comes a rocket ship! *Bzzzzzz!*" Max guided the cup toward her lips. Even though her eyelids had shut, her lips and teeth separated ever so slightly. Max tilted the cup and slowly let the liquid pour. It came dribbling out of the side of her mouth and onto the sheets. But some was going in, he could tell.

Mom gagged and coughed, then closed her mouth and seemed to swallow. But she wasn't turning colors or throwing up, so he tried another cup. Pools of amber liquid were gathering on either side of her on the bed sheets and on her pajamas. "Is any of it getting in?" Dad asked.

"Yeah, I'm pretty sure," Max said. "I think she likes it."

When the third cup went down, Max sat back in his chair. Alex came to stand at his side. He wrapped his arms around her leg and waited.

And waited.

Mom's breaths were raspy now. Her lips moved once or twice, as if she wanted to say something. The fingers of her right hand twitched. Max watched the rising and falling of her chest get shallower and shallower.

And then, as her head lolled to the side, her breathing stopped.

Max sat upright in his chair. It wasn't working. It should be working by now. "It was a lie . . ." he murmured.

"Oh, Max," Alex said, reaching out to him.

She was crying. He lurched away. He didn't want touch. Or tears.

The serum was a total lie. His trip around the world was the dumbest thing anyone had ever done in history. Everything was swirling. The Hulk seemed to be dancing on the windowsill. Out of the corner of his eye, he thought he saw the priest entering the room. He rocked back in his chair so hard the wood cracked.

As he toppled over, he let out a scream that came from the bottom of his toes.

46

"OHHH, that was a bit loud, Max, wasn't it?"

Now Max was hearing her voice. It was cruel that his mind could do that. He let his cry exhaust every bit of oxygen in his body until he was doubled over and light-headed. Then he sucked it in again and stood up next to the broken chair.

But the next cry caught in his throat.

Everything in the room had changed.

Mom was sitting up.

She was thin and pale, looking around in bewilderment. She lifted her hands and stared at the gross, sticky liquid that had dripped all over her fingers. "What is that? Did I throw this up?"

"Mo-o-o-o-om!" Max cried out. If Alex hadn't grabbed

him by the shoulders he would have jumped on his mother and maybe crushed her. "It worked! I can't believe it worked!"

"What worked?" Mom said, looking from face to face.

"Honey, how are you feeling?" Dad asked, kneeling by the other side of her bed.

"Like I just had the worst sleep in my life," she said. "Some horrible dreams. But you know, I feel pretty good now. Except for this foul-smelling stuff."

"What. Just. Happened?" Alex said.

She was weeping. Bitsy was weeping. Nigel was blowing his nose into a paper towel. Dad leaned over and gave Mom a kiss on the mouth.

"That is so gross," Max said.

"Then I'll do it again," Dad said.

Mom's body was shaking with laughter. "Will someone tell me what's going on?"

Max took a deep breath and told her everything that had happened—the confrontation with Gloria, the mixing of the chemicals. She listened, shaking her head in amazement. "I can't quite believe I'm not dreaming."

"You're not," Max said.

"Definitely not," Bitsy said.

"Nope," Alex piped up.

Honk, went Nigel's nose in the paper towel.

"Well, I'm also starving. Please, George, can you clean me up? Whatever was in that potion is absolutely foul."

Max's dad stood and pointed to the doorway. "Out, everyone! I will prepare the patient for a homecoming party that will last until the first person says 'uncle'!"

For the first time since he'd been home, Max felt fine leaving his mom in the room. He ran out to the kitchen and jumped on a chair, screaming.

Alex turned on Sonos and blasted music. She and Bitsy danced into the living room. Nigel seemed to be intensely stomping on insects until Max realized he was doing a jig.

"We did it, Max!" Alex cried out. "I can't believe we did it!"

Max began singing along with the playlist. He didn't really know the words, but he didn't care. He could make up better ones. Mom was well. She really was. That was the most important thing ever. And they still had enough left to give Evelyn. She would walk again. Together, she and he would fly. And someday, some supersmart people would figure out how it all worked and make more of this stuff. For everyone.

Yes.

Max jumped off the chair onto the carpet. From

that spot in the kitchen he could see the portrait of Jules Verne they'd rescued from the attic and hung in the living room. He ran to it and gave it a quick salute. "Thanks, dude," he said. Stepping on the sofa, he gave it a kiss on its face. Kissing a painting was easier than kissing a person.

Being a painting, it didn't react. But Max could swear it looked ten years younger.

He laughed and began to spin around like the snows of Antarctica, like the rotation of the Earth. As he spun he laughed, and he thought just maybe he would never stop.

47

MAX was going to get the chocolate cupcakes right if it killed him.

"I promise I will not set the stove above three-fifty," he said. More to himself than anyone, but both Alex and Smriti found it very funny. They were sitting at the kitchen table trying to do a crossword puzzle.

He greased the cupcake tins like he had the first time. He sealed up the chocolate-chip bag. He opened and closed the refrigerator and looked out the window. "When do you think Dad and Bitsy will be back with the milk?"

"It was more than milk," Alex said. "Your mom gave them a long shopping list. Dude, we can't start until they get back. So chill."

Max nodded. But he kept pacing. Upstairs, Mom was taking a bath. He could hear her singing softly. Later a bunch of neighbors was going to come over. Just close friends. Mom wouldn't be 100 percent for a while.

They'd all agreed to keep the potion a secret for now. That was the advice of Dad and his lawyer friends. Best to wait until it was looked at by scientists and a strategy had been devised for mass production. Then they would roll out the news in a planned, organized way.

Which was fine with Max. The publicity for their previous adventure had only just died down, and the quiet felt good.

Outside Max heard the *thunk* of a car door closing. He raced to the front door, with Alex and Smriti right behind him. The Lopez family car was parked out front, and the rear passenger door opened.

Evelyn's mom got out of the driver's seat and came around the back of the car. That was her routine, always. Get out, circle around, open the trunk, take out the wheelchair, set it up, help Evelyn out of the back seat. Every time. The family choreography.

But this time Mrs. Lopez walked past the trunk and left it closed. She stood by the open passenger door wearing a big grin and waved.

Max, Alex, and Smriti waved back.

Now Evelyn was emerging, holding on to her mom's hand. As she stood, she straightened out her new jacket and smoothed out her jeans.

"You can do it, honey," her mom said softly.

Evelyn took a step forward and wobbled. Her mom slipped her arm under Evelyn's, but she gently pushed it away.

Evelyn's second step was even more wobbly, but it was on her own. The third and fourth steps were quicker, but that was because she was catching herself. With a deep breath, she looked at Max and grinned. With one hand she took her mom's arm, and with the other she flashed Max a thumbs-up. "That's four steps! Tomorrow five! Saturday a game of handball!"

Slowly, holding on to her mom, Evelyn made it all the way into the house. It was the first time Max had seen her standing in months. As Max held the door open, Evelyn blew him a kiss. He was receiving a lot of kisses lately. He liked blown kisses better than real ones, or hugs. It made him feel loved without being too dis- gustingly uncomfortable. "This is because of you, Max. And you, Alex!"

As they passed, Max read the logo across the back of her jacket, in spangly letters:

I BELIEVE I CAN FLY

His phone buzzed, and he ducked away to take a call. "Hi, Dad!" he said. "Guess what? Evelyn is here, and she's walking. You should see her!"

"That's amazing, Max," came his dad's voice. "Does Bitsy happen to be there?"

"She's with you, Dad. Did you forget?"

"No! We drove here together. She had this big backpack. I told her to leave it in the car, but she was in kind of a strange mood. Did you know she's eighteen?"

"She's sixteen," Max said.

"Nope, she said she was eighteen. Did you also know that she was the daughter of Spencer Niemand, from an early marriage? And not of the woman they caught at the train station?"

"She's not Gloria Bentham's daughter?" Max said. "Wait. She told us she was."

"She kind of blurted all this stuff out on the drive. I don't know why she decided to tell me instead of you. Anyway, we get to the store, and we split up to go to different aisles. And next thing I know, I'm ready to go—but she's gone!"

"Have somebody check the restroom, Dad."

"I did. And the parking lot. I figured maybe she got confused. Maybe she thought I'd left, and she figured she had to walk back. So she's not there?"

"No," Max said.

Alex peeked in from the kitchen. "What's up? Are they on their way?"

Before Max could answer, his mom called from upstairs. "Max?"

"Yes, Mom?" Max answered.

She appeared at the top of the stairs, still too skinny in her jeans and floral blouse. "Did you open the upstairs safe?"

"*What?*" Max felt a prickle go up his neck.

"I thought maybe you took out the vials and the coral—"

But Max was racing up the stairs past her, still clutching his phone.

When he reached his bedroom door, he stopped.

The safe door, which he had closed last night, was hanging open. Every vial was gone. And so was the *Isis hippuris.*

"Max?" came his dad's voice from the phone, sounding tinny and far away. *"Max?"*

Max sank to the floor. There was no defining the smell that settled over him like a suffocating blanket.

EPILOGUE

NINA Cranston didn't love doing double shifts. The Greyhound station wasn't exactly party central, but money was tight.

She yawned as the girl stepped up to the counter and asked for a ticket to Boston. Her sunglasses were huge, and under the floppy knit hat, Nina couldn't even see the color of the girl's hair. "Boston's quite a trip, honey," she said. "You go ahead and swipe your credit card."

Instead, the girl slapped a wad of tens onto the counter. "I'll pay cash."

"Well, well, someone won the lotto, eh?" Nina said with a smile.

No reaction. None at all. Nina liked to think she could connect with people, loosen them up with a joke, a nice comment. After a sentence or two, she could usually pinpoint their accent and surprise them—*You're from Wisconsin, aren't you? Why, how did you know, ma'am?* It was her little game.

But this passenger was tough. Tight like a drum.

As she began counting, the girl looked away. "Family?" Nina said.

"What?" The girl seemed startled.

"Do you have family? In Boston?" Nina made change for the girl and printed out her ticket.

"I don't believe that's any of your business," the girl replied.

As she took the ticket and walked away, Nina Cranston exhaled. Only an hour left on the shift. This would be a story to tell.

At least she got a few words out of the girl.

British, Nina thought. Definitely British.